THE ENGLISH STORIES

T0162005

Also by Cynthia Flood

STORIES

The Animals In Their Elements (Talonbooks, 1987)

My Father Took A Cake To France (Talonbooks, 1992)

NOVEL

Making A Stone Of The Heart (Key Porter, 2002)

THE ENGLISH STORIES

THE
ENGLISH STORIES

Cynthia Flood

BIBLIOASIS

FIRST EDITION

Library and Archives Canada Cataloguing in Publication

Flood, Cynthia, 1940-
        The English stories / Cynthia Flood.

ISBN 10: 1-897231-56-3
ISBN 13: 978-1-897231-56-2

        I. Title.

PS8561.L64 E54 2009   C813'.54   C2009-900931-5

Readied for the press by John Metcalf.

 Canada Council Conseil des Arts
for the Arts du Canada

 Canadian Patrimoine
Heritage canadien

 ONTARIO ARTS COUNCIL
CONSEIL DES ARTS DE L'ONTARIO

We gratefully acknowledge the support of the Canada Council for the Arts, Canadian Heritage, and the Ontario Arts Council for our publishing program.

This book is printed on Rolland Enviro and is 100% PCW recycled content.

PRINTED AND BOUND IN CANADA

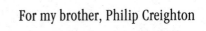

For my brother, Philip Creighton

It is rather the rule than the exception in human affairs
that the principal actors in great events lack all knowledge
of the true causes by which they are propelled.

—Thomas Flanagan, *The Year of the French*

Contents

The Indian Box

The Indian set up two orange crates overlaid with oilcloth, near the grocery but off the sidewalk so the white people need not step aside to pass her. On display were boxes and canoes of birchbark and braided sweetgrass, adorned with porcupine quills. There was also beadwork. In deerskin there were coin-purses, dolls with supplicating arms and red-feathered headbands, and brooches in the shapes of elephant, giraffe, camel, with safety pins for clasps.

The Indian woman said nothing. Nor did Mrs Ellis. Wasting no time, she looked, chose, paid. In the sunshine Amanda waited for permission to run down the hill to their car, for the drive back to the cottage. Was the Indian woman herself a mother? Where did she exist, when not with ice-cream-licking tourists, matrons laden with big wrapped roasts, and barefoot city children in kapok life jackets who'd proudly paddled into town from the family island? Such questions did not occur. Amanda just waited.

Here and there in the small rooms of the Ellis cottage, birchbark boxes stood on tables and dressers. On the Queen's birthday, when the family came up to Muskoka for the first time since Thanksgiving, a rush of sweetgrass and cedar met them at the opened door. Every summer Rachel Ellis bought more boxes as souvenirs for house guests. She wiped them with household bleach and set them in the disinfectant sun. The fragrance of sweetgrass, soon prevailing, would last for decades.

Not long before the family sailed away on the *Empress of Britain*, Amanda got a new box of her own, round, quilled in red and white. The lid had a maple leaf.

Mr Ellis laughingly set the lid on his daughter's head. "Queen of my heart!"

Mrs Ellis snapped the two of them with Amanda's new Brownie, but her father moved. When the prints came, he was blurry.

"Gerald, really! Couldn't you remember to stay still?"

Packing for England, Amanda set pebbles from Lake Muskoka in the box, and tiny lake clamshells. In went her best barrettes, three Woolworth rings (ruby, sapphire, emerald), a writing pad and envelopes, a tiny set of watercolours, her bag of jacks. The silver paper from her mother's Export As wrapped up her Canadian coins: a maple leaf, a beaver, the *Bluenose*, a caribou, and a voyageur with a scalp-locked guide. King George VI's neat haircut backed each one.

Daisy, four doors down the street, had a going-away present for Amanda.

As often, the friends were sitting under the Callaghans' front porch. Daisy clutched a small object. Amanda waited, knowing she wouldn't get anything till Daisy stopped crying.

"Mama never buys me a *new* dress. Kathleen gets a new dress, and she wears it, and then Moira wears it, and then when it's old I have to wear it. Mama's so mean. So so so mean!" With every *so*, Daisy's other hand poked a stick hard into the earth. Then she scored a circle, stabbed in eyes and mouth and nose. With her heels she kicked and scraped until her mother's image was no more – and began to laugh.

Then Daisy's other hand opened. "Here, Amanda. So you can write to me."

The little address book was in bright pink leatherette. "I've never had one! Thank you." A loop on the spine held a pink pencil. The lines in the book were pink, too.

A door opened. "Daisy, Amanda? Where are you, girls? They're ready!"

Mrs Callaghan's cinnamon buns were warm still, the icing almost sliding off and the raisins juicy. Amanda ate fast lest Mrs Ellis find her like this, with Daisy and eating out on the porch in public.

"What kind of a name is Daisy?" That was one problem with her friend. Her surname was another. In his amiable way Mr Ellis said,

14

"Yes, certainly, lots of fun at Finnegan's wake! But I'd rather not live next door to Judy O'Grady."

Mrs Ellis said, "Micks." Amanda did not ask.

Finally, Moira and Kathleen and Daisy had three older brothers.

"Six children!" exclaimed Mrs Ellis, when the family moved in. "The Pope must be happy."

"What's a Pope?"

"A meddling old fool in Rome." Her mother sent Amanda upstairs to her desk. "Do your arithmetic first. And bring your fractions down, for me to check."

The girls did not spend a great deal of time together, since Amanda was in Grade Five at public school while Daisy wore St Patrick's smart green tunic, with a white blouse, but after school they could play.

Amanda's mother never called out into the garden, "Bring Daisy in for cookies and milk." Sometimes she phoned Mrs Wainwright three doors down or Mrs Egerton two doors up, to see if Lucy or Marion could come over. Then she would appear at the back door. "Amanda, time to come in. You're going to have company."

After one such episode of social engineering, Mrs Ellis said at dinner, "I don't like the way that Irish child stares at me. Rude."

"We'll be leaving soon, Rachel." Mr Ellis took more beef. His tone told Amanda not to ask why Daisy was nameless and Irish.

"Dogans," said Mrs Ellis.

Amanda ate, and considered Marion. A dull little girl, she always brought along her doll Freda, whose china eyes had fallen back into her head irreparably after a bout of shaking. Marion would not let Amanda peer into the sockets at the lost eyeballs.

The silence at the Ellises' table went on.

Amanda herself did not speak when Daisy said, "Those rings are so pretty!"

The girls were then under the Ellises' viburnum. This was less secluded than the Callaghans' porch, but Amanda once in a while felt she had to invite Daisy on to her territory. She had brought the Indian box downstairs, to show her friend.

Daisy didn't react to the box itself, or the pebbles and shells and coins. Instantly she picked up the rings and held them to the light. "Moira likes diamonds, but these are much beautifuller!" To Amanda's annoyance, she undid the little chain linking the jewels and looked at sapphire, emerald, ruby one by one. "The red's the best. The brightest." Daisy looked up, hopeful. Amanda pulled a dry leaf off the viburnum and sniffed it. With one foot she traced a circle in the dirt, made squiggly hair on either side. Daisy replaced the rings. Amanda obliterated her scrapes.

Another afternoon, when Amanda was on her bed reading *Alice In Wonderland* yet again, she heard the signal that Daisy had decided was "theirs." A ball bounced against the side of the house, rhythmically, in time with *Ordinary, clapsy, roly-poly, backsy, high, low, heel, toe, criss-cross, away you go!* Lying still, Amanda saw Daisy as she stood down there on the thin grass, tossed the ball and made the necessary gestures and caught it, every time. The chant ended. Silence. Amanda turned a page. Then Daisy did the whole routine again, only louder and faster. After she finished there was only a short silence.

"You're there, Amanda! I saw you go inside. Come on out!"

Daisy cried out thus several times. Amanda continued to be still. Then slow steps sounded, trailing off. She visualized Daisy's pout, the shoulders down, the wistful look. When the silence was full again she went back into *Alice*.

Now the cinnamon bun's soft sweetness was almost gone. A last raisin, a last swallow – utterly delicious. Daisy's mother held out the plate.

"No thank you, Mrs Callaghan."

Daisy grabbed a second one. "I still hate you, Mama!"

At this her mother hugged her.

Amanda had also seen Daisy both hug and kick her older sisters. She had heard Daisy scream at Mr Callaghan because he didn't bring her an all-day sucker. He'd laughed. His daughter laughed back. Daisy's actions terrified Amanda. As for her father's behaviour, it was incomprehensible, scarcely to be believed.

She thanked Daisy's mother again and went home.

Mrs Ellis found the pink address book under Amanda's pillow. "Will that silly little pencil even write? And what a vulgar colour."

Amanda went out to the viburnum. There she wrote down names, starting with Daisy's, and numbers and streets in the little book. The pencil was indeed hard to work with. Even in her best small printing, each address took a full page.

To cover the bottom of the Indian box, Amanda used red construction paper. The pink book slipped under; coins and shells weighted the paper down. All her little things looked nice against the red, especially the glittery rings. Amanda thought several times about perhaps giving Daisy the ruby, as a memento.

September 1951

In England for a year that stretched into two, the Ellises planned for their whole life to be different, an adventure. Possibly even a dream.

Amanda's father was on leave from teaching English literature. He had got a thing called an inheritance, which Mrs Ellis kept insisting was "very small," and another thing, called a fellowship, to do research for a big book about the Romantic poets – specifically, Keats and Shelley. He would travel about the UK frequently. Mrs Ellis, a freelance editor, would travel too.

Thus Amanda's family did not set up house. Instead a small residential hotel called The Green House was selected, in Oxford, and a school. With delight Amanda learned that she would wear a uniform. As a day-girl, when her parents were in the city, she would thrillingly go to St Mildred's alone, by bus; the school was in a suburb.

"But I wanted a green uniform, like Daisy's." She and her mother paged through the brochure; girls wore navy tunics or blue Liberty print dresses, with cardigans.

"But Daisy was Catholic. You're going to a C of E school."

"Does that mean Country of England?"

Her mother's laconic explanation, her father's lengthy and admiring remarks found little to attach to in Amanda's head. The term *Roman Catholic* was not completely strange, for she had studied brave Brébeuf among the savage Iroquois and bad Riel of the revolting

Métis, but those people seemed far from Daisy. And why did her mother say Daisy *was*? Amanda let the matter go, to contemplate the best-of-all about St. Mildred's: she was to board there, whenever her parents went off to be badgers at libraries and archives and stately homes.

"Digging for facts," Mr Ellis said happily. "Digging for Sheets and Kelly."

"Two badgers and a boarder, Daddy." Amanda and he giggled.

At The Green House, Martha was the maid-of-all-work. She came from Yorkshire but otherwise was quite unlike Martha in *The Secret Garden*.

Smiling, curious, she turned Amanda's Indian box round and round in her hands. "You've seen them, miss? You've actually seen Indians?"

The answer was *Yes*, though a stocky quiet woman in a house-dress could not be what Martha had in mind.

"Such beautiful colours, miss. And how clever, to make such a thing."

"Do you like how it smells?"

"Oh yes miss, it's like the country fields, in August." Martha stroked the glossy red-and-white quilling and admired the braided grass – but then she must finish cleaning Amanda's room and go on to old Professor McGeachie's next door, and then clean the lavatories, the bathroom, the airing-cupboard. "Work never ends, miss."

To this Amanda found nothing to say.

Mrs Ellis said, "You shouldn't spend so much time talking to Martha. She's got work to do. Let's go out and explore."

Amanda learned the Roads – Woodstock, Banbury, Polstead. She found a little shop, for candy. No, for sweets. She learned how to cross the canal and the railway line and thus reach Port Meadows.

"I've never seen anything like it," said her mother.

The immense green expanse shone with water. Far away, horses moved in the sunlight. And cows. The horizon's curve shimmered. The first time Amanda went to Port Meadows by herself, the place made her feel as if she were in Muskoka.

Her Indian box was heavier now, with pebbles from the Windrush, Isis, Thames, and a little lump of green stone from Connemara offered by Mrs K, the widowed proprietor of The Green House.

"It's real marble!" Amanda reported.

"So she claims," said Mrs Ellis.

Also under the maple leaf lid lay a leather bookmark from Blackwell's children's bookshop, and a folded program from *A Midsummer Night's Dream* in a college garden, attended soon after the Ellises made landfall in the city of dreaming spires.

"Real Shakespeare," said Amanda's father. "The genuine article, at last."

October 1951

At school back home, Amanda had enjoyed doing maps. With pleasure she drew the sharp black outlines. Her colouring and lettering were neat, and her marks in Geography were excellent. For "The Discoverers," she got ten out of ten. This effort showed how six famed French and English and Scottish explorers crossed the ocean and then, although everywhere confronting Indians, intrepidly stitched their map-seams right across the continent. For each site of savage trouble she drew minute red feathers, without one thought of the deerskin dolls in Port Carling. The term itself, Indian, was unremarkable. The Atlantic she coloured turquoise instead of the usual blue.

Now at St Mildred's Amanda's form was mapping Britain, and Miss Lincoln Geography moved along the aisles to check the girls' work.

"Very nice, these little Welsh mountains. Look, Janet." She drew the girl in the next seat over to see Amanda's tiny green and brown cones. "Try to draw like this."

To evade Janet's sour gaze, Amanda showed her teacher – no, that wasn't right – her mistress a list of Welsh names. "How do you say these?" Arenig Fawr, Y Mynyddoedd Duon, Carneddau.

Miss Lincoln smiled faintly. "I have no idea. And Amanda, in Ireland you need only map the Six Counties."

None of this could be written down. None of this could be sent to Daisy's pink address, or to Lucy's or Marion's (Mrs Ellis insisted on letters to these girls). About what went on at her new school Amanda hadn't even words to tell herself.

By dormitory custom, boarders at St Mildred's set out knick-knacks on their dressing tables. Ceramic mares and foals were popular, as were Noddies and ballerinas, and hand-painted shells from English seaside resorts.

The first time Amanda boarded, Janet and her best friend Tessa got at her when she was alone in the dormitory. They rumpled through all her belongings and tossed them about, scorned her un-English dressing gown and her best dress with her mother's exquisite smocking.

"It's called a *frock*. Didn't you know? And what might this *peculiar* object be?" From the dressing table Tessa snatched up the Indian box, shook the contents out on to Amanda's assigned bed. Coins and shells, pebbles and paper and rings flew about. Tessa put the lid to her nose. "What *is* the beastly thing made of?"

Sweetgrass, porcupine quills, birchbark, Indians – stammered, blurted. What else could Amanda say?

"Ugh!" Tessa dropped the lid and wiped her fingers on her tunic. Then she fingered the pink address book. "Toronto. How peculiar. I suppose it's Indian, too."

Then Janet, as if playing jacks, scooped up the Canadian coins and peered at them. "Do you call this money?" She cast the bits of metal on the counterpane. Some bounced off and down to the floor-boards. "Animals, Indians, ugh!" Shrilling with laughter, the girls ran from the dormitory towards the stairs.

The *Bluenose* was still rolling across the floor, so Amanda managed to retrieve it, but the caribou and the beaver fell down the cracks and went into hiding for ever. She never found the ruby ring, either. Was it down there with the animals? Or perhaps Janet had taken the jewel. Or Tessa.

When this first experience of boarding was over and Amanda was back in her room at the hotel, she opened up her pink address book. She tore out the pages with Daisy's and Lucy's and Marion's addresses and ripped them into dozens of still smaller scraps and threw them all up in the air. Floating down, they made a brief snow-storm as the flakes landed on the bed and bookshelf and floor. At home now there would be real snow, deep and crunchy, perfect for fox-and-geese. Or perhaps a little sticky, for snowballs and snowmen. To make snow angels, the soft first fall of the year was often best. The kind of snow needed for the oblongs of a good igloo didn't come often. You could tell, using your hand like a knife, if the texture was right.

In this country, no snow fell. Resentfully Amanda gathered up the shreds of paper and put them in the wastepaper basket so her mother would not be cross.

From then on, when boarding at St Mildred's she still took the Indian box with her, to display on her dressing table, but it was empty. No one attacked it again, though. The English girls were not interested. Sometimes she took off the lid and put her nose right into the box, to inhale.

Country Life

I no longer remember, if I ever knew, why we paid this visit; such adult arrangements simply appear in the lives of children. We were to drive to a village deep in the countryside some distance from Oxford, for lunch at the home of a Miss Lucinda Jones. I was to stay with her overnight. Next day my parents would collect me, to continue our journey to London. Nor do I remember my feelings about this plan, which in retrospect seems an odd one, nor the drive, nor our arrival, nor the sherry and lemon-squash which preceded lunch. The memories start, and end, with a meal.

The dining table was a shining oval, like a forest pool rendered brilliant brown by an underwater layer of fallen leaves. On this sheen stood a vase of pussy willows. Sheathed in ice, their branches gleamed, though the catkin fuzz was dry to my touch. My mother kept on her purple suit jacket, though she wore a pink sweater beneath.

"Where do you think we're off to, Rachel?" my father had expostulated that morning. "Baffin Island?"

"Into the England countryside, to see the damn buttercups and the frozen pear tree." She put on sheepskin driving gloves. "Gerald, are you *still* not ready to go?"

Miss Jones's table napkins were deep cream, and at one corner of each a triangle of lace substituted the linen. I'd never seen such. Her placemats were not cloth, like ours in Canada, but stiff cork-backed rectangles. Their lacquered surfaces bore hunting scenes. Mine was *The Meet*. Foxhounds clustered at the feet of horses and men, two hunters drank from stirrup cups, and the Master held a horn. I peered, trying to see my mother's. On the pussy-willow stems, drops belled out but did not fall.

"The pictures tell a story," said Miss Jones. "You may see them later," as she set a roasted chicken before my father. "If you would be so kind, Mr Ellis?"

Our knives and forks were reflected in the bare wood.

"Why don't you put them on the mats?" I asked. "We do."

"The cutlery is not hot, Amanda, and will not mar the table." Gravely, Miss Jones smiled. My father frowned, tested the carving knife. He looked big in the dining alcove. Its outside wall chilled my back. Shapely slices fell from his knife on to the rosebud plates. Miss Jones brought gold-roasted potatoes and a dish of grey-leaved sprouts lying like hippos in a glutinous sludge.

"A delicious bird." My father spoke with his mouth full.

"From my neighbour. Amanda will meet him." Miss Jones smiled at me again. Her eyes were long-lashed and satin-brown, unshielded by glasses. Her blue blouse had faded to no-colour at the collar. She took a single slice of chicken, one potato.

"Where has April gone?" Miss Jones fiddled with her amber beads and ring while she and my mother discussed bud unions, dividing crocus bulbs, and whether Wordsworth's daffodils were King Alfreds. Meanwhile my father took more potatoes. My parents' mats were revealed as I helped clear the table. My mother had *View Halloo*, where muddied scarlet coats converged on an orange streak that was leaping a brook. In *After the Hunt*, hunters smiled and horses drooped as the dogs jumped for a torn tail.

"Brush," Miss Jones corrected me. She brought us each a fluted circle of pastry on which lay a glazed apricot. I ate mine in two bites, fingers not fork, and saw too late my father's disapproval. The pastry evanesced in my mouth. Evidently Miss Jones did not eat sweets. Both my parents accepted a second tart. Ashamed, I did not.

"Is the fruit your own, Miss Jones?"

"At that window, Mrs Ellis." On a brick wall, above earth cluttered with rows of chopped grey stalks, bare branches lay as if embroidered on a sampler. "A southern exposure," said Miss Jones.

"Espalier!" Delighted, my mother rose to see.

"What have you done to that tree?" I asked.

"Good. You like to ask questions." Miss Jones explained, while I carried out the plates. Her placemat was *Across The Fields*. This was a dun landscape, grey-skied and distantly spotted with the dogs' and horses' liverish brown.

As my parents said goodbye, rain fell through blinking sunlight. "Our English spring," sighed Miss Jones. "Violets. Primulas."

Pointing, she led my father towards the gate, while my mother whispered urgently. "Amanda, wear your sweater to bed tonight. And your bedsocks!"

Pink and yellow and pale blue spotted all the dark ground. The car left.

"This is Bartholomew." A marmalade cat sitting by the door sniffed my fingers scornfully. When I touched him, he whisked his tail round to cover his front paws.

"Is Bartholomew a girl? Is she having kittens?"

"A neutered male. Weight gain is a consequence." The cat preceded us inside, the bag of his stomach swaying. Miss Jones bent to rub the thin fur above his eyes.

"Can I help you do the dishes?" I asked.

"What shall we do to them?" I shrank – but there was interest in her tone. Miss Jones told me about *washing up*, and we considered why up, not down. Then we went on to dessert and sweet, pie and tart, cookies and biscuits, sweets and candy. Meanwhile her long fingers dipped one plate at a time in the white enamelled pan.

"The coffee cups live in the drawing-room, Amanda." She spread the tea towel across the pan and doused it with scalding water.

I knelt to reunite the cups with their sisters, in a glass-fronted cabinet in a small strange room. In Canada (but that house had been sold and the furniture put in storage) our living room had a ten-foot ceiling and tall windows, tables thick as middens with books newspapers ashtrays photo albums bowls of fruit, battered furniture coated with cat hair, my mother's pastels and my father's watercolours tacked to the walls, disordered bookshelves, a Mexican rug, pots of forced narcissus, their roots concealed by freshwater clamshells from Lake Muskoka. Miss Jones's room was a quarter the size. A bare-legged loveseat and two skirted chairs squarely met a patterned rug.

(Was this Persian?) An embroidery frame stood by the leaded window; along the sill, green elephants were sentinels of descending size. On the mantel above the fireplace, a gold-domed clock ticked and tinkled between pencil sketches of a church.

"I have a task now, Amanda," Miss Jones said, opening a basket with a tapestry top. "Children's books are there, on the lower shelf. Later we will visit Mr McGregor."

Water Babies, King of the Golden River, Daisy Chain, Wind in the Willows, Treasure Island – old friends. I reread Mole's homecoming, and then *Peter Rabbit*. Would I really see Mr McGregor's garden? How my mother would laugh! Next to *Gulliver's Travels* stood an unfamiliar picture book: *Struwwelpeter*. A blotchy face, splayed-out hands, long tapered grey nails, horrible. . . . Horrified, I read all about cruel Frederick and incinerated Harriet, the half-dead Inky Boys, the strange finale of the hunting hare. When I got to Suck-a-Thumb, Conrad's bleeding stumps made me feel faint. The book's flyleaf read *Lucinda, love from Granny, July 7, 1910.* I looked up.

Miss Jones was dropping an egg on to her lap, through a long brown snake. Now in and out of the lisle stocking pricked her needle, till the egg resembled a balding head. She turned the work, began to weave. Her ring made tiny knocks on the egg. When all the white had disappeared, she tipped the thing into my cupped hand. Smooth, heavy, warm. "Ivory," Miss Jones said. "From India. My uncles were there."

"The stocking looks perfect."

"We must be careful of what we have, mustn't we?" The same brown lisle stretched over Miss Jones's thin ankles. My mother wore nylons. My knee socks as usual had fallen down. "What book have you there, Amanda?"

The red-lipped tailor made the blades of his scissors meet through the little boy's thumb. "Isn't this awful?"

Miss Jones's needle danced again.

"Once when I was a little girl, Amanda, my mother went to visit a sick neighbour. While she was gone I must not open the garden gate, not even to play with Emily next door."

"Did you really live in this same house then?"

"Yes, always. She said, 'Lucinda, do you promise?' And I said, 'Yes, mummy.'" Miss Jones folded away the mended stockings and took up a hank of coarse grey wool. "Off she went. I don't suppose it was five minutes before Emily was at the gate – and off *I* went." Her solemn glance. "I did not say to myself, 'I am disobeying.' No. I forgot, but the consequence was the same. I left our garden." The darning egg now looked tiny, against an enormous hole in a sock.

"What happened?"

"Emily and I finished our play. When my hand was on our garden gate to close it, I remembered." Miss Jones threaded a wicked-looking darner. "And just then I saw my mother coming, with a strawberry ice, because I had been a good girl." The cow eyes met mine again. "I ate the ice and I did not tell."

The needle worked around the hole, solidifying the looseness at the margins before embarking across the void.

"Every night in my prayers, I promised God that next day I'd tell my mother."

"And *Struwwelpeter*?"

She smiled sadly. "On my next birthday, I read about that little boy who sucked his thumb as soon as his mother left. Then I made myself read it every night. I had to look at every page."

The pictured scissors were almost as tall as Conrad himself.

"Look at that one, where Suck-a-Thumb's bleeding," said Miss Jones. "The sun smiles at the sight. I dreamed of that." She held out the sock. "I'll show you now."

Thin needle, sprawling weave – but Miss Jones's fingers gently moved mine, showed how to hold the sock to meet the steel. We worked. A good feeling came, the one from school when I met something new and did not understand but knew I was about to. This way: that was how needle and fingers must move.

"The daily battle with the self," she said, as we drew the wool from lip to lip.

Right now, where were my mother and father? Might they see a hunt? Who had imagined the terrible stories in *Struwwelpeter*?

Bartholomew paced into the room, back arched and tail plumed, and headed for a basket by the fireplace. There he curled up in magisterial dignity.

"You look pleased, Barty. Have you been a bad boy?" The clock struck its tinkling notes. Miss Jones folded the sock. "We must be off to Mr McGregor's, if you're to see something of country life this afternoon. Do you want to spend a penny?"

This expression was familiar from school (*loo bathroom lavatory washroom*), and Miss Jones pointed up to a white door. Here was the now-familiar toilet-with-a-chain, set on a dais atop three steps tiled in Dutch blue. The room, scarcely wider than the cold toilet, contained nothing else but leaves of stiff tissue on a flowered china tray to one side. A narrow window stood open, yet there was a smell, faint, definite, of throw-up. (*Sick vomit sick to the stomach in the stomach?*)

Miss Jones and Barty were in the kitchen, by the eyeless head of a mouse.

"Where is the rest?" sternly. The cat blinked, licked a paw. Miss Jones dropped the thing into a lidded white pail and washed her hands. "I expect the head is not meaty enough." She sighed. "To kill is his nature. And perhaps it is a present, for me."

Everything was white or small-flowered or wood. None of the work surfaces or cupboards aligned.

"Where's the fridge?"

A smile. "I know that in America everyone has one. This is my larder."

Pushing aside a long flowered curtain, Miss Jones stepped down. I followed, into coolness. A stone floor. Plastered walls. White wooden shelves held jars of preserved vegetables and fruits (there were the apricots), and a butter plate was hidden by a *Tailor of Gloucester* teacup. ("Barty," she murmured, showing me.) A dusty paper bag of potatoes. Custard, in a pan covered with a screen. Two oval plates sandwiched a fish. "Here we keep our larder, / Cool and full and dim." Not full, this one. Back home in Toronto, we had to take things out of the fridge in order to get at other things.

"Do you know this fish, Amanda? On our way, I'll tell you a story."

In the front hall, Miss Jones took up two thin books in half-leather bindings, dull green ("Accounts") and a manila folder of papers scrawled with numerals. We left the house, closed the garden gate. Was Suck-a-Thumb already savouring his own flesh?

Just as I do not remember the journey to Miss Jones's, so I do not remember how we reached Mr McGregor's. Was it far? What did we see? Only her tall thin form is clear, her regular steps, her skirt moving tidily. (My own skirt insisted on rotating so the pleat was wrongly placed.) I can hear her voice's serious warmth as she told of an old and honoured scientist who in youth had gone for training to a great scholar.

On a table near the scholar's study lay a dead fish. "Examine it, and then describe it to me." The gifted youth was left alone. "How stupid, how simple," he thought, quickly observing length, width, thickness, colouration. He reported back. The scholar listened. "There is more to tell than that." The young man returned to the fish. This time he checked its filmed eyes, its gills and lips, the shapes and colours and textures of its scales, the number and placement of its teeth. He reported. "There is more to tell," was the response. Standing by the fish, the young man sulked. Then he pinched his lips and went at the creature. He measured. He counted. From end to end he listed, described, classified, and as the afternoon faded went into the study and spoke at length. "There is more." The scholar pointed to a dissecting knife. The student was about to shout defiance – but then the young scientist took up the knife and went eagerly to the fish.

Mr McGregor's voice was wheezy. I still hear it, oddly high for a man. "Yes, hatching. She can see that, right off. Then pigs." I was a girl beside a huge man whose sweater came right up to his chin, like an extra neck. One boot of his was bigger than my two shoes. He limped. Miss Jones, my parents were not there. A loose smock covered Mr McGregor to the calves; his deep pockets bulged and clanked.

The eggs lay on rough splintery plywood set on sawhorses. Boards nailed to the edge formed a wall; I held on tight. About a dozen eggs. Bigger than hens', streaked and stained with red, brown, green. Some whole, several cracked open. From these protruded blind wet lumps tipped with beaks, set on necks like cooked asparagus. The heads feebly bobbed and poked, while the puny bodies thrashed about. Eventually the calcite prisons split, fell off, were crushed, and the exhausted newborns slumped on to the plywood. Spastic, the rubbery feet struggled for traction against air. The goslings emitted unending frail cries. There came another sound, a faint tapping.

"What is knocking?"I blurted out.

Mr McGregor's forefinger, big as the pork sausages my mother cooked for Sunday breakfasts in Canada, touched an egg.

I bent close. The blows of the gosling sounded against the walls of its home. *Tap tap.* Silence. *Tap tap tap.* Pause. *Tap.* Fissures appeared. *Tap tap*, and a patch of shell broke off, revealing not a blind head but a whitish veil over frantic movement.

"Membrane," said Mr McGregor. My cheeks heated, because that sounded much too close to unknown menstruation. Desperate, the head tore at the veil.

"Not seen hatching before?"

One egg barely moved, while others now disgorged their living contents. What was wrong with that one? The young scientist – his fish was safely dead. I leaned close to the still egg. *Tap*, faintly. A long silence, then a barely-there *tap*.

"This one can't get out! Can we help it?"

"No sense in that," the farmer wheezed. "A bird that can't peck its own way out isn't strong enough to live. One is no matter." From a pocket he took grain and flung a handful among the birds. They cried and pecked and snapped at each other's legs. That young scientist's fish could not flap or scream at him. "Now the pigs."

Their sty was a bigger world, walled so high that Mr McGregor threw down a block of wood for me to stand on and see. On their neat hooves the piglets rushed about, tiptoe, dancing, grunting, butting, snouting at each other, tight eyes winking, hairy triangles of ear fluting tipping twitching as the ridiculous twiddles of tail flipped up and down by their *hams*. The piglets circled and circled a wooden trough, empty, glossy along the edge where their snouts had wiped and wiped. Were the trout's scales slimy? Did the young scientist's hands smell bad?

Mr McGregor carried pails heaped with grey sludge. The piglets fought for place, shoving and squealing at his legs. He set one pail on the wall of the sty. Taking the other in one hand, he slung its contents in one cast along the length of the trough. The food vanished under the struggling pigs. "Here," he said, "give them the rest." Using both hands, I could scarcely hold the bucket. The food-smeared snouts were upturned as the pigs set their trotters on the empty trough's edge. Distracted, I took my right hand off the handle and reached for the pail's bottom, but my weaker left hand uncurled. As the thing began to slide, his huge fingers took it from me, just in time.

"Hunger can't wait, lassie." Splat – and immediate diminuendo. If pigs purred, that would be the sound. I wiped my hands on my skirt.

"Come see their old mum." He lifted me over the wall and set me down in piggy mud. In the dark warmth of the shed at the back of the sty, something slumped, like a huge pancake with silly little legs. The swollen edge nearest me erupted in coarse tall nipples. The sow's head lay half-obscured by a flopped ear; Mr McGregor scratched it with a stick, smiling. "A grand girl. Here, give her this," and he reached into a pocket. A bruised apple. At home, my mother's *Joy of Cooking* showed a suckling pig with a peach stuck in its roasted mouth. The tailor in *Struwwelpeter* had those red red lips. Now the sow's big hairy head was up, curious, her snout wrinkling, button eyes focussed on my hand. When I dropped the fruit she made one bite of it, looking at me.

"No more now." The sow nosed at his smock. He struck her, and his pockets jangled. "Get on with you, my girl."

Then, I think it was then, after goslings and pigs, before cat and kitten and hen, there was the fragrant farmhouse kitchen. Scorched currants, yeast, caramelized sugar.

"Here we are, mother, and here's the sums all done." Mr McGregor took the account books and the folder from his pocket.

Mother? Wife? A small old woman whose face I scarcely saw. Her work stood to cool on a scrubbed-to-whiteness table, its edges bevelled by decades of hands. Cottage loaves, brown bread, scones, and what at school was called a Chelsea. A mug of milk was tepid at my lips. Residual cow-warmth? I couldn't drink any more, then.

"Same milk as in town, girl." Mr McGregor sat down heavily. His limping leg stuck out straight, and then the woman scurried away. Was she frightened? Why?

On our way to the barn the silence between me and the farmer worried me, remembering the conversational grace of my mother and Miss Jones, at lunch.

"How did you hurt your leg, Mr McGregor?"

"War."

In the hayloft, warmth – or was that the shame of having asked such a bad question? *He said there was a mother cat up here.* Straw scratched my neck, stuck in my clothes. Dust coated throat nose mouth. The barn's rafters and the streaks of sun between them were as beautiful, as hard to count as those in our cedar cottage at home. In Canada and in England, if I lay just so I could feel the stripes of cool shadow and thin sun. Cow smell, horse smell, an occasional stamp, a jangle of harness and click of hoof, the regular scrapes and dumps as the farmer wielded a pitchfork in the gloom below.

In that placemat story Mr McGregor would not appear, unless the hunt crossed his fields, did damage. I must have hurt his feelings. A farmer would not study that scientist's fish. He would gut, behead, scale. (*My father – critical, sceptical – read from the map the numbers of faraway roads, and pointed sharply: "Now Rachel, to the left."*) Where was the mother cat? Where was Miss Jones? She would handle the fish dextrously. (*My mother drove fast between tall flowery hedges, steering, gesturing. Where?*) I stretched, and the mother cat's claws raked the length of my forearm.

Jerking back, I hit my head on a post. My skull sang. Lynx, wildcat – a madly-patched calico with tufted ears and flaring copper eyes and every tooth on display, framing her scarlet gullet. A small thin cat, fur furiously on end. Between her legs squirmed curls of orange and black and white. She raised her paw: rampant.

My voice was a continuous murmuring softness, and, though I wanted to hold my bleeding arm and my head, my hands stayed still. What lovely kittens, what a clever cat to have them, how proud you must be, and they're so beautiful because you are. . . . I wanted so much to stroke her coat of many colours, but that animal resisted everything that a childhood full of cats had taught me. (Tiger and Willow were now with my uncle in Hamilton. Were they happy?) She did eventually sit, and her crazy fur subsided. She abruptly licked a kitten but stayed on guard, glaring.

"A fine mouser," came Mr McGregor's voice, below. "Won't talk to you, eh?" The tines of his pitchfork glinted in the dim hallway, scored with gutters running the length of the barn. Stalls and storage rooms opened off. Glossy horse-rumps shifted back and forth. Tack and tools, bundles and stacks and tanks and barrels, fodder mash grains seeds swill. In this world, the calico in her patchy camouflage would prowl and rush. She sliced mouse-squeaks in two. Thin and strong, she leapt to her babies with the juicy crunch clenched in her teeth, the tail stringing out. How would it be to hunt? To ride thundering over hedges and brooks, mad with the hounds and the frenzied fox? To be the fox? At home, once kittens could stagger about, we set out a plate of thin pablum and held a dipped finger to a small curious mouth, edging towards the dish, luring the young tongue to the strange not-mother-milk that was good, so good.

"Don't you feed her, Mr McGregor? She's so thin."

A wheezy laugh. "Barn cat feeds herself. Milking time she gets a good drink."

On the floor near his jabbing fork, drifted over by straw, lay something, dust bunny? hair-combings? A tiny head. Motley black and white and orange.

"Mr McGregor, a kitten by your foot! It's fallen! Is it all right?"

Wheezy laugh again. "Long way down."

"I want to see it, please, Mr McGregor."

The mother cat hissed. Only when my feet were on the ladder

did she stretch, drop, curl round her kittens and expose the rippling colour of her belly. Gated within her legs, the kittens clung and climbed for food.

The dead one's ears were minute round folds, its eyes sealed. From the fuzz of belly-fur sprouted a thread. The body was not putrescent but dried out, nearly weightless. Its left side, on which the tiny cat had met the floor, was flat as a bookend.

"Bin's there," said Mr McGregor, pointing. "Then we'll be along to the hens, get you an egg for your breakfast." He clashed his pitchfork into the rack.

The henhouse is a single memory. Underneath a living bird, my hand was caressed by fluttery softness. Then came a squeezing convulsion. Diarrhea, dirty? I wanted to pull away, but feared that wheezy laugh. The hen clucked, nudged. There was an opening, wet and wrinkled, and here was the egg. Warm, dry, hard, curved. Pale cocoa in colour, the egg's powdery surface was speckled in chocolate, lovely as the Ukrainian painted egg that came one Christmas, back home.

Then we were on our way back to Miss Jones's house.

Carrying six eggs in a small basin, I was afraid of stumbling and walked head down, staring at the stone-pocked mud.

"Now, lassie. If I took those six eggs to market, how much would I come home with?" Naming a price per egg, Mr McGregor began waiting for my reply.

Pounds and shillings and pence still bewildered me. There was also a thing called a guinea. The farmer's impatience was visible. My mother did English money easily, my father too. But why must I be questioned, as if at school? I gave up, offered an answer.

"I'm surprised at you, a girl in school and all."

That young scientist had not been required to do sums in his head. He had been good at science, had wanted to know more; that was why he had come to see the old scholar. We walked silently. I must not fall, not fail. Mrs Wilmer at St Mildred's said, "You simply don't try. Such a clever girl, but you won't add two and two." These dun fields ached for colour; a million hollow stalks left from last year's harvest had toppled everywhere, like pick-up sticks. Mr

McGregor's long limping strides took him way ahead. I must hurry. My socks were muddy. Where was Miss Jones?

"It would be different money over in Canada, I'll be bound. But you're not there now, are you?" Mr McGregor smiled.

Thousands, yes, thousands of miles of map-blue ocean swelled between me and my country. Meanwhile my father was digging in some library and my mother View Hallooing at all she saw. I had not understood what absence from her might entail. After recording any fresh insights on Keats or Shelley for his book, my father would note the day's tiny travel stats in his diary.

Somewhere Miss Lucinda Jones in her miniature and spotless house was waiting, but I was stained and sticky with egg, blood, hen-dirt, pigswill, sugar, straw, mud. Her strange green ring had sailed the sea. So had her uncles, to India, to Ireland. She, never. Even Mr McGregor had got as far as France, to bring back a wound. A dead kitten had lain on my hand, my fingers had touched a hen-hole, my arm and head hurt. I could not empty a pail or gentle a cat or multiply pence into shillings. Unlike that young scientist, I could make no good report. Who was this man that limped ahead no matter how I hastened, this man whose clothes clanked? Did the red-lipped tailor-man have pockets? Was this the way to Miss Jones's house? How would I know?

She was smiling just inside her garden gate, Barty in her arms. The cat smelled my fingers, jumped down to smell my shoes, put his ears back.

"Such lovely brown eggs, Mr McGregor. They must be Betsy's, Bertha's?"

"Right, both." He smiled.

"You have seen something of country life, Amanda." The satin eyes took me in.

"Didn't do bad, for a town girl."

"For you." Miss Jones handed over a pile of work socks.

(*Good gravy, Amanda,* my mother said. *Listen to this, Gerald. Barter! For God's sake. Genteel poverty of the gentlewoman. Can you believe the English?* And my father, *Now Rachel. They have their stations in life, both of them. They recognize each other. There's respect.*)

"I'll be off then. Milking."

"Thank you for showing Amanda, Mr McGregor." She glanced at me.

"Thank you, Mr McGregor." *(But what for? He just did what he was going to do anyway. I was just there.)*

Miss Jones's bathroom was as white as her larder.

Steam rose from the tub. Afterwards, the cold in my room struck through all my nightclothes to my skin, and I hurried down to the fireplace. Bartholomew purred in his basket. Nearby stood a little brass coal scuttle. In Canadian December and February there were snowy dawns when *the coal came;* thousands of black nuggets tumbled down a chute into the cellar. The sound here was of a light spring rain.

Miss Jones and I ate our fish before the fire on a gate-legged table. Our knees knocked, and we laughed.

"It's like playing house with Emily," she said.

The fillets lay neatly brown and white, with home-dried parsley sifted over top and a dab of sharp sauce on the side – utterly different from the bony wet-your-pants glue served on Fridays at school. The sweet flesh shaled off in curves, like ripples of sand at the edge of Lake Muskoka. Miss Jones served me twice. Then she brought in (a breath of chill air from the larder came too) the dish of custard, plus a perforated silver sugar-shaker and an odd metal thing. We coated the custard with brown sugar.

"Now, Amanda, put the salamander in the flame." Lovely word! The circle of closely-set wires turned scarlet. If we held it too near the dish, the sugar collapsed and burned; too far, nothing happened; just right, the stuff relaxed into caramel.

"All you need is practice," said Miss Jones, inspecting the blotchy *crème brûlée.* We laughed. She gave me a second helping and told me the legend of the salamander, which lay dark and cold on the tray while I stroked Bartholomew. His fur was hot.

My bedroom was like a playhouse, too. Sloped ceilings and dormers were familiar from home, but there the attic spread out wide and high. Here, the bed's pillow end was in the middle of the room; anyone sleeping the other way would hit her head if she even turned over. To see in the mirror, I must bend. Dresser, chair, and wash-stand stood tight in the only possible nooks.

A last eye-blink showed Miss Jones setting my slippers neatly on the rag rug.

Hours later, the little room was moonlit. The rain had stopped. I needed the bathroom. Fur warmed my right hand. *Where am I?* Bartholomew's purr told. I went to the door, en route hitting my head. *I'm too big for here*, though wherever I looked was lovely, curi-ous, perfect. Outside the window were all the stars, and on the sill stood other tiny things: a worn silver thimble; a tiger, its woodgrain emulating stripes; a lump of amber (the moon had bled its colour); a Dresden shepherdess. I could take handfuls of this stuff, handfuls, and all would fit in my Indian box. Another small thing fell at my touch, a hollow sphere of fragrant sandalwood inside which rolled another carved ball. The cat skittered after it into under-bed darkness.

Cold passage. Cold toilet. Should I flush? Would Miss Jones wake up? If I didn't flush, would she be appalled in the morning? Cold. That odour again. How the ice on the pussy willows shone, at lunch! Back home we skated by moonlight at Varsity Stadium. The band played "Blue Danube" and "Take Me Out to the Ball Game." Perhaps the moon shone on those branches now. Did the table's satin pool reflect the stars? Down the stairs I went to see, with the warm bulk of Bartholomew's curiosity brushing my leg. The dark hallway led to moonlight, and the iced pussy willows made a shining filigree on the wood.

Miss Jones sat at table. Her napkin was tied round her neck so the lace triangle lay on the middle of her flat chest. Her rosebud plate, piled high with chicken, potatoes, fish, sludge, rested atop her hunting scene. The *crème brûlée* and a big spoon waited. Miss Jones's knife and fork were balanced in her long thin digits. She gobbled noisily. Her eyes glittered like the branches. They glittered with tears.

The Margins Are The Frame

E arly in the English time, I was taken to see a church whose clock tower was ringed with statues. Rotating as the chimes sounded, they wound into an invisible place and out again, as they had done for centuries. From all the angles of the building, gargoyles protruded.

The Green House too was old, with doors everywhere, named, numbered, closed to conceal other closed doors, or stairs or halls – no, *passages*. Things everywhere were covered – the piano in the lounge, the lavatory paper, the dinner gong in the lobby. Except for Miss Clyde, the residents were mostly old ladies, obese or skeletal. Shining jet hung on Miss Apple's dress. Just like Dickens's Miss Murdstone! Miss Orr, Mrs More. Mrs Bracegirdle, whose son lived in Manitoba. The Talbot twins, Milly and Tilly, had dressed to match for seventy-seven years. Daily they raced through *The Times* crossword. Dr and Mrs Ledington, lemurs in glasses *spectacles*, peered shyly from dim corners. Mr Penrose stood tall and prim. His scarlet knuckles looked painful.

Mrs K, the proprietor, was all knobs and elbows, talk, smoke, abrupt gestures. She twisted her cardigan-fronts till they hung like rags, while her black cat Pinky clawed at her buttons. "Get away, beast!" He flinched at her thrust cigarette. She told stories.

My father wondered if there had been a Mr K. If so, where was he? "And how that Irishwoman does murder the King's English!"

"*Murther*," my mother replied. They laughed.

Next to my tiny room in the hotel was Professor McGeachie's. Eleven years old, eighty. His body: a jar of Greek on the centuries' shelves. For decades he had tipped the tongue into younger containers, then retired. At his privileged seat in dining room or lounge, print pen paper were always near. "The tools of his trade," my father admired. The Professor's hands shook, showing jagged nails. He spilled, mopped sloppily. Tobacco stuck to his waistcoat. Mrs K said, "Professor, your waterglass, it'll tip, then where will we be? Finish your potatoes. Give me that disgraceful tie." Later she came upstairs with the faded strip smelling of benzine. Once, when he whispered a question, she snapped, "Special services, special rates, Professor. I'll hear no complaints." Martha the housemaid's room was near mine too, off a passage labelled *Staff Private*. She served at breakfast luncheon dinner, made beds, scrubbed loos. (I must never say *toilet*.) She washed up, hoovered (another new word), distributed laundry, hung towels on heated racks, polished brasses, and on Saturday at eleven brought to each resident's room a cup of horrid bouillon. She had buck teeth. In the presence of any man, she hardly spoke. Everyone called her Martha. She said Mr Professor Mrs Miss. Fair tendrils curled out from her hairnet, and she smelled sweet.

Always, Martha had only a minute to talk. "O today Mrs K's in such a bate about the dustbins!" She meant garbage cans. "Old witch." Old older oldest. In The Green House there were no other children. Martha was perhaps nineteen, twenty.

At coffee hour I reported the gibberish of St Mildred's house names – Alpha, Beta, Gamma, Delta – to my parents.

Professor McGeachie's head snapped up from *The Scotsman*. "The Greek alphabet," he reproved. "Don't you know that?"

"At least I'm not in Epsilon. It's the unpopular house."

"The beginning of learning, alpha beta." The Professor, teaching now, was affable. "The first step to Low Goes." The old ladies and the lemurs and my parents all laughed.

My father said, "Amanda, look." Smiling, he wrote *logos* on a back page of his Sheets & Kelly notebook. "*Word*. Isn't that Maynard woman teaching you anything?"

"*Maywood*, Daddy. Latin. We juniors don't learn Greek."

"What about 'In the beginning was the word'? You know that, surely." He and the Professor then went back to the recent decipherment of Linear B. To be ignorant – what could be worse? At St Mildred's, *baby* and *know-nothing* were common insults. Back home, we'd shouted *iggeramus*.

On weekdays as I left for school, Mrs K knelt at the front door with her tools alongside: lemon oil, ammonia, paste for the tile floor. A cigarette stuck to her lip, oozing smoke. She scowled. "Tell you a story, later." Pinky skulked about.

Unlike my father, who was ceremonious in his rare storytelling, or my mother, who read aloud vividly, Mrs K just said flat out what happened at the Irish castle where she'd worked as a young girl. *At first snowfall my lady's diamond necklace disappeared. Not stolen, not lost. You could see it inside one of the huge icicles hanging outside the dining hall. Then, at first thaw next spring, the necklace was back in that blue velvet box.* To hear this aloud, not just to read its like in the *Green Fairy Book*, the *Yellow*, the *Red* – entrancing.

"Rubbish," said my mother, at coffee-hour.

My father sighed. "Irish flim-flam, Amanda. Not even real romance."

When Martha came in to collect the tray, the Professor asked for more coffee. Wordlessly she tipped up the carafe to show that it was empty.

"A sweet lass," he said, smiling, as she left the lounge. His old mouth was loose, quivery. Mrs K's lips met in a tight seam, Martha's pouched out over her teeth.

Was there a Mrs McGeachie? "Long gone," my mother said. "They were divorced." This ugly new word went on the list at the back of the notebook designated by St Mildred's for Practice Work. Mrs K's own history, though, stayed hidden. *Once at the castle,* she said, *a woman's arm in a long white glove slid down the banister. At the newel post, the hand stopped. Stretched, as if the lady fitted her fingers more comfortably. Full day it was. I was at my dusting. Then it disappeared.*

My mother rolled her eyes. "Dusting, forsooth!"

In Practice Work I wrote down Mrs K's stories, embellished with the longest words possible. Could I fill all the pages, make a real book? The list grew. *Amaranth, ignoble, crystal, vicissitude.*

The clock strikes one
They've just begun

One Saturday morning, I was following Martha about from room to room.

"Take this bouillon to the Professor, please miss? I'm behind, and she's ratty."

His room was all papery litter, books, journals, typescripts. A smell of tobacco, of scorch. Toast? And of something nasty, but surely that couldn't be.

"A sweet frock, Amanda." The old man smiled. I got out. Back in my own room, I lay on my bed to eat a Crunchie and re-enter *The Queen Elizabeth Story* and thus get away, away. The Professor's soup-cup chattered annoyingly in its saucer, but I was too comfortable to get up and close my door.

There came a hint of cigarette smoke, and then Mrs K hissed, "Dangerous, Professor! See this sheet?" Flap. "Ruined. That electric fire. Warned you and warned you, I have. Are we all to burn in our beds? If you go on like this you can't stay." A deep inhale. "Who'd take you in? Who'd put up with you-know-what?" Exhale.

Soon the Professor would attend a College Dinner. The gargoyles and the lemurs and my parents enthused about the gown he would wear, the special velvet hat.

"He'll walk into that historic Great Hall. Built in 1513, Amanda. Imagine!" My father yearned. "He'll walk in the procession of his peers."

Sometimes Martha did not serve at dinner. Then Mrs K's anger smoked through the swing door to the kitchen. "Made every allowance. Thinks she can run off. A girl in her situation."

"What does she mean, Mum?"

"Get your arithmetic prep, Amanda. I'll go over it with you."

"What does it mean?" That was when the Professor read Greek aloud to us.

"I'll translate, dear girl." His dirty thumb inched along the twiggy shapes. His mind ate up the Greek, and English came out of his Scots mouth. Bewildering. Only *Ajax* made any sense. "Thursdays," he said finally, "poor Thursdays. The ugliest man." He set down the text. Word-eater. Logos-eater. At the back of my school poetry book was *The Lotos Eaters*, but "Lotos" wasn't even in the dictionary.

"But what does it say?"

"Not now, Amanda." My father and the Professor began to discuss *Cymbeline*.

That I did recognize, for Miss Pruitt of Literature and Composition had made us memorize an alphabetical list of all the plays. What or who was a *Cymbeline*, though? Iggeramus. Back home in Canada, my social studies text had shown a painting of feathery naked Indians who knelt amazed and dazed before priests dangling written scrolls. The word of God. *Vaulted, diapason, engraved, harmony.*

* * *

Lord receive us with thy blessing
Once again assembled here.

So we sang, on my first day at St Mildred's.

I laid out my History notebook as taught to at home, with *The Renaissance and the New Learning. September 17, 1951* centred on the top line. "Your page is a picture," my Canadian teacher had said. "The margins frame your text." I left a white border all round and wrote double-spaced. Now Miss Trout, not teacher but mistress, not fishy but red-fleshed with a chin full of blackheads, glared. "In the colonies perhaps you can waste paper like this. We've been through a War. Bonny, show her."

This girl was a smug-smiling nail-biter with braids. No, plaits. Her page was filled single-space to all edges and headed *Renesonts*. Unpopular Bonny looked up then to smirk at popular Tessa Janet Helen. These three – Pretty, Spiteful, and Tall – were the powers of the Third Form. That language I knew. Though we all spoke English, no one else spoke as I did. Either their speech was strange, or. Soon the bell rang for the end of History.

The clock strikes two
They're kissing like glue

Unexpectedly, Miss Pruitt took in our Practice Works. Already I was grateful to her for her rose-lipped smile, and for reading aloud to us a wonderful book about a cat called Jenny, and for pointing out the long hard poems at the back of our poetry book. (My father approved of "St Agnes' Eve" but of "To A Skylark" he declared, "Too predictable.") Shockingly Miss Pruitt wrote, in capitals, clear across my word-list, "Use plain English!" She studded Mrs K's tales with red interrogation marks. Worst, in front of the whole form she wagged her finger at me. "The Irish are notoriously superstitious, Amanda. Don't waste time on fantasies."

Yet another surprise came when, on a day seemingly like any other, no girl at St Mildred's would talk to me. No girl even looked me in the eye. The hours ached with their length. Sent to Coventry – I'd read about this, in school stories. Arithmetic was the day's last lesson. English fractions were as bad as Canadian, English money a cruel enigma. Then my mother was waiting for me in the school's courtyard. At home I'd always liked it when she picked me up, but now, smiling among the English mothers, in her purple tweed suit, she was clearly all wrong.

"Such a strong colour." Next morning, pretty Tessa's voice faded out in falsely-polite regret on the word *culla*. Helen just stared. The other girls waited, stared.

"Not really *quite*." That was spiteful Janet, with Bonny nodding. Quite what?

On my way home that day, I got off the bus and drifted through the Children's Bookshop and Woolworth's. A violent and novel urge to steal burned in me.

The clock strikes three
She's on his knee

In an early Latin lesson, Miss Maywood went round the form-room to identify all the girls whose names had roots in the great language.

"To be loved," she said. "A gerund, girls. You will study those in the Upper Fourth. A sweetly pretty name, Amanda."

"TBL," giggled Pretty and Spiteful and many strangers, at Buns-And-Milk. Soon though they abandoned that game and began pinching each other.

"TBL," chanted Bonny. "Oh I say, sweetly pretty TBL. So funny, isn't it, Janet? Isn't it?" But the trio had moved on, leaving Bonny alone on a remote periphery.

On another day Miss Maywood paced across the front of our classroom and pronounced, "*Ambulo*. Helen, come here, please." The mistress tucked gangly Helen's arm under hers, covered in nubbly maroon wool. The two began to pace. "*Ambulamus*," said the mistress, "*ambulamus.*" She let go. Helen sat down. From the blackboard, we all copied the utter strangeness of *ambulo ambulas ambulat ambulamus ambulatis ambulant*. Helen copied a few words only. Then she snickered. Everyone laughed, not at her.

"Girls," said Miss Maywood. Silence. Bonny still laughed and peered about for approval, but the lone sound failed. "Girls, observe the stem."

At lunch, big girls speculated about those maroon nubbles. Did Miss Maywood's titty-tips fit right into two of them? Or was there a bra? A prefect reported, "I can only see her petticoat straps, but her bosoms are enormous. Surely?"

Vibrant, pinions, contemplative, squander, squalid. For some days *stem* was unclear to me, like *stodge, prep, ST* said in a furtive tone, and *tuckshop*. Soon though I learned *sweets*, not candy. *Crunchies, Mars Bars, Flakes*, I bought and tried them all.

"You must have a lot of pocket money," Bonny said.

"Would you like a bite?"

"Ugh, where you've bitten already? Tessa, isn't that disgusting, Tessa?"

"You're disgusting, Bonny. We all know your father only pays half-fees, because he's a clergyman." Hearing this I felt hot, radiant. Stealing a Crunchie at Woolworth's that day brought even more radiance.

Latin, History, Geography.

To come top in anything at St Mildred's was not possible because of my handwriting. The mistresses disapproved of the vertical script taught me in Canada; they set me to sloping. To maintain my own way did not occur to me. I tried leftwards. "A shopgirl's hand," ruled Miss Lincoln, Geography. "Vulgar," seconded Miss Pruitt, her pink lips pouting, but when my round letters tried to lean rightwards they wobbled. The downstrokes wouldn't align. Marks evaporated from my exercises and tests.

"Pity," remarked Helen, by the noticeboard where the fortnightly class standings descended like flights of stairs. Bonny elbowed in, giggling. Spiteful and Pretty paid no attention. "Composition, first, not Amanda. History, ditto."

Bonny cried, "Jolly good, Janet, you're fifth in Latin." Helen turned away, her aquiline nose indicating contempt. Her own name was well down on all the lists.

In Geography we studied Australia – thank goodness, not Canada. The big world map was just the same as at school back home, but there my own country spread out solidly around me. Here, I was away. The slender capitals of ATLANTIC OCEAN made no solid bridge between Ireland and Newfoundland, though the pretty script resembled that on Sweet Marie chocolate bars. Regularly now I stole candy, even from a little shop whose owners knew Mrs K, knew my mother. The place was dark and crammed with goods, just as in *Alice Through The Looking-Glass*. Sometimes with my illicit handful of boiled sweets I walked further down the Polstead Road and on to Port Meadows on the city's western margin. Its unfamiliar beauty comforted me. Back at the hotel, I hid my treasures on my bookshelf, behind a hot-water bottle in a flowered case.

Needlework. Science. Religious Knowledge. A girl called Ruth once called it Scripture, and right away a blush rose through Miss Flower's pale skin. "I'm afraid that is the Chapel term," she whispered, pink as Northern Rhodesia.

Winnowing, Saracen, repugnant, nocturnal, lipless.

* * *

As Martha set down the coffee-tray in the lounge, I got up.

"*Ambulo.*"

"*Ambulas, puella,*" the Professor approved. My parents smiled. To study the classics was good – yet my father had said *that Maynard woman.*

"*Ambulamus,* Martha!" I took her arm, laughing.

We stepped awkwardly. Soon she pulled away. "What is it then, miss?"

"We walk!"

The clock strikes four
They're on the floor

In the lobby, Mrs K was scowling at Martha. "She's off to see her baby *brother*, Amanda." The proprietor exhaled. "Lucky you are, to have a place like this. Many a girl in your situation hasn't."

Martha's hair shone in the wet lamplight as she unfurled her umbrella. "But it's natural, to be with a sick babe."

Mrs K flicked ash. "Time's long past to think about natural, Martha. Your day off is *not* tomorrow. Consider yourself warned."

The maid covered her teeth. Flap, her umbrella flared up. *Puella. Femina. Mulier.*

Near the castle, Mrs K said in the dark of my small room, *lived a woman whose husband died in the dead of winter. You know, Amanda, how a window must be opened after a death, to let the soul out? The widow's cottage was frozen shut, though, and the snow heaped up so she couldn't open the window. Not even a crack, all the night long. The neighbours found her next afternoon, but by then she wasn't right in her wits. He'd been a hard man, mind you.*

My mother said, "This Catholic claptrap goes too far."

"Amanda just takes it as story, Rachel. A little cheap romance. Nothing to worry about." When I lay awake retelling Mrs K's tales, his words returned. Sometimes they weren't enough. Then I got up to wander alone about the nighttime quiet of the hotel.

Next day, near dinnertime, Martha and I met at the juncture of our two hallways. She was rain-wet, breathless with haste. We hid. Mrs K berated the Professor.

"She's not here. You must wait." A long murmur. "No complaints! I've a heavy load, not a soul to bear it with me, and the girl's gone gallivanting while I've nine tables for dinner. Stop. Or I'll tell. Yes, I'll tell those Canadians you're so fond of that you dirty yourself like a baby." Slam. Footsteps, heading downstairs.

Then Martha plodded wordless to her room. I moved around the passages, hearing through the residents' doors the murmurs of their boring unintelligible talk or the tinny sounds of radios. Boring. . . . I knocked at the maid's door. She took me by the ear and marched me to the sign. *Staff Private.* "Can't you read? I'm worn out. Soon I must face her. Leave me be, miss. Leave me be."

Corrupt, ember, asphodel, sanctity.

Martha plodded. Mrs K moved as silently as a snake. Before you even noticed, she could be standing right there, but nearly always the telltale smoke gave her away.

Clutching his stick, Professor McGeachie tottered to the pillar box at the corner to drop in small manila envelopes. Their contents came back transformed into booklets thin with text, huge with footnotes. "A fine monograph, sir!" my father said warmly. "I hope to have one of my own ready soon. Early thoughts, on the correspondence."

Sometimes other post slipped under the residents' doors.

"Mrs K's raised the rates all round," my mother reported. "The poor old boy."

My father threw up his hands. "What a harridan!"

"I'll speak to her."

From the landing I saw my mother approach Mrs K's glass-fronted office. An official smile, a listening look, a frown, a head-shake, words, words.

I went upstairs to look up *harridan* and to hide my candy, because Martha was about to give my room what she called *a good turnout.* To dust she took all the books off the shelves. Putting them back, she sorted by size, so paperback *Swallowdale* stood by paper *Five Children And It*, not by its sister *Great Northern.*

"Mum, has Martha got a baby brother?"

"Martha had a baby without being married." The words seemed

hard to say, as if my mother were pushing a heavy door. "A son. Mrs K is very kind to employ her."

Mrs K told about *a bad girl, who had a baby that she shouldn't and left it on the church steps in a freezing December. As she walked away, the baby cried. Poor mite! From then on, every year on the baby's birth- and death-day, that girl had to come back there, had to sit on the stone steps to hear the chimes and the baby's cries. No matter where in the whole wide world the girl was, that day, she had to come.* This story I did not share.

The clock strikes five
They're feeling all alive

"But Mum, where is he?"

"In the country. A woman who does that kind of work looks after him. Martha spends her Mondays there."

"A classic tale of female foolishness," said my father. "To learn too late that men betray, etcetera."

"Gerald," said my mother. He fell silent.

Tuesday was laundry: delightful ritual. On my unmade bed I set my list (*Blouses 5, Pyjamas 2*) and my piled dirty underclothes, socks, towels. When I got home after school, magically in place of that messy pile lay last week's donation, fresh, ironed, starched, and wrapped in shiny buff paper.

Now there came another and larger list of clothes, from St Mildred's, because soon my parents were off to the Lake District to do research. Then they would go north, to Edinburgh, carrying letters of introduction from the Professor. At last I'd be inside St Mildred's. A boarder, I would walk in the procession of my peers. Briskly my mother counted pairs, half-dozens. We sewed on Cash's name tapes.

"What on earth is a liberty bodice?" This item was listed under Senior Girls.

"A bra." Shame, that I knew but my mother did not.

"Say *brassière*, dear." In Canada the big girls said brazeer; she didn't even know that. "Well, that's one thing you don't need." My mother's look was loving. "I'll write lots of letters to you, dear. Remember what your name means."

Friday, by St Mildred's timetable, was Out Early day. For me it meant theft. At Boots, I got Yardley's "Lily of the Valley." Such a pretty bottle! I set it on my dresser.

My mother shook it in my face. "You said you'd spent your allowance. No stories, now. How did you buy this perfume?"

"*Pocket money. Scent.* Mum, does Martha get a lot of money for working here?"

"Don't try to change the subject. Of course not."

"Is Mrs K rich?"

"Answer me!"

"But Mum, Martha has a baby. She walks miles. Mrs K's mean to her."

"Stop whining. I'm taking this perfume. I have no more to say to you, Amanda."

Then she went out to tea with Miss Clyde, a strange choice of companion. The lady accountant looked exactly so, with her rimless glasses and all-fawn clothes. She never seemed to smile, yet my mother said appreciatively, "She has a wry humour."

Thus I was left behind to sulk in the lounge while the lemurs blinked and the gargoyles knitted sipped. Martha brought in hot Eccles cakes that oozed butter and sugar; my father and Mr Penrose teased each other about who could eat more. The maid bent close, smiling at me, to point out a specially crisp cake.

Unthinking I asked, "What's your baby's name?"

Did everyone hear? Yes. Of course. Bright red, Martha hurriedly took the empty platter out of the lounge. Desperately I ran upstairs, grabbed Maltesers and *The Woolpack* to fill my mouth and eyes, and tried to get away, away.

A key slid into my door. Pale Martha, hissing.

"Save your sweets, don't you?" She nodded at the bookcase. "I heard them talk, I did. 'O, Amanda wouldn't steal'" – and she parodied my father's fond tone. "And your mum, 'She had no money.' I know what I know, miss. Sweets, scent. I'll bide my time." She left. My mouth was empty. I couldn't read.

The clock strikes six
Dix to dix

On Saturdays, Martha changed the linen and collected paper refuse. Big wicker baskets stood along the passages, awaiting their burdens.

Drifting behind her into the Professor's room, I scanned his Greek shelves and fingered the greenish coins stacked on his desk. To touch: that was how the pleasure began, the pleasure that ended in taking. His laundry list lay by the money. *Cloths 24.* "Snooping again, miss?" Martha rinsed a white metal pail at the tiny sink. "Tell me, what does this say?" At the foot of the list was a handwritten scraggle.

With some effort I made it out. *"Less starch."*

"Old fuss-budget." She tipped disinfectant into the pail. Then while the green coins poured in a pretty waterfall from my left hand to my right, she shook out the wastebasket: typescript, manuscript, newsprint, aerogrammes, onion skin, book jackets, fluttering paper speckled with crossword anagrams and Greek. Logos-eater. "Money!" Martha snapped. "That's your ABC, that's the be-all and end-all." Her teeth showed. "Dirty old man. And stingy. Mr Penrose, he's different. He has a kind heart."

A leather bag of money, said Mrs K at the end of a wandering tale of robbers and grief. *Underneath the floorboards. All those years of hearing the footsteps, all the years of shame, and there was the money. More than enough for everything they wanted, but of course too late.*

"What's a be-all, Martha?"

"Hush." She listened. "There's the witch, shouting." She brushed past me, smelling of fields.

Parallel, multitudinous, contemptuous, carcase, Samarkand.

That night was the Professor's College Dinner.

Towards dusk, the proprietor stepped to his room and rapped smartly. A whiff of smoke glided under my door.

"Damn it, woman, I can't go. I'll shit myself."

"Nonsense! A grand time it'll be. You've taken nothing all day, and you've been to the loo a dozen times I'm sure. Martha's wrapped you well. Enjoy yourself, man! Think of the port. It's past the century mark, I'm told."

A long sigh, and then the Professor's quoting tone: "*Thursday's body is as good as Ajax, When neither is alive.* Poor Thursdays."

"The taxicab's waiting. No more time! Here's your hat."

I slipped out of my room and downstairs, to join the audience in the lobby.

Robed and descending, the Professor looked tall. Scarlet flared out from the blackness of his rustling gown. One hand gripped the banister, the other his stick. His hat was a squashy black velvet square, tilted. My father's eyes shone. At each downward step, my mother patted her heart in relief and then tensed while his next foot felt the air.

Reaching the lobby, he smiled at me. "*Ambulamus?*" He crooked his arm.

My parents poked at me. Horrid old baby! As his robes brushed my thigh, I felt thick padding. Did Martha lay him legs-in-air to change him? Were there pins? Were there rubber pants, knickers? I cringed and pulled my arm away.

"Amanda!"

The clock strikes seven
It's like heaven

Very quiet The Green House was, in the middle of the night. I couldn't sleep, though I'd finished *Pigeon Post* again and had imagined several of Mrs K's stories.

A girl I knew at the castle had worked in a house where there were two ghosts. In the pantry, she'd be lifting down a jar of cherries from the shelf, or some groats, and there would come a presence. Cold, like a cloud in the room. A sad feeling. A maid had died there, years before. And the other was in the garden by a holly tree. Evil trees those are, Amanda, with their drops of God's blood. On autumn evenings a young man leaned his hand on the trunk of the holly, moaning. My eyes felt gritty. Unbearable, to close them. So – I went wandering.

Light edged a few of the silent doors. Did the old people sleep with their bedside lamps lit? Or had they died, reading? Down the stairs, alone, on my nocturnal route. In the kitchen, the stoves and the cold flagstones looked huge, and so did the shrouded tables in the dining room, as if giants cooked and ate there. To the side of the lobby, Mrs K sat in her glass-frosted den. Sometimes at this hour she wrote but more often clacked at an adding machine. Pinky snoozed. A cigarette smoked in the ashtray. All as usual – but the proprietor's hands hid her face. Her shoulders jerked. The papers before her were dotted with red. Crying over sums – well, I knew all about that.

Pinky put his ears back, hissed. Mrs K looked up. Such a gargoyle, distorted, creased, gaunt. "Stupid beast, get away!" She threw crumpled paper. The cat ran. So did I. At the top of the stairs stood Martha. Her arms were tight, her wrapper fragrant.

"There, there now," she crooned, "the old witch can't get you."

Soon I was warm in my bed. "Martha. I'm so sorry."

She smiled so her teeth showed fully. "He's William, miss. My sweet boy."

* * *

At St Mildred's, many girls picked on the stranger with the strange tongue, but everyone picked on Bonny, even though not a few other girls were as dull, myopic, and bad at games as she. In Singing, Helen Tessa Janet generated such laughter at *Speed bonny boat / Like a bird on the wing* that Miss Munro had to abandon the forlorn prince and smash into *D'ye ken John Peel*. At lessons, Bonny's books disappeared, her inkwell toppled, burnt umber and vermilion vanished from her paintbox. The girl who sat behind Bonny daily, patiently, unstitched her tunic's hem. In the dormitory, the trio jeered repeatedly at the photo of Bonny's parents by their vicarage, gazing mildly at the camera, and at Bonny's own plump self on a pony at the village gymkhana.

Yet Bonny persisted. She followed Janet Helen Tessa about, pushed elbowed agreed echoed applauded until the trio brutally drove her off. Still back she came, and courageously back again, determined to come in from the cold margins. It was as if she believed herself spellbound to tasks imposed by the superpowers. Her faith was sure that, her trials once completed, she would pass into the inner world of the real story, the world of acceptance, and be able to slam its door in my face.

Bonny's hair was stringy. Mine was much too short.

"Dear, it'll grow in no time," my mother said. There was none. School was now. Her own hair curved in a pretty French roll.

"Really quite a boy's cut, Amanda's, isn't it, Helen?" Tessa was combing her curls before the mirror in the daygirls' loo, a space that the boarders invaded at will.

"I guess so." Helen used my *peculiar* Canadian idiom, not looking at Bonny or me but gazing out the window at the flower beds, faded now, brown with autumn. She twisted at a lock of her own lank hair.

Bonny cried, "Say I *guess*, Amanda!" and looked about eagerly.

Janet's sharp voice rose from a cubicle. "Ooo, someone's not wrapped an ST." Her hand flipped over the cubicle's door, holding a white thick twist, bandage-like, bloody. Screams erupted. "Ugh, ugh, putrid!" The thing flipped out of sight again.

"I *guess* Amanda doesn't know what it is."

"Nor Bonny. Look at her silly face!"

For us two to share the same bewildered look was intolerable. Not to speak was worse than to speak and be laughed at.

"I do too. It's because of babies." First bell sounded. The trio screeched, laughed, ran, Helen with a surprised and curious glance at me. Bonny followed, in tears.

Happy because I was not an ignoramus, and with minutes in hand until second bell, I took up *The Far-Distant Oxus*. This familiar title had welcomed me in the junior common room, on whose shelves Anne Emily Jane Marigold Pat, Mary Laura Carrie, Meg Jo Amy Beth did not appear. No STs appeared in books, either, not in Canada or here. I opened the book and got away.

The clock strikes eight
Doctor's at the gate

On my first night as a boarder, when I slipped into bed my legs couldn't stretch out. Puzzled, I kicked. The sheet ripped. From Bonny, loud giggles. From Spiteful and Pretty, distant amusement as they chatted on Helen's bed. Apple-pie – I'd read of this too. Bonny laughed until Lights Out. Then Helen said, "Stop that row. Stop."

I lay awake. To make up a story about Bonny, to tell it abroad. . . . To the dormitory prefect I said that the sheet had torn when I had a nightmare.

Molten, saffron, pageant, zodiac.

While boarding I could close no door for solitude, so I wrote about Bonny during prep, and on Sundays after the hour in which we produced our compulsory and censored letters home. Puce shreds of erasure silted up the gutter of my notebook as I sought the meanest, most horrible words. A discovery – if I stared for a bit at Bonny's pigtails and fat legs, the next sentences would go well. The pages thickened with pencil. I didn't fear Miss Pruitt would read them, either, because I'd got my mother to buy an extra Practice Work notebook that I kept separately in my desk.

She wrote to me from Windermere and Edinburgh.

"Your mother *types* her letters to you?" Janet was disbelieving.

At the mirror, Tessa tightened the belt of her tunic. "How peculiar."

My mother's handwriting was a joke, alike among family and friends and her editing clientele, but it hardly seemed the moment to explain that.

"You'd think you were a shop." Janet.

"It's quicker," Tessa supposed. "*My* mother says the nicest time in her week is the whole morning she spends writing to me."

"Isn't it peculiar?" Bonny. "Does your mother *work*, Amanda? In an office?"

An illegitimate Bonny, an adopted Bonny – this vision arrived. My story would be a million times better. How soon was prep?

"Does your father type too, Amanda?"

"Bonny, you are so utterly wet. Men don't type." Helen stalked off, nose in air.

Bonny's story did fill all the pages. It was a real book.

The clock strikes nine
Nappies on the line

Rejected by her unmarried mother, who detested her child of sin on first sight, she lay for months and months in a squalid orphanage. The contemptuous staff wanted her to go, but the would-be adoptive parents always chose better-looking babies.

When Bonny had grown into a fat ugly child, at last an ignoble pair did choose her. They were utterly wet. Also, they only adopted because a childless married vicar would be peculiar, and because Bonny was old enough to be out of nappies. Soon they sent her away, to St Mildred's.

Here I hesitated, wanting to put *because she smelled and was deeply repugnant to them.* Older girls sometimes did smell. Each boarder had an enamel wash basin, but none would expose her body to the view of others by daylight. Only one ten-minute bath per girl was scheduled weekly; the tubs were scored with a low line above which water must not rise. Mistresses patrolled the lockless bath cubicles, checking. However, like me, Bonny did not yet bleed, so I had to leave out *because she smelled.* Satisfaction welled up from a long way down. My words were pictures, my margins were the frame.

One afternoon after games I told Bonny, "I know a secret about you." There. The words were out, unrecallable. We walked down the hockey pitch to sit sweatily behind the goal. The story, I said, was based on a magazine article on adoption that I'd read back home in Canada. Surprised, I'd realized recently that I was at the same school, even in the very same form, as the featured English girl.

Together we read my text. She turned the thick pages. "Were there photos?" Bonny sobbed, scrubbing at her eyes with a snot-caked square of Irish linen.

The answer arrived at once. "Yes, that one of you at the gymkhana." Bonny cried harder. Removing the book from her hands, I got up. "I haven't decided about showing it. To Tessa, I mean. And Janet, and Helen."

The end of term neared.

At mealtimes, I stared at Bonny across the Dining Hall until she turned away from me, her red eyes bulging under thick glass. I ate extra everything.

While we sat in our form room awaiting our History test, Tessa asked, "Amanda, what did you do to Bonny?" Girls looked at us. At *us*. "It must have been jolly good."

"*Jolly* good." Janet giggled.

Helen's look was thoughtful. I shrugged and gazed hard at Bonny. She was crying already. Bells chimed, the strong figures rotated around the clock tower and disappeared into the inner sanctum. Might I truly go in?

That night I treated myself to Callard & Bowser and *The Voyage of the Dawn Treader* in the flashlit warmth of my bed, but at our dormitory's far end Bonny cried on and on. Because of the noise, Lucy and Aslan did not become real. I couldn't get away.

Loudly next morning at chapel we all sang, "Lord, dismiss us with thy blessing." At lunch there was chocolate stodge with custard. Then it was time to leave.

* * *

My parents were to return from Edinburgh next morning, so the afternoon, the evening, the night were all solitarily mine, in The Green House. No one anywhere need know exactly what I was doing. Wonderful . . . but time got stuck. I could not find Martha. There was no one to talk to, no one to follow about. Tea with lemurs and gargoyles – too tedious a prospect. As for Mrs K, her head ached, and she was cross enough to slap Pinky so he yowled. When after hours and hours I peered at the clock in her office, dinner was still far off.

At the Children's Bookshop I put Enid Blyton's *Five on Treasure Island*, one of a series I despised, into my coat pocket. Then at Woolworth's I found that pretty "Nuit d'amour" was just waiting for me. The scent bottle was a black die with scarlet pips, its cap pure gold.

Back at the hotel, the Professor's door stood open as I carried my treasures to my room. He sat at his desk. The Greek coins were there. In his ashtray a pipe rested. That was all right. Martha stood by him. She held her feather duster, tool of her trade. That was all right too. His left hand shook under her unbuttoned overall. Cold old fingers touched her titty-tip. In his right hand crackled paper money. My eyes went wide. The woman and man turned slowly, like figures on a clock tower, to face me. Their eyes widened too. Her teeth showed, not in a smile.

At dinner I sat awkwardly alone at our table. In welcome, the Ledingtons beamed at me, and Mr Penrose stopped by to shake my hand. Cool Miss Clyde nodded. The Talbot twins bowed, nearly dipping their bosoms into the parsnip potage.

Mrs K's head was better now. "I'll see you later, Amanda, tell you a tale."

As he left the dining room, Professor McGeachie gave me a packet of Maltesers. "I'm told," pause, "that you're a lass who likes her sweets."

Wordlessly Martha served everyone.

Mrs K came to my dark sugar-scented room. Her stories seemed only a few of many, their fearfulness normal on the shelves of her brain.

A man who didn't love his rich wife. He killed her, but her scent filled his nose if he even kissed another lady. He couldn't do anything. All the money just stayed in the bank.

A couple who made a beautiful garden, but in one flowerbed nothing would grow. Digging, they found a woman's skull, cracked by the right ear and missing two teeth. "These," said Mrs K, tapping her canines. *Left on the grass overnight, the skull next morning had been smashed to powder. Soon the couple sold that house and moved far away.*

A girl who had to take a certain train. Why? She didn't know. She was so alone, so frightened, but she simply had to put her foot on the carriage step. Then an invisible hand pushed her in the small of the back. Pushed hard, it did. She almost fell into the train. No person was in that carriage. Just a strong smell, like mildew, or mould. Something from underground.

At last, Mrs K butted her cigarette. "Nighty-night!" Alone with two murdered women and a rotting invisible arm, I lay awake.

For Professor McGeachie my parents brought a handsome Aran pullover. Opening the parcel, he blushed. Water pooled in his horrid rheumy eyes.

My present was Edinburgh Rock, but my mother hesitated to hand it over. "My goodness, you've gained weight! We must deal with that during your vacation."

"*Hols. Holidays.* Mum, I don't like the Professor."

"But dear, he's a wonderful old man. A famous scholar. He was thrilled that you did so well in Latin."

"I wasn't top."

"You can't have seen him much, anyway," my father reasoned. "You were at school. What are you staring at, Amanda?"

Bonny's fat eyes protruded in my brain.

On that celebratory night of my parents' return, as we all emerged from coffee hour in the lounge, we heard Mrs K pronounce, "I'm not well." Her voice came from above. Stepping down from the landing, the hotel proprietor held Martha by the ear. The maid in her drab uniform whimpered, stumbled. "And weary to the bone," Mrs K continued. "I've been patient, God knows, but theft I won't stand for. Don't deny it, girl. Who'll believe you?"

The women reached the lobby. Mrs K let Martha go and stood arms akimbo. "She'd left her door ajar. Her handbag, on the bed, open, so careless, I thought to close it. And what did I find?" She held out paper money, crisp and fresh.

All stood still. Mrs K waved her cigarette. Pinky, curled on the hall table, twitched as smoke reached his nose. "You're a thief, Martha. I never pay you in new notes." She inhaled. "You're dismissed, but before you go I mean to know whose money you've taken. Tell us!" She rapped the table. Pinky jumped off.

Into the huge silence I whispered, "Martha didn't steal that money."

The Professor's eyes shone old hate. My father's look was puzzled, my mother's angry. Martha's yearning glance was soft, soft. Oh that ring of eyes! Bonny, Maltesers, "Lily of the Valley," Crunchie, "Nuit d'amour," *Five on Treasure Island*. Bonny. Belief. Betrayal. The gargoyles and lemurs, goggling all. A procession of my peers. My parents. Martha's sobs. The Professor's old fierce mouth would eat me up.

I quailed and I cried and I ate my words.

My mother put me to bed. "You're exhausted, darling. We'll talk about it tomorrow. How about a cosy hot-water bottle?" She reached for the flowered case.

"No, I hate that rubber smell!" Too late. My treasure hoard was exposed.

Before sunrise I was at Martha's door, but she was long gone, filled neither with Greek nor with knowledge of her own mother tongue but with love of her baby. Rows of Martha stood on the centuries' shelves. A classic, she ran far away in the procession of her peers: women who will endure all to be with their babies, do anything to keep them safe.

Slowly the days passed until the new term began. My parents puzzled that I did not want to walk in Port Meadows, drive to Burford for tea at Huffkins or dinner at The Bay Tree, even go up to London for the day. When they drove away together to these delights, the sound of the Morris Minor crunching over the gravel in front of the hotel made me cry. Relieved, I stayed in my room. The mirror showed that my hair was longer now, softer looking, but the face was still a gargoyle's. Seizing *The Silver Branch* and *The Tree That Sat Down* and *The Story of the Amulet* and *Six Cousins at Mistletoe Farm*, I read as hard as I could and tried to stop my ears to the sounds of crying.

On the first day back at St Mildred's, I told Bonny the truth. She stared. What must her hols have been like?

"I'm sorry. I'm sorry." My voice was doubly too late, here at loud Buns-And-Milk, there by the maid's silent room.

Still that stare. "Live and let live. That's what I say."

The clock strikes ten
Start all over again

The doors did not open for me, for our form's rulers could smell that I had lost my hold over Bonny. She suffered less that term, though. One new girl had hysterics in Needlework after four days of Coventry; on the floor, she thrashed and drummed her heels. Another new boarder wet the bed every night, and even the day-girls knew.

Early In The Morning

At lunch on the rainy February day the King died, the sweet was custard and stewed damsons. Not all the stones had been removed. Miss Pringle entered the Dining Hall late, at the end of the meal. As she walked stately to her place, her pallor was remarkable. She struck her waterglass with a knife. The liquid shook. Tearful, she spoke. We all – two hundred girls and women – shuffled to our feet for an interminable silence, spotted by nose-blowing. The mistresses at High Table stood stoically aligned with Miss Pringle while their tears dropped on their smeared plates.

As we waited our table's turn to file out of Hall, gangly Helen muttered, "He wasn't even supposed to be King. He wasn't ordinary, either. He stuttered. If his stupid brother only hadn't met *her*."

Pretty asked, "Whatever do you mean? Who's *her*?"

Spiteful tittered.

Because of Helen's big nose, a frown looked fiercer on her than on other girls.

"When will the coronation be, I wonder?" Kay looked up to the crowns and haloes in the stained glass window behind High Table. "A young queen, imagine! In a beautiful satin dress."

"I say, Kay, you're awful." Spiteful Janet glared. "Our king's not even buried yet. You've never lived here. You don't know."

Kay Singleton was a strange day-girl, everyone said. Her skin was sallow, for she had lived years in hot dangerous India. Her father's circumstances were unknown. For some reason, she was excused from field hockey and lacrosse. She walked toes-out.

As for me, my Canadian speech and ways precluded both popularity and rejection. I'd settled into the familiar route of a minor planet, not as peripheral as the weepers who didn't have a clue and threw balls poorly, nor as the other foreigners orbiting still farther out – the girl from the Orkneys with an accent so peculiar that she scarcely spoke, and the Irish girl suspected of Roman Catholicism.

Pretty Tessa wiped her dry cheek and stuck out her tongue. "Amanda, you can't possibly understand how we feel, either."

A prefect turned to see who was talking. Janet pointed at Kay.

Lessons, games, practices were cancelled. All afternoon we sat about, aimless, because of the cold king at the core of the stone palace far away. How many black-veiled queens would join the funeral procession? Three – no, four. Five.

Months then passed, months and terms in which Kay and Helen and I exchanged not a word.

In December of that year, Janet and Tessa and Helen fought over their roles in the School nativity play. (It was a question of angels.) Split, the trio fell. Now Spiteful and Pretty worked as twin agents in the new power dynamics of our form, but Helen moved about alone, frowning. I had grown as tall as she.

Once, during hockey, I sought out her sceptical glance and showed my own.

Then the Games Mistress chose us two to help tidy a storage shed. Amid cricket and tennis balls, lacrosse and hockey sticks, Helen held up a racquet in one hand and a wicket in the other. "What is it all for? Why do we play?"

"You have a task, Helen," said Miss Fielding. "Finish it."

In Needlework, our form was knitting an afghan for the African needy. At least half of the blanket was Kay's, her squares smooth and error-free.

"I've had so much practice! On the ship from India, Mummy and I knitted all the way." She knew crochet too, for joining the squares. Miss Michaelson smiled.

Unlike Kay, I and others produced holey rhomboids of wool. Our mistress said, "If a thing is worth doing, it is worth doing well. Kay, show Amanda your method of casting on. And Helen too."

Agreeably Kay did so. Still Helen did not complete even one square, and enquired, "Who asked St Mildred's for these things?"

As we three returned from the sewing room to the main school building, each of us walked alone through the chilly mist.

Then one day, in Geography, Miss Lincoln most unusually read aloud to us from a newspaper. In London now, we learned, air was not air but murderous fog. People choked. They fell down. They lay in hidden bedsits or in hospitals, and they died.

"Awww," rose in the classroom as she read.

Miss Lincoln went on to read of Smithfield Market in London, where Britain's best cattle were gathered for the Fat Stock Show. Overcome by the filth in their lungs, eight beasts had to be slaughtered. Three had died on their own.

Louder came the mournful hum. "Awww."

"Perhaps the very ones who died would have won prizes and medals," Kay said urgently. "Blue ribbons. Pictures in that newspaper."

Helen burst out, "But *people* are dying!" She gripped her desk.

"Remember our classroom manners." Pretty and Spiteful snickered, but Miss Lincoln nodded in response to Helen's now properly raised hand.

"People dying – that's worse. And by chance. Probably some were only in London by chance, shopping for Christmas." Helen's pimples stood out red.

I raised my hand. "At least they went to London on their own. They weren't sent away. Driven, like those cows."

Helen for the first time spoke directly to me. "But what about the people who live in London? That's their home. They're dying there!"

"Now no one can ever know who was Best Of Show, who was exceptional." Kay nodded emphatically at me and at Helen. "The best might have died."

"An animal is a which, not a who." Miss Lincoln folded the paper.

Helen raised her hand again. "Does *The Times* say why it's happening? What makes the air so bad?"

"We have moved on now. Do pay attention." Titters, nudges.

Over the Christmas holidays, the *Illustrated London News* printed a photo of a sturdy heifer at the Fat Stock Show. Above the sack tied over her muzzle, her mild stare met the camera. A man in a white coat smiled beside her, and the caption explained that the sack was soaked with whisky to help the cow breathe. When school re-opened, I did not think to mention this repellent image to Kay or Helen. They did not yet feel necessary to me.

In mid-February, the term met that period of stasis when everyone and everything at a school is profoundly boring. At morning break, girls counted the currants in their buns and fought over them, snatching and tearing at each other's breadstuffs. The Orkney girl wept in a corner. Some girls' ties were torn from their necks, dipped in ink, smeared with Marmite. The Lower Fifth got Mr Greene, Visiting Specialist, to lose control completely. Miss Trout had to take over his History lesson.

One morning Pretty and Spiteful began to snigger at me. Others took up their mood. I looked about. Nearby, Kay gazed out of the window at the melting snow, while Helen stared at her shoes. Simultaneously the two became aware of the mockers. They moved towards me, and then we three laughed to find that we were friends.

The surprise was like finding a door to a new room in a well-known house. Those aching stretches between lessons, after meals were happy now, and eagerly awaited. Among us, Helen could ask and ask as many questions as she wanted. Kay showed us a photo of her father, in India, and one of herself in a tutu. I told them both about Muskoka. My marks in arithmetic began to crawl out of the red. Mrs Wilmer gave me a look not far from a smile.

Later in the spring, we three knelt together on a patch of chill damp earth. The plot, set out behind St Mildred's kitchen garden, had been allotted to us in a draw organized by Miss Gregson in Science class.

Kay held out seed packets bright with colour. "Look! Mummy gave them to us. We can plant them."

At home in Canada, my mother made our garden. On summer evenings my father admired her work, as the two sat together in the fragrance of her roses. But I only played in that garden, or drew it. I knew nothing about growing things. Of my painted flowers, Mrs Tonelli of Art always said, "Amanda, you need more control."

As for Helen, she never spoke of mother, home, family. She and I watched Kay's deft hands flip through the packets.

"Sweet william, and bachelors' buttons. And here, johnny-jump-ups."

"Why are they all boys' names?" I asked.

"I don't know. Aren't they pretty?"

"There must be a reason," Helen insisted, her big spotty features set in their habitual frown. "What is a garden for?"

Kay drew her fingers over the pictured petals. "They will be so beautiful." In the cool spring light her smooth cheeks were not sallow but tawny, sown with golden hairs that shone. She wore a dark green cardigan that was not part of our navy uniform. "Wait till you see the pansies and the heartsease!"

We took hands, laughing as we jumped and danced around our garden. Short Kay was wonderfully stretchy and straddled the plot's width easily, far better than Helen or I for all our height. She did not boast of this, nor of her skill in Gym, where she walked on the balance beam as if on the broad floor. Nor did Kay join me in the crowd eager to see the marks posted fortnightly for each subject – First, Second, the ladder sinking right down to Nineteenth. Later, alone, she scanned the board to confirm her high standings. Helen never looked at all.

The next day I remember at our garden was a Wednesday, still later in the spring and much warmer, for a freakish hot spell had overtaken Britain. Helen had a cold and sucked one pale green Sucret after another. Kay said we would plant the seeds now, arranging the flowers in graduating heights from the back of the plot.

Helen scanned the seed packets. "They all say *flowering masses*. But Kay, the term will be over before they bloom. Ten weeks? Two months?"

"Last year was so sunny that everything was early," Kay countered. "It's certain to be the same this year, because of the Coronation. You'll see!"

Helen took up another packet. "What is *variegated?*"

I got out my pocket dictionary.

Helen frowned. "But how will we know which seed is which, to arrange the colours?"

"We can't! It'll all come by chance," Kay answered in delight.

With Helen's ruler, we measured the depths and spacing required. We buried the blank seeds, big and wrinkled as grapefruit pips or small as shaken spice. The earth was warm on top, then briefly tepid, then chill. Next were the pansies; Kay's mother had helped her to start these at home. They were in cheesecloth bags, soft little purses, and fitted in at the front of our plot. The green leaves were small, tight.

I said, "These aren't really masses, Kay."

"They will be. And Mummy has some in full bloom, right now." Kay's voice was eager. "Come to my house and see them! Tea, on Sunday?"

"I'd love to!"

"It's not an Out Day." Turning away, Helen blew her nose. "I couldn't."

"Mummy will ring up Miss Pringle," Kay assured her. "You'll see. You'll come."

We all smiled as we sat quietly by our garden.

Supposing that these English girls would know, I asked, "What shall we do, the day the queen is crowned?"

"We should make special souvenirs. Amanda, you could paint a picture of this garden. Our garden." Kay shivered and drew on her cardigan.

Helen was solemn. "We shall always remember that day."

A statement made by Miss Trout came to me. "Elizabeth will be queen in her own right, not for being married to a king. We should do something special."

"A time capsule!" Kay cried.

Oh perfect! To hide our own record among our own flowers – the concept thrilled us. Radiant, Kay sat back to rest while Helen and I tidied up the torn packets and put away the trowels before the bell rang for netball.

"I wonder who'll find our capsule? In what century?" Kay buttoned her cardigan. "We can sit in my bedroom on Sunday after tea, to plan it all out. We'll need a special box, won't we? Perhaps Mummy has a pretty one."

I was about to say, "I have a special box," but then I thought of the red quills and the sweetgrass buried here in England. My mouth shut itself.

"And I'll show you my things from India," Kay said happily.

"Aren't you hot?"

The green wool of her cardigan circled Kay's neck. "No. But I'm tired."

"You're getting a cold, just like me." Helen gave us each a Sucret, and we went off to netball with the sugary acid thick on our teeth.

Miss Fielding played us hard that day, for the School's teams were to be chosen shortly and she was alert for talent. "Come on, Kay, jump. I know you can. Jump!"

"Is it good to jump?" Helen wondered.

"Kay ought to be able to," sounded Janet's voice. "Look at her muscly thighs."

"Ugly!" Tessa agreed.

Helen and I then made more than our usual minimal effort. Several girls cheered Kay's leaps and throws. Leaving her hands, the ball repeatedly slipped through the net without touching its rim.

Eagerly that night I told my mother of Kay's invitation. It was a first in my experience of the School; she hugged me. Perhaps I would take along my Indian box after all, just to show my friends. They would understand.

On Thursday, Kay and Helen were both absent from school.

On Friday Helen emerged from the San, red-nosed but breathing more freely, in time for lunch. Together we savoured grey potatoes, fish drowned in scorched white sauce, and stodge with caramel. Could school food go in our time capsule?

The Head then rose to speak. The school stilled.

"You are all aware" – this was not so – "that with the unseasonably warm weather has come another wave of occurrences of poliomyelitis. Our area of Britain has mercifully been spared so far, but no longer. I deeply regret to inform you that a young girl has been stricken. At St Mildred's." I knew the coming words. "Kay Singleton."

Helen and I would not be with Kay at home on Sunday. We would not meet her mother, see her room, the pansies, her Indian things, a pretty box.

Miss Pringle recommended the Christian virtue of hope, and of course prayer.

After lessons, Helen and I went to our garden plot and discussed the Head's statement that Kay was in an iron lung. Of this we could form no picture. We poured water everywhere, and weeded. The pansies were taking hold; even we could see that.

"Helen, let's go visit Kay. I'll get my Mum to ask Miss Pringle, so you can come out too. Do let's!"

"But we don't know them, Amanda! I mean her people. We couldn't just ring up." My un-English mother could and would, I knew. But Helen would not consent.

That night my father explained what an iron lung did, and all the while he stroked and stroked my hair.

On Sunday, my mother won Miss Pringle's permission for Helen to come on an outing with us. At first my friend embarrassed me, tongue-tied, eyes down.

Cheerfully, Mum gave her the map of Oxfordshire. "We're driving to Bourton-on-the-Water, to see a model village. You can navigate." Helen actually smiled. It wasn't long before Mum was hearing all over again about Kay, the garden, the time capsule.

In the model village, the tiny houses in their warm Cotswold stone were wonderful. So were the shop signs, pillar box, bridge, school, war memorial, the church with its tower and minute gravestones.

"It's one-ninth actual size," Helen read from the official brochure.

Wonderful, yes, wonderful – yet all the time Kay's-not-thereness was palpable, as if the Sunday-that-might-have-been were running like a river alongside. Even as Helen noticed ecstatically that the model village itself contained a model, my peripheral vision kept showing plum and violet pansies, clustered, and lemon pansies, and lavender, with Kay's fingers bending back the petals to show their inner velvet. Yes, models within models until further smallness was impossible, but no dolls. No people.

"Why was it made?" Helen asked, as we left. "What is the point, really?"

After we took her back to St Mildred's, my mother said, "One day that girl will be a handsome woman."

Kay's white bed stood in a small room, I imagined. She was tiny, one-ninth actual size. Her green cardigan was buttoned to the neck. A huge iron creature straddled her, leaned its life-sustaining weight on her chest to help her breathe. Smiling men in white coats circled motionless Kay.

The heat wave continued.

Kay was not back at school on Monday or on Tuesday or on Wednesday. Helen and I talked and talked of what we three would do on her return, but by Thursday the scenarios felt thin, false, the way things do when they are imagined past bearing.

In History, Miss Trout assigned trios of girls to prepare speeches about the Coronation regalia. Helen and I were a leftover pair.

The mistress said, "You two must be ready to do the speech on your own. We don't know when Kay will be back, do we?"

Our topic was The Orb. We learned that there was a special Orb for queens, a pure golden ball to be held in Elizabeth's left hand. The sceptre would be in her right.

Daily, Helen and I watered our garden and observed the pansies' stiffening stalks. Their leaves were unpleating. Tongues of lush colour showed.

Cool and grey and quiet – that was the atmosphere of St Alban's, the small church down the road where St Mildred's community gathered to pray briefly each weekday and at length on Sunday. Time there was peaceful, except for the nudging and shoving because no one wanted to sit by the Irish girl or anywhere near Patricia the bedwetter.

At Friday's service, even before we had sung "Early in the morning / Our praise shall rise to thee," Miss Pringle stood at the lectern that was a squashed brass eagle and told us Kay was dead.

"As you are all aware," said the Head, "she was an exceptionally gifted dancer. With great reluctance she and her mother had left her father, Major Singleton, in India, so that Kay might advance her training here in England. She was their only child."

We stood for one minute of silence. Helen's cold hand filled mine, mine hers. Girls stared at us and whispered. Before we left the church, there were reminders about netball team practice and about a special watercolour class.

Our first lesson was arithmetic, a test. Helen did a few sums and then sat staring. Mrs Wilmer did not reprove her. I could not bear to be so different, and tried each question until the mistress gently took my paper from me, saying, "It doesn't matter." Tessa and Janet saw to it that our form shunned Helen and me until the funeral was over. No information reached us about the event, only that Miss Pringle had attended. Somehow also word spread in the School that Kay's father had flown to England from hot dangerous India and had arrived before her death.

On the morning after the service, before lessons began, Helen and I went to our garden plot. We each picked the blooming pansy we thought most beautiful, and with her pocket knife we sawed off bits of our hair. Flowers and hair we wrapped in a sheet from one of my notebooks.

"Kay Singleton made this garden," I wrote. "1941-1953. She was our friend." Helen put the date. We signed our names. The packet fitted perfectly into the Sucrets box. We buried her.

The Usual Accomplishments

When their father was dead at last and the Second World War was over and they were sixty-five, Millicent and Matilda Talbot put their small house in the country up for sale and came to the city. They walked the streets. In their thick flannel coats-and-skirts, so old the fabric had felted at the jacket corners, in their cotton combies and hairnets and wool and lisle and much-polished leather they walked, stepping as one, their toes turned out like hens'. At last, they found The Green House.

Tilly sat on a loveseat in the lounge, *The Times* crisp on her grey worsted lap. Amanda squeezed in by her; the twins were big ladies, Tilly the bigger and younger. "Just five minutes after Milly!" She was also hard of hearing and favoured her left leg. Milly, whose humpy back dominated her appearance, faced her sister. Tilly wore a rose jumper, her sister raspberry. On other days the colours might be celery and olive, or cream and biscuit. Sometimes, the twins spoke in unison. "We were so sad when Daddy died," and, "City life is so lively," and, "That was after Mummy," and, "We do like a man to smoke a pipe." This last smilingly referred to Professor McGeachie, who suggested they might term themselves sororal rather than fraternal twins.

After breakfast, custom reserved the lounge and a copy of *The Times* for the Talbots. Mrs K didn't begrudge it "to the poor old souls. A little fun. They don't get about." She herself, proudly, hadn't slept a night away in fourteen years.

"Those two are formidable, Rachel," said Amanda's father. "The Professor says they do the crossword without filling in the boxes. But where do Englishwomen find these awful shapeless sweaters?"

"Jumpers," said Amanda. "Remember, Daddy? Or jerseys."

"Milly's a wonderful knitter," insisted her mother. "And good wool wasn't available for years, because of the War."

Now Milly took *The Times* from her sister – snatched it, really. Amanda readied herself to listen. She'd had flu, was recovering; to be present was a treat.

I. The Anagrams

"We do these first," I said, but that ignorant girl did not even know what they were. Of course Tilly had to baby her by providing an example.

"Amanda, what could T E A turn into?"

A silence. "*Ate?*"

"I say, isn't that jolly good, Milly?" Tilly cried. "*Eat*, too!"

Recently I told my sister she was *a greedy girl* because of the cream buns at tea with the Ellises. Not that I named those buns. I needed only to remind her of that vicarage tea when we were little. So much cream made her sick. In the shrubbery she tore her sash. Tilly has always been careless and greedy. If we return from a walk to find Mrs K lugging in string bags of food, she's all smiles. "Oh, may we hope for one of your wonderful tarts?" Or if the fishmonger pulls up to the tradesmen's entrance, Tilly must see his wares. A haddock can excite her. "So fresh!"

Tilly didn't speak to me for hours. I could have gone longer.

This morning, all the anagrams were Down clues. I read aloud an easy one. "Twenty-one Down, *Masters turn to current affairs.*" The child looked blank.

Tilly simpered, "Amanda, watch, I shut my eyes to move the letters about." She always does. It looks so silly.

I was not willing to wait. "*Stream*. As in *current*. Surely you see it, Amanda? Now, *Trots wrongly*. Easy." But she didn't know *torts*, either, though allegedly a great reader. Tilly as always wanted to smooth over a failure, and urged me to go on.

"Whose turn is it to lead today, Tilly? Mine, I believe. Six Down, *Mutt! Hen needs accommodation.* Seven letters."

My sister came right back with, "*Hutment.*"

So much for educating Amanda! Tilly only wanted to even scores with me. I threw the next at her instantly. "Fourteen Down, *It's choler, maybe, if they don't suit.*"

"Why are all the anagrams Down?"

"The which, dear? What a clever girl, to notice! Why, Milly?"

If there is anything I cannot stand, it is unwillingness to concentrate on a task. A puzzle requires full attention. "The mind of each crossword-maker is unique, Amanda. This is Torquemada." Not that the name would say anything to the colonial child.

"Such hard work it must be, to invent them!" My sister giggled, wanting the girl to giggle too. I could tell. And pray what could Tilly know of real work? She has no experience. She lived always at home, first helping Mummy, then looking after Daddy and a little house and garden. The girl's silence pleased me.

"*Clothiers*, obviously. Now, here is the final anagram. *Regal tour.*"

"Oh, regal makes me think. . . . No! I'll tell after." Wits to the winds, again.

"*Regulator,*" the girl said. Is she less stupid than I thought? Sometimes Tilly is. However, my sister then became excited and vocal. When her cornucopia of praise was empty, I was about to go on as usual to the word-plays, but Tilly actually reached over to take *The Times* from my hand.

"Look, Amanda, right here on the front page. The Aga Khan! *Because of a slight indisposition . . .* Perhaps he's had the flu, poor man, like you, dear . . . *will be unable to attend to correspondence for the next three weeks.*"

"What's an Aga Khan?"

"An Eastern potentate." Tilly's voice softened dreamily.

"A foreign prince, Amanda, who has a London residence. Tilly, let us continue."

"And this advert," she said, in her annoying way poking at the newspaper so it crackled. "Milly, couldn't this just have been us? *Woman graduate (28), married, living in London in NW direction, seeks post. Some experience journalism, usual accomplishments, wide interests, especially people.* Not that we were graduates, Amanda dear. Or married, of course, or journalists. *Write Box 1636.*"

"I hardly think we'll need that number, Tilly."

Her face fell. "Milly, I was only remembering what it was like, at the beginning."

Of what? She never did anything.

II. The Word-plays

"I'm afraid my sister is somewhat absent-minded."

So Milly said, when at an appointed hour Amanda knocked at the sisters' door in the hotel. Tilly had promised to start her on embroidery, which Miss Michaelson at school refused to permit for anyone "so utterly incompetent with her needle."

The two had twin beds, ha ha! On Miss Talbot's dressing table stood old photos: a woman like Milly, a man like Tilly. Her table had china giraffes. The sisters shared bookcase and escritoire. Near one bed was an embroidery-stand where a crimson dragon writhed in a round frame. From his whorled nostrils, silver steamed.

"Where is St. George, Miss Talbot?"

Milly emitted a sound like a laugh. "This dragon is not English but Chinese."

"Has Miss Tilly gone to China?"

"Don't be silly!" She collected herself. "My sister has had the opportunity to read widely, Amanda." The dragon's scales were smooth as glass. "You admire it?"

"Oh, it's beautiful. It's kind of strange, too."

On Tilly's wall hung an oblong of bright orange weaving, a mediaeval world map, a scroll on which a waterfall trickled past plumy trees. Milly's held watercolours of Ely Cathedral and Derwentwater, exactly like those on Amanda's school paintbox. Six framed photos showed a formal garden, black and white.

"*Kind of?* I suppose that is a Canadianism." Shrugging her hump, Milly closed the door. The lock clicked decisively.

Once, at coffee-hour, Amanda showed her Indian box to the twins.

"How clever!" cried Tilly. "What is their needle? Bone?" She held the box close to her eyes, peering at the red and white.

Milly took it from her, fingered the brilliant quills. "Remarkable. One might think they were porcelain." She picked up her knitting again.

"I see you use the European method," said Rachel Ellis admiringly, watching the needles exude a smooth panel for a skirt, in oatmeal wool.

"For a time we had a German governess, Mrs Ellis. The Germans were not then the enemy. I make clothing only," Milly added. "My sister's handiwork is decorative."

Now as Amanda sat with the Misses Talbot (her father said that was the right term) to do the crossword, she rubbed her aching forehead. "Does that lady want a job?"

"We do not say *job*, Amanda. We say *post*. Now, if you and my sister have quite finished your little chat, let us start on the wordplays."

Milly shifted her thick legs. Tilly's were as thick. What colour was the sisters' hair, before? Iron-grey and ashen, now. Their ringless hands were large, the bare nails ridged. They kept their gloves on during the holiday excursion from the hotel – Rachel Ellis's idea – to see Alastair Sim's new film *A Christmas Carol*. In the theatre they sat thus: Amanda's mother, Tilly, Amanda, her father, Milly, the Professor. Now it wasn't Christmas any more. Amanda's head hurt. Her clothes felt thin, yet she was hot.

"Listen carefully, now." Slowly Milly read out, "*Makes a tremendous impression, but not in the circus.* Two words, five letters and four."

"Think, dear." Tilly was all eager. "At the circus, what animals?"

Back home in Canada, after a trip to Barnum and Bailey's, Amanda had pretended that the cats Tiger and Willow were panthers, lions, fabled Siberian snow leopards. Blinking, they crouched in the dirt ring Amanda drew by her mother's roses. The old cats purred, slept in the sun. Now they were with her uncle in Hamilton.

Were they happy? What other beasts? Monkeys. Penguins. Elephants. Performing seals. As they danced in the water their whiskery noses stuck out, the magic nostrils flared and sealed. Kipling's white seal Kotick did the fire dance. For him, sealers were death, but Amanda's mother canned greengage plums and applesauce in sealers.

"What *impression* did the circus make?" asked Tilly, and could wait no longer. "*Great Seal!*"

Amanda then recalled Miss Trout's reverential commentary on this object. A new one was made, she told the Third Form, for the ascension of each monarch.

"Can I write *Great Seal* in?" Amanda reached for the paper, but Milly gripped it.

"We used to, dear," said Tilly. "Such fun, the squares filling up! But too easy."

"Far too. You *may* write in the answers, Amanda, when we are done. *Superfluous to 9 it, though some do.* Nine letters. Elegant!" Milly's tone told; she already knew.

"But how do you *nine* something, Miss Talbot?"

"The reference is to Nine Across, which is *Hoist*."

"I wish I could see the page!"

"It is good mental training, to listen, Amanda. To read words in your head."

Tilly's giggle said she knew too. "Dear, what's another way to say *hoist a flag*?"

"*Run up*, I guess."

Milly tsked. "What an odd expression! Well? What does one not need to run up, though foolish children often do?"

"You oughtn't to be so peremptory, Milly. The child's not well yet."

"She's well enough for this simple clue. We mustn't be slackers, Amanda! *Escalator.* Now Tilly, if you are in such haste, try *Not a summer blazer.* Four letters, three."

"*Yule log*," Tilly spat.

Milly snapped, "*Pen that sounds like a fleece.* Nine."

"Not a writing pen, Amanda," warned Tilly. "We must always enquire whether a word has multiple meanings. Easy, Milly! *Sheepcote.*"

"Too easy. Try this now, *Paddy's periodical.* Four, five. Amanda, don't look so blank. Use your brain!"

"Not the funny Irish Paddy," Tilly warned. "Not green or fairies or lace. Not lovely potatoes. Think of China, of Japan. Isabella Bird went there – did you know?" Her voice yearned, as when speaking of the Aga Khan. "Imagine! She even spent time among the Aino. Now Amanda, what must the poor people in those countries eat?"

"*Rice paper* is the answer." Milly was both certain and nervous. Amanda saw her wince as Tilly stamped and stamped on Mrs K's new treasure, the fitted carpet.

"Milly! How dare you! It is my turn to give the answers!"

"But Tilly, you and the child are so slow!"

Sunny watery fields, bright clouds reflected in green water, everywhere people reading: to look at that picture calmed Amanda, as the sisters' voices rose.

Then came a loud *rap rap!* on the door of the lounge. All three startled. Mrs K peered in, like a warden into a cell. A cigarette was pasted to her lower lip as usual. She carried wax, oils, rags, brushes, sponge. Behind her, the Hoover stood guard.

"Off to do my bedrooms, ladies. Then I'll bring your Ovaltine." The door swung shut, wafting the scent of Players across the room.

"Dear Mrs K! Really, the Irish are so hospitable."

"Bog Irish, I should say." Milly sighed. "Tilly, the Ovaltine and biscuits are ours. They are stored in the pantry, and Mrs K simply serves them to us." Upstairs the Hoover blundered and thumped. "Let us proceed. *The hat you eat.* Four, three."

"Pork pie!" Tilly and Amanda called out, and laughed.

"Indeed, and so simple. Only two word-plays remain. *They are not the runners.*" Milly emphasized the pronoun and noun. "Four, five. Come along, girls!"

But Tilly had lost her rhythm, and Amanda had none. They were silent.

"*Race goers*, of course."

Amanda's mother had gone. To be back when, when? She was meeting one of her authors, to explain again the distinction between corrections and alterations to proofs. That evening, she would act out their talk. The twins and the Professor and the Ledingtons, Mr Penrose and Miss Clyde would laugh and laugh.

Then they might play the new game, *Scrabble*. Tilly would smile at her own tiny words. Milly would fight hard. Later Amanda's father might say, "Formidable! But broad-beamed women shouldn't wear skirts like that. Don't they know how they look?"

"Milly couldn't find proper lining fabric, Gerald. The War." And Amanda's mother would sigh, "What I'd give, to get those two into decent girdles!"

Tilly's bulk, just now, was squeezing Amanda against one end of the loveseat. It felt hard to breathe. Was that still the flu? Her body felt uneasy, itchy, chilly, warm.

"One more. Tilly, this should be easy for you. *No Grand Tour.* Five, four."

"Me? Why, I haven't even crossed the sea to Ireland. The opportunity never arose. Amanda, what are other words for *tour*?"

"*Journey? Voyage?*" The Ellises had sailed to England on the *Empress*, across liquid green beauty. On maps, the seas were blue. Would an empress have a greater seal?

"Lucky you, dear, to travel on an ocean liner! *Trek*? No, that's South African."

"*Trip*?"

Triumphantly the Misses Talbot cried, "*Cheap trip!*"

That must be English. "Please, what are *usual accomplishments*? Doesn't *accomplished* mean *all done*?"

III. The Straight Equivalents

Dear me! I was quite taken aback. Of course Milly knew how to respond.

"An educated young person's accomplishments are what he is capable of doing, Amanda. Speaking of an older person, one would mean what he had done with his life." With her pencil, Milly drew a line through the clue for 9 Across. "We already have *Hoist*. The two others in this category are *Put out* and *Lisping song*. Each is five letters."

Dear Milly! She can think clearly about two things at once.

French – that is an accomplishment. For Milly it was useful, too, with the military at the Colonel's, and with Mrs Brocklehurst's Continental friends, and at Cambridge.

And dancing, certainly. Our lessons were held at the vicarage. I never danced well, but that did not matter, since few occasions of dancing arose in later years.

Needlework.

Music. The piano is always nice. Milly and I loved our duets. Such fun! At least I did. We still know our pieces. The crossword man at *The Times* isn't a bit musical. Pity.

And, well, being able to run things. A dinner party. A sale, for the church. Flag Days – dear Queen Alexandra. That girl at Box 1636 might find a post with a charity. Or she could be a companion, like Milly. Such opportunities to meet people!

Skill at cards.

Not long after the Canadian family arrived here, at coffee-hour Mrs Ellis suggested we play. "What shall it be?" she asked in her energetic manner. "Bridge? Hearts? Canasta? Gin? Five-card stud?"

I was quite bewildered. Milly explained that while she enjoyed bridge with the Professor and the young people, something simple would be better. Milly has played a great deal. At Cambridge with the Dickinson girls, she often made a fourth. They gave her a handsome book about the history of bridge, as a souvenir of their years together.

Mrs Ellis got a card table from Mrs K, and that kind Mr Ellis went upstairs to their room to fetch port and Lucozade and some glasses. We all played "Continental." A form of rummy, Milly told me later. Naturally she played without hesitation. I was so proud! I dithered and giggled, and Amanda became my consultant.

"The which, dear?" How often did I say that? We all laughed so!

"There's another bottle upstairs," Mr Ellis said, tipping steeply into Milly's glass, "and the wine merchant is still in business, I believe. So no holding back, ladies."

They are a generous pair, those Canadians. They enjoy things in a way that makes me want to move away from them. A little. I am afraid though that I did not hold back. As the game went on my cheeks became hot, and doubtless bright pink. Next day my head hurt. Milly said that I should have stuck to the Lucozade. Of this I was aware.

"*Lisping song*," my sister said. "That is *Thong*."

To hear a child laugh is a pleasure, but again she was invading my territory.

"*Expel* – that will be *put out*." Indeed Milly looked put out. I couldn't help giving a tiny giggle. "Now Amanda, have you heard of the silly man who wound up the cat and put out the clock?"

She had. "And Miss Tilly, do you know about the moron who threw the clock out the window?"

I didn't. *Moron* is a harsh word, on the lips of a child.

IV. The Hiddens

Above the three in the lounge, the distant Hoover growled away.

Milly stared silently at *The Times*. She set it down, drooped so her hump showed more. "Tilly, there is a difficulty," she quavered. "Seventeen Across. I'm not receiving."

Her sister gave a small gasp. Deliberately then she settled herself.

"Dear, we both know. It sometimes happens." Tilly's speech was incantation. "We shall simply. Go on with our work. And. The word will come." A pause. "Now, Milly?" Miss Talbot straightened. "The hiddens." She blinked. "Amanda, pay careful attention. Join the end of each word to the beginning of the next. *Result from having eaten suet pudding*. Five letters. Think now. Does any combination mean *result*?"

Ultfr, omhav, ingea. No sense, nonsense, dizzy-making. The lounge was airless.

"Buck up, Amanda! *Ensue*." Neatly Milly pencilled out the clue.

"Daddy always loved treacle on his suet-pudding," Tilly noted.

Amanda whispered, "What does Miss Talbot mean, receiving?"

Perhaps Tilly's pale blue gaze saw nothing. "My sister will know.

She always does. But as yet she does not know that she knows. The feeling upsets her."

Milly sniffed. "*Material insects that are striped.* Nine letters. First, Amanda, think of synonyms for the first adjective and the noun. Then use the same technique of joining. A longer process. Still simple." She found her handkerchief, wiped the tears away.

"Name some insects, Amanda dear."

"Spiders? Beetles? Dragonflies? Bees? Ants?"

"Ants!" Tilly chuckled.

"Silk ants? Satin ants? Cotton ants? I don't know!"

"Spiders are not insects, Amanda. Think. Don't shirk."

Silence. The Hoover stopped. Mrs K's footsteps sounded as she lugged the machine down the stairs.

Tilly burst out. "*Sergeants!*"

"But why are sergeants striped?"

Tilly was going to explain, but Milly shushed her. "The child wouldn't know. The colonies didn't really go through the War."

"Lots of Canadians were at Dieppe."

The French town issued from Amanda's sour mouth only because, long ago when she was young, she'd seen her mother crying over a newspaper. Amanda ran, terrified. In the garden, she hid under the mock-orange. Later her mother spoke at her father in a loud rough voice about slaughter, the butchery of boys, no, of children.

"Dieppe was not the whole war, Amanda."

Ovaltine, soon. Amanda's head ached more. No, the flu was not over. Did she need a pill? Where was her mother? In strange England, both pills and books were at Boots The Chemist's.

There, Miss Tilly was buying corn-plasters, while Amanda was once again borrowing *Swallowdale*. They walked together back to the hotel, their home.

"I'm a steady walker, but not quick," said Tilly. "My sister is afraid of falling. Her brittle bones." In the loose raincoat, she resembled a limping tent. "Milly's teeth are not strong, either. Today she is visiting the dentist."

"Miss Tilly, did you read Arthur Ransome when you were young?"

"The which, dear? Oh no, I'm far too old," comfortably. "But I know why he is so popular. I've always loved reading about adventures, when I could find the time."

Miss Tilly and Amanda now stood at a zebra crossing on the Woodstock Road and pointed. These civic features were new; people wrote to the newspapers, pro and con. Milly and Amanda's father followed the debate. She had a letter printed.

Cars stopped. They crossed.

"I always think, Amanda, how surprised a zebra would be, to find himself here! I had to read aloud to Daddy, you see," Tilly went on. "Mummy always did. Of course I couldn't do it as well, but with the eye strain Daddy couldn't. So he was accustomed."

"What was your father's job?"

"His – ? Why, Daddy was a headmaster. A boys' prep school, small, but well-respected. As was he, I believe. Wonderful how Daddy lasted! Twenty-three years after Mummy, till his retirement. Then another twenty-three at our little house, still near the school. I'm afraid Milly found it small and shady, after Mrs B's. So frail, though. After breakfast I'd settle Daddy in his study and read aloud till he dozed off. And after his afternoon nap. And sometimes after dinner, though he did like the wireless then."

"What did you read to him?"

The old woman and the girl passed by large Victorian houses that loomed far back in dark dank gardens edged with towering laurel. Rain slid off the slick foliage. Might a zebra's pale blue excited eye peer out from the glistening leaves?

"Trollope," promptly. "Really, I felt as if I knew Barsetshire better than Oxfordshire. Wasn't I a silly? We read right through the *Chronicles*, every decade. I could draw a perfect map, still."

"Did you like those books?"

"I love Mary Kingsley," said Tilly, and she twirled her umbrella like a big black flower. "Of all the lady explorers, she is the very best writer. *Travels in West Africa*. Oh, the first time! Never forget. In the garden. The peas shelled for dinner. An hour to myself." Stopping by a pillar box, Tilly waved as if conducting an orchestra. "Listen to this, Amanda. *When we got into the cool forest beyond it was delightful;*

particularly if it happened to be one of those lovely stretches of forest, gloomy down below, but giving hints that far away above us was a world of bloom and scent and beauty which we saw as much of as earthworms in a flower bed." Tilly's eyes gleamed. "Fancy! Then Daddy called." She resumed her uneven trudge.

"Did your father like Mary Kingsley? I never knew there were lady explorers. Where did they go? Like Drake and Raleigh?"

"The which? Oh, all over the map. Harriet, of course," Tilly enthused, "she got to America and the East. Lady Ann Blunt, in Syria, Saudi Arabia, Egypt. Such a life! Such a nice man! A good writer too, though not like Mary. As for Lady Hester, all was not well with her mind, Amanda dear. Very sad. The Lebanon. But her descriptions! And Isabella went simply everywhere. To every mountain. A cold person, but such courage. Oh, I stayed up to all hours, reading their books. Alexandra David-Neel. Alexine Tinne." She sighed, as she and Amanda approached The Green House.

"Those explorers kept me hopeful. Brave ladies, travelling to unmapped lands!" Snowdrops bloomed by the doorstep. Tilly shook her umbrella at them and resumed her quoting stance. "Listen, Amanda. *Here and there the ground was strewn with great cast blossoms, thick, wax-like, glorious cups of orange and crimson and pure white, each one of which was in itself a handful, and which told us that some of the trees around us were showing a glory of colour to heaven alone.*"

Tilly pushed open the hotel door, fitted her umbrella into the stand and clapped. "*Glorious cups! Each one a handful!*" She limped to the oak settle and sat to rub her ankles. Her feet were boxed in black shoes. Cocoa-coloured lisle was visible to mid-calf, then a fawn hand-knitted costume with horizontal crenellations.

"Would you like to travel yourself, Miss Tilly?"

Just then Celia, the new housemaid, came out to strike the warning gong.

Tilly sniffed. "Mrs K's good potato soup! Do you know, Amanda, we gave a dinner for every new master at the school. Fancy me opposite Daddy, in my best dress! Only a few new ones were married." She re-tied her laces. "All those dinners I cooked, all those men saying the same things." Mischief tightened Tilly's wrinkles. "I used to laugh – oh, not aloud! But I would imagine the table talk of my brave ladies. Jungle dinner, desert dinner, dinner at Gondokoro or on the bounding main." She heaved herself up. "I must let my sister know that I'm home. She worries."

That evening Tilly sat alone at table because of Milly's pulled tooth. Afterwards, in the lounge, Amanda's father enquired, "How is Miss Talbot?"

"Thank you, Mr Ellis. She is reading an article by Mr C P Snow. Milly has such powers of concentration! And very wide interests. Her post at the Colonel's suited her so well. Meeting rajahs, running up to London for research. So stimulating."

Tilly set down her empty coffee cup at a careful distance and brought out her embroidery bag. Layers and layers of crisp white paper emerged, unpleated, and finally an altar cloth appeared. A surgeon, Tilly worked on a small exposed section of sacred tissue. From her needle's point, the letters *IHS* grew glossy and full.

"And my sister is so precise. So exacting. When she came home to visit Daddy and me, she always wanted to cook. I'm afraid I always let her."

"Why afraid?" asked Mrs Ellis.

"Milly would insist on using recipes. No substitutions! Impossible, in wartime. I simply cooked what Daddy liked, or what was in the garden. And after Milly went away again, if I made a favourite for Daddy, rice pudding perhaps, he'd tell me, '*That's* the way.'" Tilly's smile was fond. The embroidery needle drove into its hole. "My sister so much admired the kitchen at Mrs Brocklehurst's."

"Perhaps Miss Talbot would have liked to run a kitchen?"

"Oh Mrs Ellis, who could *want* to? Such a fuss. Boiled eggs just right, shepherd's pie every Tuesday for forty-six years. Then the fish. Fresh were hard to come by. And Daddy never understood rationing. He would become very cross."

Tilly rethreaded her needle with the silvery-white silk and began a lily.

V. The Literary-and-Historicals, Round One

I am not one to eavesdrop, but the child spoke so loudly.

"Daddy, why did Miss Talbot leave home and Miss Tilly stay home?"

"Primogeniture," said Mr Ellis. "Miss Talbot is the elder. The son, as it were."

To hear from the mouth of another a thought held private for decades, and that other nearly a stranger, and not even English: a difficult moment. Mercifully those two were crossing the lobby on their way out. No spoken words were necessary.

Someone had to earn.

Daddy's salary at that wretched school was minute, his pension scarcely visible. Mummy was ill for years. Then we were three. Daddy died at ninety-six. Tilly always declines to face the meaning of inflation. Like other great worldly forces, however, it wields power whether understood or not.

In my experience, men take little interest in how a woman spends her time, but Mr Ellis did ask, "Miss Talbot, what was the nature of your work for the Colonel?"

"I performed the usual secretarial duties, Mr Ellis."

This was during Sunday luncheon at The Green House, when the few guests present all sit at one table for a scratch meal of cold beef, vegetables from tins, and beetroot with salad cream. Tilly likes everything, of course, and eats hugely. For sweet, Mrs K invariably offers tinned pears.

I described to Mr Ellis the Colonel's book on his years in India, and the high standards he set for both of us in its preparation. A full decade, that project took. Sometimes still I wake at night because my fingers are poised over the coverlet in the correct position for typing, and they are cold. Also, the volume's supporting elements – photos, captions, maps, legends, index – consumed much time, as do all tasks requiring attention to detail, and perhaps especially one of which a military man is in charge. The Colonel's book finally appeared in 1936. Unfortunately General Franco revolted in the same week, so these English recollections of life in India received little attention. In a peculiar way, though, the book's defeat seemed to me appropriate. The Colonel never had a good strategic sense.

"Miss Talbot, was it well-written?" asked Mr Ellis.

Startled, without intending to I repeated my thought aloud. "The Colonel lacked a strategic sense." I had never said this to anyone.

"Indeed!" Mr Ellis clearly had more enquiries, so I suggested he borrow a copy of the book. Thus I protected myself, but later was fatally careless in my choice of which copy to lend him. Such embarrassment. Tilly does not and cannot understand.

Now there she sat on that loveseat by that conceited child, smiling and chuckling as though we were all at a picnic. We were not. The work was not on schedule – and then Mrs K burst in again. She set lemon oil, a chamois, and our box of Peek Freans on top of the piano, and grinned right at me. So impertinent.

"Enjoying your puzzle, ladies? Kettle's on. I'll just do the downstairs lav."

"That woman! Amanda, customarily we complete two-thirds of the puzzle before our break. Here is One Across. *Risky to hoax a sea-captain.* Nine."

Then I glared at my sister, and I began to count time, and my smile grew.

Tilly spoke loudly at Amanda. "I'm only allowed fifteen seconds for the literary and historicals. Milly always knows them right off. Not Seventeen Across, though!"

I spoke at the girl too. "Have you heard Admiral Nelson's last words?" She had no clue, of course. "Kiss me, Hardy. So, *Foolhardy.*" To get back at Tilly for her sneer, I lifted my chin and stuck it out. When we were little, she hated that. She still does.

"Another clue, please," my sister said then. Why so meek?

"Three Down, *A pilgrim by name*, seven letters."

Tilly actually counted on her fingers. Hopelessly childish. "Christian. Faithful. Evangelist. Worldly-Wiseman, no no. It must be *Hopeful!* Always be so, Amanda dear! Like that girl at Box 1636, hoping for a place in the world. But Milly, really, when I think of it, there are very few women in the *Progress.*"

I should have expected it. Not meekness. Only indifference. Failure, criticism, judgment – they all just roll off Tilly. There's no way to make her realize her limitations.

"Bunyan's great work describes a journeying soul, Tilly. Its sex is irrelevant. And that girl can't be making much of a wife."

"I suppose you would know, Milly. The Professor does not lack for female company, does he?"

"And what do you mean by that?"

"You thought it ever so clever, how you sat next him at the cinema."

"Do you not remember all your Mr Hopefuls, Tilly, in the old days? Every term, it seemed, you wrote me about some new master." This sally I regretted at once. My sister will fling it back at me when next we are alone. There will be a scene. Therefore I sat upright and said as calmly as possible, "Tilly, at this rate we shall never have our Ovaltine. And you know my worry about Seventeen Across."

"Yes, Milly."

"Then forward march! *Novel signpost reader?* Five. *Diana*, of course."

Tilly blinked. The girl gawked.

"*Of The Crossways*. Meredith."

"Wasn't that Mrs Brocklehurst's name, Milly dear?"

"Meredith? No, it was Diana."

"I meant Diana."

"You weren't plain, Tilly. So often you are not plain."

"Why didn't you let us try that clue, Milly? That wasn't fair to us, was it dear?" My sister actually patted that stupid girl's hand.

I kept my stiff posture. "Try this. *What Elsie, Lacie, and Tillie drew.*"

"Treacle!" those two cried, giggling again.

"Dodgson had a Tilly," my sister said, inevitably and with pride. "Tillie at the tiller!" She shifted her bulk on the loveseat. "You've seen his snaps of the Liddell girls, dear?" No clue. "Slender little pretties, sometimes with no undies. Why, Milly?"

"It is a work of fancy, Tilly. Those lucky girls were noticed by a well-known man. Otherwise, who would remember them? *One pre-eminent in woodcuts.* Three, six."

I could tell Amanda was counting to fifteen. She counted again. Tilly pouted. Really, she looked about eight years old.

"I thought that would keep you light on your toes, Tilly!"

"You mean I'm fat. Mean Milly!" She becomes tearful so quickly. "You think he fancies you! You talk softly so I can't hear, but I know. I know he'll never ask you!"

"Leave the shouting to Mrs K, Tilly." I turned to the wide-eyed girl. "The answer is *Top sawyer.* Not *Tom.*" That allusion Amanda did recognize, so I continued to address her while my sister snivelled. "The Professor and I occasionally enjoy working *The Observer's* crossword. Most amusing. And have you seen him blow smoke rings?"

The kitchen door slammed. Mrs K was imminent.

"Tilly, you are not at your best today. *Biblical queen's anaesthetic.* Five."

"I lead tomorrow. Then you'll be sorry, Milly."

I ignored her. "Amanda," I said, chin up, "I presume you know the Biblical story of Queen Esther? Very well. Then, anaesthetic. Is not *ether* common? And ether is the queen minus her *s*, as suggested by *an*, Greek 'without,' and *aes.*"

Mrs K pushed open the lounge door. She carried a tray of steaming cups.

"Lovely Ovaltine!" Tilly smiled and clapped. "Lovely biscuits, Milly!"

Mrs K did a circuit of the lounge, tidying piles of *The Lady* and *Punch* and *The Countryman.* "Just making a start. Let me know when your little puzzle's done?"

"Do not open the tin yet, Tilly. One more! Amanda, you have visited St. Paul's? *O Sir Christopher is possessive.* Five."

"*Owner.* Oh, don't be cross, Milly. Here, Amanda. Do choose." Happily, my sister proffered the Peek Freans biscuits.

VI. A Break for Ovaltine

Mrs Ellis sometimes bought Peek Freans because her husband and daughter liked them. The Swiss Mochas disappeared right away, then gradually the Fruit Cremes and Sandwiches, Nice Biscuits and Digestives, until the Arrowroots lay forlorn.

Amanda's father looked sadly at them.

"Really you are a child, Gerald!" said Rachel Ellis. "Just open the new box. Me, I'd hand over all those pasty things for one good gingersnap from *The Joy*."

Amanda sat on her parents' bed, towelling her newly-washed hair. It was nearly her bedtime. Together, they had been looking through the Colonel's book. The photos showed him with various animals, some dead, and with personages in unusual clothing. Now her mother was skimming the text.

"A standard *My Twenty Years In Poona*," said her father. "Bit of a tyrant, the old boy. Made her retype a whole page if he so much as changed *and* to *so*. It wouldn't have seen print without her, that's for sure. Seventeen years she spent with him."

"Sounds like a fairy tale, Daddy."

"That it was not," said her mother, setting *Poona* down and starting to comb out Amanda's hair.

Her father began to examine the book's maps and index. "*A great empire and little minds go ill together*," he said. "Is that Mill? Or Disraeli?"

"Ow, Mum! Not so hard."

"Or perhaps Gladstone."

"Miss Tilly visited Miss Talbot at the Colonel's once," said Amanda, yawning. "She took three buses and a train, to reach Torquay. She'd never seen the sea before."

"Yes, probably Gladstone," said her father, and re-opened the book to read the back flap. A yellowed clipping fell out. "Good Lord, Rachel, listen! *Mention must finally be made of the admirable index prepared by Miss Millicent Talbot. Detailed and accurate, it is the more noticeable within the context of the work's general quality.*"

"What does that mean?"

91

"That the book's a stinker but the index is good," said Rachel Ellis. "Not uncommon, that. Do hold still, Amanda. Only a few more tangles."

"High praise, from *TLS*," said Gerald Ellis dreamily.

"What's *TLS*? And why does Miss Talbot have that hump?"

"Osteoporosis. From the Greek." Her father explained.

Next day the Ellises, as often on weekend afternoons, were driving out to explore Oxfordshire. Amanda helped her father to navigate.

"Rachel, what about that Brocklehurst woman Miss Talbot worked for?"

"What about her?" Amanda's mother exited smartly from the roundabout at the city's north end. "Diana, her name was. Miss Talbot said, 'To use her Christian name was a mark of distinction, in her circle.' Which didn't include Miss T, natch. What a country! Years of *Yes Mrs Brocklehurst, No Mrs Brocklehurst, Milly do this, Milly do that*."

"What did Mrs Brocklehurst do?"

"She had money."

"She was a lady, Rachel," my father protested. "That's an accomplishment."

"Gerald! You are too much in love with England. She was rich, period. Except that she made a garden. Not that Mrs B lifted a spade herself. Beautiful, yes. You've seen those photos in their room, Amanda."

Lawns, terraces, borders, swaying walls of roses, vistas overarched by trees – these were in all the Ellises' minds as the noisy little car sped past fields like the green silk of the balloon in *Wizard Of Oz*. Gradually, though, the charm of villages and views and jumping black lambs took over. Not till hours later did the sisters reappear in their talk, after the little car turned to head for tea at Huffkins and the hill of Burford High Street fell away before them. On all the trees, vigorous pollarding had been performed.

"Dreadful deformations," lamented Gerald Ellis, as the family tucked into clotted cream, cottage loaf, butter, jam, crumpets, honey, and large striped cups of tea.

"Only gardeners understand the necessity of pruning," said his wife.

"Delicious." He took a third crumpet. "We've nothing like this in Canada."

"Did Milly lift a spade, Mum?"

"Oh yes. Mrs B thought her touch essential for the roses. The bulbs. The pruning."

"Milly was a valuable assistant, then," said Amanda's father.

"Not only that. She was a designer. She envisioned gardens."

"Strategic planning."

"She's kept some of her plans, along with Mrs B's obituary. Scale drawings with tissue-paper overlays. Elevations, layouts, the Italian garden from the east. Sequences of tulips and irises and lilies that lasted months. Always colour, always fragrance."

"Is that an accomplishment, to make a garden?" Tilly hadn't even done that.

"It wasn't Milly's garden, though," said her father.

"Mum, Miss Tilly said when she visited, Mrs Brocklehurst sent a Rolls Royce to meet her train. It had vases, for fresh flowers every day. The chauffeur told her."

Amanda's mother sighed. "Other people's houses, other people's lives."

Her father said, "At least Tilly has some social life. Her Mothers' Party."

"Mother's Union, Daddy. But why, Mum? Tilly isn't a mother."

"The group's for all the church ladies." Rachel Ellis snorted. "*And* she took care of that big baby for decades. Old fool. Old tyrant."

"But Milly," Gerald persisted. "Crosswords, bridge, knitting, letters to the editor. Chaperoning those girls at Cambridge. Jilly, Janie. With a brain like hers?"

"Daddy, they were Jocelyn and Josephine."

That night at coffee-hour, the Ellises described their outing.

Tilly exclaimed, "Poor trees, murdered for those silly electricity wires. Was the jam damson or strawberry?"

Everyone laughed. Gerald Ellis was next to Milly, talking to her about the big Turner exhibition at the Tate that he and Rachel had

seen recently. She was leafing through the show's full-colour cata-
logue. Her own laugh was both short and dry.

"You heard, Mr Ellis? From murder to jam. One cannot reason with Tilly. Her *brave ladies* all had independent means, or no
responsibilities, or odd husbands, or all three. Such advantages!"
She glanced at Tower Bridge, a blue mist beyond. "As for their
travels, Tilly will tell you how the West-African waterscapes
reminded Mary Kingsley of Turner. She can even draw you a map
of Mary's peregrinations." With evident disapproval Miss Talbot
inspected an apricot sunset. "What is the point of going to Africa,
if all you see reminds you of an English painter?" She handed back
the booklet.

"Miss Talbot – your sister and your father – had they a garden?"

"Of a kind." Milly's voice sharpened. "Small, though Tilly's
complaints would make it seem as large as Sissinghurst. And shady."
She sat up as straight as she could. "So much might have been done,
Mr Ellis! Sometimes I lose patience. It was all the wrong way about.
When I had to leave Mrs Brocklehurst, when Tilly was, was not well,
I did what I could. But she had made all the major decisions, and they
were incorrect."

"Did you and Miss Tilly ever think of moving elsewhere, to start
fresh?"

Milly's blue glance hardened. "My sister had no wish for further
domesticity."

Gerald Ellis paused. "You didn't lose patience with the index for
the Colonel's book, Miss Talbot. My compliments to you, on that
TLS review. High praise!"

Trouble flared in those eyes. They widened, glistened. They
looked desperately to and fro for a hiding place, and Milly began to
wring her hands. "I did not know my sister had put that there. I did
not know." She cried out, "Tilly! Tilly!"

After escorting her sister upstairs, Tilly returned, with apolo-
gies. "My sister is shy. It is hard for her to meet people, so hard. And
I never went anywhere!"

Now the two elderly women sat across from each other, with
Ovaltine and biscuits before them, and the Canadian child irrele-

vant, and *The Times* laid aside although solutions to seven clues remained AWOL.

"How many cookies can I have, Miss Talbot?"

"*Biscuits*, Amanda. *May* I."

"How sensible! At your age, I always wanted to know. *She* said it wasn't proper." Tilly glared. "We take three, a plain and a not-so-plain and a fancy."

"But Tilly, Mummy would have corrected Amanda for saying that."

Tilly ignored her sister and eyed the Peek Freans avidly. "I'm afraid I love my chocs. Daddy always gave me his." She bit largely into a Swiss Mocha. "The which, Milly?"

"Mummy always corrected us," in a pleading tone. Tilly stilled. She set the remaining Mocha on her saucer.

"Dearest Mummy," the sisters sighed in unison.

Then Milly was crisp once more. "Whilst we're having our break, shall we finish up the Down clues?"

"Up the downs," Tilly giggled. She and Amanda peeled off the yellow fillings in their Creme Sandwich Fingers and rolled them into cylinders to nibble separately.

"If you two are quite ready? *Wish for an annual letter.* Five." Milly's tone said that the answer sat ready on her tongue. Amanda's tongue and whole mouth felt furry.

"To wish for." Tilly spoke longingly. "How do we express that, Amanda?"

"Or consider the reference of *annual*. You are studying Latin, I believe?"

"Is it *yearn*?"

"Jolly good! Another biscuit, dear?"

But the dry disks of jam, the sugary glazes held no more appeal. In any case Milly was proceeding. "*Musician's large reward.* Seven."

"Why, *fortune*."

Mean Tilly had not even waited for Amanda to try. "Doesn't *fort* mean *strong*?"

"Substantial. Such nuances come later, in the study of any language."

Mean Milly. Amanda contemplated her own minimal accomplishments, and the mockery at St Mildred's for her lapses in English
usage and accent. She would never learn the language, not entirely.
Never.

"Then Miss Tilly, what are your accomplishments?"

"The which, dear? Oh, hardly anything." Tilly chuckled. "I kept
Daddy happy."

"Onward!" cried Milly. "*Not the same as an E, however.* Seven."

Tilly cried, "See, dear? Not like lonely or sickly. Think of a word
like repart*ee*."

"Toffee? Coffee?"

"You must listen, child. Seven letters, I said."

"But well tried! With *toff*, you're getting warm."

Truly, she was warm. Or chilly? Some word began moving
towards her mouth. Her eyes closed to see a toff, who showed off,
was spiffy and smart and grand.

"*Grandee!*" As she rose, excited to have got there, the sisters
laughed to see the Peek Frean crumbs cascade in all directions.

"That will greatly annoy Mrs K," said Milly.

VII. The Literary-and-Historicals, Round Two

The Canadians also are sometimes so direct.

At coffee, Mrs Ellis and I sat side by side. I was embroidering,
working the last lily in a row. She was looking at but not touching a
corner, where the lily leaves start.

"Why no thimble, Miss Tilly? That's a thick callus on your
forefinger."

"A thimble always seemed to hold my hand back, Mrs Ellis. I felt
so even as a child. I only used one in my fifties. I worried about stain-
ing my silk."

"You had a hard time with the change, Miss Tilly?"

Mrs Ellis is so friendly, and her lively ways have brought such
interest to The Green House, that I felt I must respond.

"The hard time was Milly's. She left Mrs Brocklehurst and came home, so I could care for her. Five years. Then she took up her post with the girls in Cambridge."

"Two people to care for!"

"Oh, Daddy was so happy to have her home, Mrs Ellis! He was so proud of her."

"And were you happy?"

"Milly enjoyed working in our little garden. She dearly wanted a pond, but the space didn't allow for it, let alone the expense. So she designed an elegant bird bath." Dear me! I felt myself running on, as Milly says I do. "Such trouble, keeping cats away! Then that wonderful chance, to go to Cambridge with the Dickinson girls." I peered at my silk, straightened it again, again, but still Mrs Ellis watched and listened. "A chance for her to live amid all that learning! My sister is very intelligent."

"So are you."

"Oh my goodness, Mrs Ellis, I'm the one who stayed home."

Wasn't that silly? If only my sister would turn from her chat with Mr Ellis to frown, or even to signal silence at me! She did not. I started on the lily's golden stamens, hoping thus to indicate to Mrs Ellis that we would move on now.

"What exactly did Miss Talbot do, for these girls?"

"Why, their parents thought it unsuitable for them to be alone there, especially with Jocelyn's mathematics. Not one other girl read maths in her year. Milly was their companion. Charming rooms, they had. When I visited, there was a party. Delightful!"

"Did you and Miss Talbot go to university?"

"The which, Mrs Ellis?" I did ask that, I'm afraid, though I'd heard her perfectly. Just to gain a moment. "By that time Mummy wasn't well, and it wasn't really thought necessary. For girls. The expense. Then Mummy died. And we couldn't leave Daddy." Gabble gabble. I'd taken so few golden stitches that the poor stamen scarcely showed yet. "No, we really couldn't."

"Miss Talbot did."

Mr Ellis and my sister laughed then, concluding their talk.

He turned, no doubt to look at his pretty wife, and rose to join us. I was so grateful. My needle began to move. As always I was briefly away, inside my work, till the rhythm established itself. I came back to find Mr Ellis sighing.

"Cambridge, Oxford. An impossible dream, for us. Amanda will just have to put up with a Canadian university."

"Really, Gerald! They're fine."

That little Canadian girl, so full of herself and so confident, would have that privilege denied my sister. To Amanda it would seem natural.

Jealousy is my great fault, Milly says. Or do I mean envy? They burned in me again this morning, as we set down our empty cups and returned to our crossword.

"We're not finished with you yet, child." My sister smiled sourly. I smiled too, to hear her tone. "*Make farms and foes*. Five letters. Well?"

To see Amanda not answer was a pleasure. Milly spoiled it. "*Yield*," she said, just as if she had the right to, and went on as if she were leader. "Three more. All difficult."

"And one is Seventeen Across!"

She winced, but my sister and I are strong. She pursed her lips, re-opened them.

"Eleven Across. *Fifty enter without Tudor collars calmly*. Nine."

I laughed. "Eleven, Fifty, Nine – quite a party!"

Glancing at each other, we decided to show that tedious child what we can do.

Milly mused, "Let us see. A Tudor collar is a ruff, is it not?"

"The fifty are ruffless," I replied.

"Or unruffed?"

"Indeed. In Latin, I do believe, fifty is *L*."

"*Unruffled*." We said the word together into her blank stupid face.

"Two more!" crowed Milly. "Six Across. *Not the Bohemian girl*. Five letters."

"It won't be the eponymous opera."

"True," Milly agreed. "Musical clues are rare, in this crossword."

"Think of Bohemia, child," I urged. "Do think!" But she only frowned.

"John Huss," said Milly.

I stepped closer to my rightful victory. "The Hussites."

"Narrow Calvinist thought, Amanda. *Hussy!* Isn't is obvious? Can't you understand? Don't you know anything?"

Mean Milly! The child looked sick with shame.

I snatched *The Times* from my sister. "Again you took my answer! Very well, Milly, let's hear you find Seventeen Across. *Van of the broom display.* Five letters."

Amanda counted the moments, on her fingers. I did too.

"Second asking, Milly. *Van of the broom display.*"

We went on saying numbers, slowly, but my sister's lips were closed.

"Last chance to show off, Milly! The third time of asking. Just like banns."

Silence.

VII. The Final Round

Tilly pouted. "You've spoiled it, Milly! We can't finish. Our time's up, and Mrs K will be here directly to fetch the tray."

She threw the newspaper down. The pages flapped and slid about as they settled on the floor: *Winston Churchill Ideal Home Exhibition Thomas Beecham.* And also *Coronation Stone Yorkshire Colliery Fire The London Library Grand National.*

"Don't grizzle, Amanda! It is often not possible to accomplish what one wishes. You will learn."

And *Quo Tai-Chi Egyptian Parliament Hoa Binh.*

Tilly chuckled. "One becomes accustomed to disappointment."

Saskatchewan. A disease of cattle had broken out.

At school in Canada, Amanda's class first drew maps of the whole country. Then they coloured British Columbia green for all its trees, and the Atlantic provinces four shades of blue. Unusual Quebec was purple, Ontario red, while the prairies got brown, yellow, and orange. The Territories were left blank for later study. Saskatchewan: that was the nation's granary. It had all straight borders, the only one. Amanda's class had used their rulers carefully. That name on the English page, the English fitted carpet told her that though she had never travelled there, she loved, she loved Saskatchewan. Her heart and mouth were full.

* * *

At the New Year's party at The Green House, Gerald Ellis took off his jacket and tie, to put full vigour into galloping from Aix to Ghent. Reciting the poem was his *party turn*, a curious Canadian idiom. Was it an accomplishment? Amanda wondered, amazed to see her father thus. At home he went tie-less only at the cottage, in the air fragrant with warm raspberries, pond mud, clover, skunk, pine. Here in Oxford, a rare deep snow had fallen. The English were excited.

Mr Penrose read aloud the final scene of *A Christmas Carol*.

Miss Clyde did card tricks and made everyone laugh.

In an unexpectedly true voice, Mrs K sang *Quite Early One Morning*.

Professor McGeachie blew smoke rings. He also told a classical Greek joke. Days later, Amanda's father was still trying to explain it to her.

Then came a slide show: English birds. As the colours flickered on the wall of the lounge, Mr Ledington said gently, "Grebe," or "One of our many coots." For a small brown bird, Mrs Ledington's thin voice suddenly offered, "Our poet Hardy puts it so well: *An aged thrush, frail, gaunt, and small / In blast-beruffled plume*."

Amanda's laughing mother carried in a pudding-basin of fresh snow, looped hot maple syrup all over, dished it out. The puzzled English spooned up Canadian winter.

Next, the twins. Over the piano, Mrs K had draped red velvet. Tilly beamed, Milly smiled, in their knitted dresses of dusty rose and cranberry. The piano bench scarcely contained those two broad beams.

"A duet," Milly said. "Schubert."

"A rousing piece! *Marche Militaire*."

Their fingers moved. Quickly the files of notes executed their manoeuvres, while in their bright uniforms, with epaulets and harness and instruments glinting, the band played. The horses wheeled. The soldiers stepped about their square, flourishing their tiny courage. The music ran up clear and high, unstoppable, and Milly leaned back from her agile fingers; then it fled downward, sounding for depth, while Tilly's sensible shoe pressed like a lover on the pedal and her torso bent in weighty urgency over the keys. At last, the sound returned to the blending centre and to the miniature pomp, half-humorous, of the appointed melody.

"Bravo!" Everyone rose, clapping and clapping. The twins bowed happily. Tilly's hem caught on the piano bench; Milly freed it.

Later, Amanda was curled up half-asleep in her bed while her parents sat by her, finishing their nightcaps.

"Vivian Clyde was lively tonight," said her father. "She's good company."

"I think she should marry Mr Penrose," her mother replied.

Amanda opened her eyes.

"Good lord, Rachel! Whatever for?"

"If Vivian doesn't marry soon, she won't. She's at that point in life."

"Have you said this to her?"

Rachel Ellis laughed. "We talk about everything!"

Amanda and her father gazed, astonished.

"But what about Penrose, Rachel? Do you know – "

She laughed again. "They'll do as they'll do." She tasted her brandy. "Soon we'll drink to the New Year, Gerald. To the completion of your book. To going home."

"I don't want to think about all that, Rachel."

Amanda's mother turned her glass in her fingers. "Now – can't you just imagine the twins at the turn of the century? The young Misses Talbot, playing for company. Hair up. Long pretty dresses."

"Those figures, in bustles?"

"Gerald! Don't be rude."

He sipped. "They played that same piece fifty years ago. Milly told me, over the punch – which wasn't up to much, by the way. Mrs

K has a woman's hand with the spirits. Here's to you, Rachel. You look very pretty tonight." Amanda's parents touched glasses. "Another thing," said her father. "When Milly was in Cambridge with the whatsit girls, yes yes, Dickinson, her sister visited."

In her tent-like raincoat, Tilly had trudged among the colleges.

"The girls put on a *musicale*. For friends, dons, tutors. The twins played *Marche Militaire*." Amanda's father drank again. "And Rachel, she said they had *quite a little triumph*." His voice skidded upwards.

"What else did Tilly tell about Cambridge?"

"The mathematical girl should have won a certain prize, but it went to a young man. In 1943 she abandoned her studies. The other married." He emptied his glass. "Such lives. Rachel, do you suppose either of the Talbot girls ever – ?"

Magnificat

The spring term in which Kay died and Constance disappeared from St Mildred's and I broke my glasses featured a school-wide obsession with mealtime talk of sex. Lessons and the church-bound crocodile also provided the essential audience of authority, but the Dining Hall was richest in metaphor: tapioca, leaking sausages, fried-egg bosoms, mashed-potato bosoms, baked-apple bosoms, fish lips, the thin stream from a water pitcher. Everyone, even juniors like Helen and me, understood some of the jokes, but I also giggled at many mysteries, hoping thus to avoid teasing. Danger and hunger went together in Hall.

Each Sunday, egg-day, Helen and I anxiously read the new seating plan posted by Miss Hodgson, Assistant Head. Would we sit together? Would the big girls be cruel or pay no attention to us? Would the prefect (an older girl vested with minor authority, a kind of colonial governor) exert humorous and friendly control over the table? Or would she herself be tormented? As a Canadian I was no social asset. I hoped only to be seated near Helen, and a window. Waiting for the breakfast gong, Helen and I peered into Hall at the two hundred stony white plates and two hundred yellow eggs, plump and cold as toads. Once inside we peered out, for the old narrow window-panes had devitrified and opalesced. Everything out there – the Great Lawn, drive, trees, birds – looked differently brilliant.

When alone, Helen and I spoke little of sex, although, before polio took Kay, she'd talked teasingly to us about dances at the nearby boys' school. She even speculated as to which girls in our form had older brothers. Kay also explained, without laughing at my ignorance, what ST stood for. And of her parents she said, "They love each other a lot. Honestly." I did not think of my parents in such terms. Helen never spoke of her home. At quarter- and half-terms, no relative came to take her out.

After Dining Hall, some mistresses used lesson time for reproof of our behaviour. Silent, we stared at our desks. During the meals themselves, a few sixth-formers frowned at our salacious snorts of laughter. "Honestly!" they sighed with distaste. Other seniors appeared indifferent. Such was the daygirl Constance Moore. Not short, quiet or loud, not brainy or fat, Constance seemed one of those girls of whom classmates, school photo in hand only a few years later, say pettishly, "What *was* her name?"

The Games Mistress, Miss Fielding, taught Health. She herself was a rosy, vigorous, big-limbed woman who liked lists. For prep she set us always five words, both spelling and meaning. When we got *groin*, the prefect supervising us that evening barely kept order. Next day, no girl would admit knowledge. "It's not in my dictionary, Miss Fielding, honestly." Puzzled, she said, "Why, look – by our thighs," and stood legs apart, hands right *there* on her gabardine skirt. Writing the word calmed us, but then Miss Flower in Religious Knowledge showed slides of groined Gothic ceilings. We groined our stodge, at dinner. Semi-hysterical, we bathed the slabs in sweet sauce.

One day Miss Fielding, after explaining that we each contained a lifetime supply of eggs, described what would happen to most of them. Hearing the M-word spoken was unendurable. At the lesson's end, Helen's task was to erase Miss Fielding's brisk diagrams on the board. She dropped the chalk brush twice. I startled. My glasses flew off my hot face to the floor, and I stepped on them. One lens shattered.

Miss Maywood of Classics liked us to "See the Latin, girls, smiling through our English words!" Our names were examples – Caroline, Vicky. She enthused too about Mary but cautioned us against any drift to Mariolatry, a term she did not define. We then confronted the day's new Latin vocab, watchful for twin or triplet meanings.

"*Nudus*, girls. That is obvious, surely?" We would not shape our tongues to that, not in front of her. Close-mouthed, we met her annoyance. "Why *nude*, of course!"

When I flipped ahead a few pages in my Latin text, *month* came at me through my remaining lens and my bare eye. The pages fell closed. I did not tell even Helen.

At dinner, spluttering, we peeled our vegetables to make *carrotas nudas*. Our prefect frowned, shushed weakly, blushed. When the rice pudding came, we went back to names. What would we call our first baby? Charles of course, for the little prince. Or Michael. Or James. Warm jam filled our mouths. And then if we had a baby sister for him? O Hilary, Rosamond, Claire. None of us liked her given name. My gangly Helen hated hers even more after Miss Maywood told us about Troy.

"I like my name," Constance said. "I always have."

How odd. *Constantia*. Girls looked away.

Or Sally. Or Alison. At this refined discussion, our prefect beamed.

"I'd call her *Labia*." O what did that mean, who said it? I couldn't see. A terrible shock in the grey April air, then laughter. "Honestly!" Then anger, noise, bad, fingers to lips, a very bad silence, the prefect striding out of Hall, driving a silent stumbling dirty girl before her, the Assistant Head flapping her napkin and rising from her cover to pursue. Before my eyes the hunt went in and out of focus. When talk resumed, Constance alone did not gasp or gesticulate.

That night, Tessa and Janet walked along the row of bath cubicles whispering loudly, "*Puellas nudas!*"

Ham was served once at dinner that week, and a girl at our table tipped over the sauceboat. Cumberland pooled out, soaking the parched Irish linen. Our prefect sent the clumsy to the kitchens. Although milk stains might stay, sour-smelling, the full week till a new cloth came, and so might the mild marks of tea or fallen Brussels sprouts, this scarlet was something else. The kitchen maid arrived. As our prefect conferred with her, a whisper sounded: "The table-cloth looks like a giant's ST." O who said that? Who was reddest? Our table erupted so that the whole Dining Hall fell silent.

In the deep quiet, the School's Head Girl rose from her place at High Table with the teaching staff (only their window had stained glass, dark old purples and oranges). She spoke to our humiliated prefect. We were forbidden to collect the sweet for our table from the serving hatch. While everyone else ate apples and custard, we silently beheld the clean rags spread by the maid over that great red stain. Constance stared.

Menstruation: no one spoke this word from the Latin *menses*.

Storytelling, however, was frequent.

One girl's sixteen-year-old sister lay resting as her Mummy mixed a pudding in a bowl and chatted with a neighbour. "'Is Jill sick?' 'O it's only her monthlies,' Mummy said, and she went on beating! As if it was nothing!"

Another hid in the pantry while her sister and aunt talked, washing up after lunch. "Andrea asked, 'Is the smell very bad?' And Auntie said, 'Nothing that a sponge bath wouldn't take care of, dear. Make it a habit, at that time. Men don't like it, you see.' Then Andrea cried ever so."

And another girl, shopping at the chemist's with her mother, met a neighbour. "Her box of STs was at the top of her string bag. Everyone saw. With the apples and eggs and Lux!"

Lux soap was ninety-nine point ninety-nine percent pure, said *Woman's Day*, stacked in our common room. The polluted point one did not show. *Showing.* At lunch an Upper Fifth girl told in hilarious disgust how, in chemistry, a classmate had shown all over her seat. "A filthy red pool, honestly!" Constance and Helen turned away.

Helen's breasts now pushed out her tunic. She hated them. She hunched. Miss Fielding nagged, "Posture, Helen! Stand up straight!" I was flat as the Canadian prairie, so she had nothing to say to me.

Weekly, a mistress and a few girls went into town to do errands. I was taken, my smashed specs in hand, to perch in the eye-doctor's fusty room with a black cylinder rammed into my eye socket. Lenses spun before me till my tear ducts spilled over.

For these shopping trips, each dormitory submitted for screening a list of desired items. Once I asked for *Astral* hand cream; I'd seen the name in *Woman's Day* and liked it. Miss Maywood, the expedition's leader that week, conducted the interrogation.

"*Nivea* is what we usually purchase, is it not? *Astral* is presumably one of your American products, Amanda." As with many at St Mildred's, Miss Maywood's confusion about my provenance persisted. In class, she chalked up both words. "*Nivea*, snow-white. Do you see the association, girls? Soft skin, pure as snow. And *astra*. *Per ardua ad astra!*" Then wartime reminiscence took her to the lunch bell.

One day our form crowded all together into the junior girls' lavatory near our classroom. By each toilet stood a white lidded pail. In my early days at school I had opened one, seen the heap of white twists sheathed in gauze, stained red-brown. Now we overturned the pails. We picked up the sanitary towels, laughed, pretended to vomit. We inspected them for eggs but saw none, waved the towels at each other, shrieked, threw them about. Most were dry or damp, but a saturated one streaked the cold wall tiles with red. Screaming, we saw the lavatory door open. No prefect, only Constance. Why would a senior girl come in here? She saw our game and left.

Miss Maywood held forth, low-voiced and disapproving, on Mariolatry. Then, changing her tone, she spoke of the Virgin's commendable acquiescence in God's project. Our Lady (a term we must use with care) had right away answered the angel Gabriel, saying, "*Magnificat anima mea Dominum.*"

The next week in Dining Hall placed me near a window. Peering, I found Helen's *Roman profile* (so said Miss Maywood) three tables away. She looked sullen. That morning as we walked to church, the Classics mistress had told about Cornelia's jewels: her beautiful children. Now Helen's smile to me was brief. Glancing about for other recent tablemates, I found all but Constance.

Also I saw, through my one glazed lens, that the rainy trees were coming into leaf. Tiny green points ruffled out. The supercooled and iridescent liquid of the old windows revealed branches and trunks most curiously slanted, magnified, like moving river water. Happy, I spent mealtimes tilting my head so as to see in different ways.

The following Sunday, Helen and I were reunited in the Dining Hall. We looked about. Again, or still, Constance was absent. We had heard of no crises or accidents, but from our form to the heights of the Lower Sixth was a long way.

Enquiring, we found that rumours angry as infected flesh ringed the name of the daygirl Constance Moore.

"Happier elsewhere, really. Not quite a St Mildred's girl," said Miss Maywood.

"Left."

"Expelled."

"Honestly, yesterday I was in the stationer's with Flower, and Constance went by. I don't think Flower saw. She'd have had a bird!"

"Is she, you know?"

"Ever so. Showing."

"Too shaming."

"Poor Constance has made a terrible mistake." Miss Flower teared up.

At my school in Canada, an older girl named Elspeth had worn an aura like a devil's. Girls' glances slid or sliced like figure skates over Elspeth, then quickly away. Her green eyes stared. When we girls knelt in the gym to have our skirts measured, hers was always too short. She had to lower it over her slim legs. Once Elspeth was sent home to remove nail polish, and shockingly did not bother to return till the next day.

After Elspeth left the school, her legacy a name resonating with badness like a transformer, my mother and I one day stopped at Woolworth's lunch counter. It smelled of Javex as Elspeth, rag in hand, wiped down the stained formica. Did she smile at me? Her waitress's uniform was tight over her stomach. What should I say to this older girl, here? She brought our sandwiches (peculiar taste of restaurant egg salad). My mother did not have coffee, and she held her lips in the way that meant anger.

"Constance has sacrificed her future," said our Head, addressing all two hundred of us in the Dining Hall. Egg-filled, egg-drained, bleeding, dry, we waited in silence for specifics that Miss Pringle never spoke. "We shall move on now, girls."

Mrs Tonelli of Art tore up my watercolour of a window framing leafy branches, blurred and swollen, or sharp, or wavily distorted. "You can't show everything simultaneously, Amanda. Try a still life."

She gestured to a pot with sticks in it, on a table in the Art Room. Showing.

Helen said, "I like your picture, Amanda. Honestly."

Who did it to Constance? Who did Constance do it with? With whom?

To us, no answer was thinkable. The only man living at St Mildred's was sullen clumping Fitzgerald who mowed lawns, moved desks, carried trunks up to the dormitories. A big Irishman, he was someone to whom girls never spoke. There was a regular Visiting Speaker, desiccated Mr Greene the historian, who went on and on about Home Rule, Iran, the Renaissance, the Yew Ess Ess Ah. Sweaty meaty Fitzgerald, withered Mr Greene – with Constance? But after all she had come to our suburban school daily from the city. What men, what boys lived there? Our imaginations shrank back, to a vividly baby-full Constance.

My new spectacles arrived. For the first few hours I raised my knee high with every step, like a trotting horse, unable to see the distance to the ground.

Gradually Helen's and my vision drifted further away from Constance, to the upcoming Easter holidays, and then to the new music mistress – she was old, and farted often (perhaps her eggs had rotted?) – and to tennis in the summer term. Then, in the holidays, my parents and I were happy. We had missed each other.

With September our form moved up. Not being the youngest in school any more was strange. Some girls had started their monthlies. They huddled, hissing of pains and blood. We others disliked and envied their smell. One girl had seen her sister kiss a boy. Another claimed to have been kissed. "It was all slimy, ugh! Honestly."

At night I set my glasses upside down, by my Indian box, to reverse any pooling that might have occurred during the day. Helen and I heard talk of *dirty nights* in our new dormitory; the older girls whispered. By torchlight, we would watch girls *do it* and ourselves be watched. Helen's difficulty in speaking of this prospect, or of her summer holidays, was extreme.

"I'll be with you," I said.

Shopping with Miss Maywood in the rainy city, Helen and I escaped her discourse on *ad*vertising ("Girls! See the Protean quality of Latin prefixes!") by offering to go to the chemist's. There we located lozenges, tooth powder, Epsom salts, Nivea, fat transparent globules of cod liver oil. We gazed then at the stacks of square boxes, wrapped in dun paper with a faint stripy sheen, and unlabelled, that contained STs.

"Amanda! Helen!"

Constance wore a smart green coat. A flowery dress showed underneath. Curls framed her face, her red lips smiled, she met our eyes. "Look!" She turned the pram. "Isn't she wonderful?"

A baby. Round face, blue wandering eyes, arms that waved towards my glasses, a sweet damp smell. What should I say?

"What's her name?"

Helen tugged at my arm.

"Jane." Constance spoke as if she had invented it herself. "Her name is Jane."

Constance's eyes radiated love. Helen pulled at me again. Jane wore a pink wool cap with ribbon inserts and a bow under her chin. A blanket covered her. Beneath, within, her eggs were ready, wet, blood-heat, abundant, full of power.

"What a nice bonnet," I tried, hating our petty silence.

"I knitted that," Constance breathed. Her stroking fingers moved over the wool to the baby's cheek. Jane turned her head, and her delicate lips sucked eagerly.

"Go now! Don't let Maywood see!" Helen whispered urgently.

As we walked back to St Mildred's, with the Classics mistress safely up ahead between two girls from the Lower Fifth, the rain stopped. I took off my specs to wipe them. "Helen, I'm afraid the glass will go thin and runny, like the windows in Hall."

"Let me see." Helen turned them over in her hands as I walked beside her, feeling her presence there, and the light directly on my eyes. "They're all right, Amanda. Honestly." Then she said, "Amanda, I hurt. Here." Through the thick navy of her school winter coat, Helen pressed her groin.

We glanced at each other repeatedly. Tears fell from Helen's eyes. Through our silence we heard the other girls chattering with Miss Maywood about *Ad*vent and the Nativity Play. Each year the mistresses chose the most beautiful Sixth Former to hold the plaster of Paris baby. Who might this year's Virgin Mother be?

Back at school, Helen and I joined the line for the Dining Hall just as its doors swung open on fatty mutton, gravy, marge, stodge, tea.

A moment's silence always came after Grace, a silence bookended by our collective *Amen* and the harsh scrape of our chairs. Into this space moved the fading winter's sun. Flowing through the panes, the full pale light made radiant all two hundred daughters standing there. Magnified, we were: we were magnificent.

A Civil Plantation

I am the only man in this English school, the only one, and I am here because I cannot teach.

Why did I give the girl that mark for her picture? O what have I done? What would my mother say? And the fragrant lady, and Fitzgerald?

The child had drawn the English settlers planted up to their waists, their necks, in the black earth of Munster. They were in tidy rows. Their mouths were open with scream. Crumbled earth crusted their red faces. Eyes bulging, they tried to push up from the soil. A woman held her dirty baby above her own half-buried head. Where did Amanda find such images?

Where shall I go tonight? I could stay here, lie in this bed and bite my nails, my nail-beds, till morning. I hold no key to any other door.

No. I shall get up and review my Notes for the history of the Irish plantations, the history that I shall never write.

One reason why the English failed to create in Ireland the plantations they envisaged was that they could not control the people whom they planted. Relatively powerless though the tenants were, and though many did take root and so displace the native vegetation, as a crop they were not what the London corporations and the ex-army officers and the minor nobility had had in mind.

Some tenants married Irishwomen. Many complained about the quality of the land assigned them. Others were unsuitably lethargic about their Protestantism, or adopted reprehensible Irish agricultural practices such as tail-ploughing and creaghting. *Hibernia hibernescit. Caoruigheachta*: the creaghts (i.e., the herds and their human attendants) moved about frivolously from pasture land to

pasture land. Some tenants even solidarized with the uprooted Irish
– though not so far as to vacate their land. Ungrateful and quarrel-
some, homesick but land-hungry, their tenants caused endless problems for the planters. Such contradictions persisted even unto the
sixth, eighth, eleventh, fifteenth generations of English plantation in
Ireland. The tenants loathed the place but wouldn't go, refused to
leave but hated to stay.

Where shall I go?

Every night, quite late, I leave the grounds of St Mildred's
School – or of St Stephen's or Miss Rammell's as the case may be, or
The Gates or Fairways or Hillscott House, any school as long as it is
not for boys – to breathe a more spacious air, move in a wider world.
I am, after all, Mr Greene: Foreign Affairs. When I return, perhaps
an hour later, all the windows are muffled. Who sleeps where? The
tall paired windows at the southwest corner belong to the Head, I am
told, and Matron holds a room near the San, but I do not know
where lies loud-voiced Miss Trout, snobbish Miss Lincoln, lovely
Miss Flower of lovely Religious Knowledge, widowed Mrs Wilmer
of Maths. Where lies that fragrance? Needles of light, at the edge of
curtains, illuminate the slanting rain.

Earlier today I was with the Third Form, being Mr Greene:
Specialist in History. During the hour I returned their work.

Their assignment was to draw the brave colonists sent to Munster by Queen Elizabeth – the first, that is. Only a few weeks ago, on
23 September, George had a lung resection, and although his progress is reported, by his wife herself, to be good, we must not, says
Miss Pringle, echoed by Miss Hodgson, underestimate the direness
of the situation, nor must we delay prayers for the young woman des-
tined soon to be the second Queen Elizabeth and doubtless to win,
too, her honorific title of Gloriana. Also the girls were to write a
paragraph about Elizabeth I's excellent plantation scheme.

Amanda's art was not confined to her notebook's left page but
overflowed the margin of the right, reserved for her paragraph. (To
the latter at least no exception could be taken, for it quoted almost
verbatim what I had dictated to the Third Form.) Her mark seemed
the only possible one. No other could be borne. Severe criticism was

114

due, though the drawing admittedly, undeniably exhibited vitality. Critical assessment had not been easy.

Contemporary analysts of the plantation schemes – *contemporary* covers a parade of centuries – refer often to the poor quality of the English and, later, Scots who were taken or sent to Ireland to be planted. Not all critics were as damning as Fynes Morrison, who exclaimed that the English settlers "were generally observed to have been eyther papists, men of disordered life, banckrots, or very poore . . . by which course Ireland as the heele of the body was made the sincke of England, the stench whereof had almost annoyed very Cheapside the hart of the body" (Canny 21). A later and more laconic commentator described Ulster as settled by "the scum of both nations" (22). Many under-tenants were in fact unemployed, or had been discharged from the army, or were destitute, or knew no trade, or had no experience whatsoever of farming and were in short plainly desperate.

My own mother's ancestors stood or rather fell into this last category. Certainly Mother scorns any touch of hands to earth. In her little shop she sells tobacco, sweets, newspapers, ice creams, and postcards for trippers. Hating Ireland and the Irish, she was and is pure English always – but this has no place in my Notes.

In the present day, the day-girls of St Mildred's come and go along the drive. Mistresses leave for errands in the city. Vans bring laundry and bread. The post arrives. Fitzgerald, the School's factotum, rides his bicycle to fetch white paint for the ruled lines and boundaries of the playing-field. Occasional taxicabs bear parents, anxious or angry. At night, though, all is solitary, or so I thought until three nights ago. It was my belief that only I broke the order of School to move about in darkness.

My shoes crunch, until the gravel of the courtyard gives way to the damp hard-packed earth of the drive. Does a curtain move? Does some woman envy my masculine nocturnal wanderings? In the dark there is no need to hide my bitten nails. On either side of the drive rears up a twelve-foot rampart of hollies and rhododendrons, the foliage sometimes freaked with moonlight, now slippery with rain. I smell wet earth. My scalp is damp, under its scurf of faded red. To imagine hiders in that glittering dark green is easy. Scrambles, chirrings are audible. Rats? Snakes? I walk on the crown of the road- way. *Kern in the woods?* At the drive's mid-point, any walker is invisi- ble both from the school and from the suburban road. I stop to listen – nervously, foolishly. The factotum Fitzgerald is one of the black Irish, strong, with a coarse lantern-jawed face, but I am the slight red kind. However, I sense no footfall or hot breath.

Both red and black appeared in Amanda's picture of the Elizabe- than plantation. Dirty hands protruded from earth, thick tongues from mouths. None of this did I have in mind. No other girl drew any like image of the second Munster plantation. Amanda – misun- derstood. Of an adult we would say, "He has distorted," or "has falsi- fied." Where did her vision come from? A Canadian. A child. Perhaps she simply does not know where power lies. My first decision was, therefore, to give the girl three marks out of ten. She may not know, but must learn. She must learn shame.

Blaming the planters themselves, rather than the tenants, is of course much less common. Who writes history, after all? However, the documents do uneasily show that many planters resembled mod- ern land speculators; they bought, sold again quickly, then high- tailed it back to London to spend the profits. Some neither ploughed nor sowed nor reaped but simply logged off all their trees, acquired more land, logged it off, etc. (Canny 43). More than one English planter vomited his way across the Irish Sea to inspect his property and, like Snailholm in 1610, looked once in disgust at the rooty fibrous soil and left forever (Perceval-Maxwell 120). As for me, on my seasonal visits to my mother in the 1920s and 1930s and 1940s and now in the 1950s, I am invariably (out of dread, going over, and relief, coming back) seasick on the Swansea-Cork ferry.

Of those plantation-holders who did stay in Ireland, many failed to build the required, extensive bawms and outbuildings. Many failed to plant the right numbers of single males of the right ages who rep- resented the right numbers of families. From their financial masters in England, these procrastinating undertakers faced threats of forfei- ture of their lands. These further shrank their motivation to plant and build, which intensified the threats. . . . Locked in this dialectic,

thousands of fertile Irish acres (acres that the official English survey-
ors took years to realize were not the same size as acres on the big
island) lay fallow first, then neglected, then in wild ruin.

Civilized order characterizes the grounds of St Mildred's
School. Turning south at the gates, I begin my nightly peregrination.
A broad pathway, well-kept and smoothed by Fitzgerald, hugs the
great rectangle of low dry-stone wall that surrounds the School. On
Sundays all the girls and mistresses follow this same pathway, clock-
wise before matins, counter after evensong. Soundlessness is the
ideal. The girls are exhorted to walk lightly, like ladies, around their
temporary home. Such is St Mildred's to me also for a week in each
term, yet I do not join the sacred crocodile. I am the only man in the
school. With whom would I walk? Difficulty charges any answer.
Not to pose the question is preferable.

In the life of various schools, I am not only the only man but also
Guest Lecturer. I am Mr Greene: Foreign Affairs, or Mr Greene:
Current Events, or Mr Greene: Specialist in History. Why does Mr
Gaitskell think we must tighten wage and price controls? I can
explain his ideas in terms that little girls can understand. To the
Lower Fifth, I unfold the first-quarter drop in net gold and dollar
earnings of the sterling area. Then I lead the Sixth to see why we
must be firm with Iran about the Anglo-Iran Oil Company, and very
firm with the Soviet Union about the peace treaty with Japan, and
positively rigid with Egypt about the Suez Canal.

When I perform my Guest Lectures, a mistress stands by me. In
Amanda's form, Miss Trout plays this role. She stands too close, her
rumpled solidity juxtaposing my rather thin neatness. There are giggles. I clasp my hands so my bitten nails curl under.

This week, my topic was Renaissance England. Led by her daring explorers and soldiers, she transformed the mapped world. Perhaps I dwelt on this point too long, for with her pointer Miss Trout
struck Ireland emphatically. To proceed was a pleasure, however, for
I like to tell Munster's story, naturally not that of the lamentable first
plantation nor of the shocking Desmond years, but of the second,
begun in 1584 as a favourite project of Elizabeth's, and of its healing
effects upon the Irish landscape.

As usual, Miss Trout concluded my talk with "Now girls, ques-tions?" Blank silence is customary. Amanda broke it. "Mr Greene, did the Queen ask those Irish people if they minded? If it was all right to come and live on their land?"

I could have said, "Amanda, that question was and is considered irrelevant by all the best authorities." I could have told how Robert Blair in 1623 spoke of the need of the truly faithful, i.e., Protestants, "to *plant* religion [emphasis added]" in Ireland (Perceval-Maxwell 270). To impress upon Amanda the bravery involved in planting right religion, I could have told her how, more than a century later, when a Methodist preacher "first *invaded* [emphasis added] the county of Monaghan[,] an attempt was made on his life by a man who had screened himself among the bushes" (Phillips 33). But I said no such things. I said nothing. My knowledge is in my Notes. There I keep a quotation from another Methodist, in the 1750s, who described himself in Ireland as "almost continually in danger of hav-ing [his] brains beat out" (34).

Here, beating the stone bounds of this girls' school, I am inland, covert Irish at England's centre. Westward over the Irish Sea is my mother, also inland, covert, Methodist in the Republic. No one here knows she is there. No one here knows I come from there. When the mistresses and I walk and talk on the Great Lawn, rolled in green rules by Fitzgerald, our conversation is of Attlee, Bevan, Bevin, Churchill, George. Once, Miss Gregson of Science men-tioned Walton's shared Nobel. Miss Lincoln of Geography won-dered at De Valera's Spanish name. On neither occasion did I mention Ireland. My habit of saying little, unless lecturing, hard-ened long ago.

I have heard the child Amanda call plimsolls *running shoes* and say *laboratory* with the stress on *bor*, and then witnessed the laughter. One word can kill. Vowels alone can inform just as well as a wrongly-emphasized syllable. Miss Pringle and Miss Hodgson are irreproachably Home Counties, but Miss Lincoln's speech is too carefully not northern, while I suspect that Miss Flower's gentle voice overlies an origin involving coins, counter, and till.

When I was shipped to my English school, ridicule met me too.

I also wore the armour of silence, but then I turned out to be that oddity in this land, *good at languages*. Irish as Paddy's pig, I cracked the code and achieved a flawless accent. Amanda's is certainly better than last term, though she is not talkative, and her sudden blunt questions to me have been startling. *The* Canadian girl, the others call her, or *Our*. She does smile. She has a good friend, too. Would that I could say the same. Thus, until her drawing lay before me, I had supposed her content.

Crude. Amanda's drawing was crude. Of her form's nineteen pictures of Munster, only hers merited more than one look. She used rather strong, in fact very strong colours. She did not even try, I believe, to stay within that red ruled line of the margin. Surely disobedience merits punishment? Ignorance of the law excuses no man, no girl. Resistance surely is pointless for either of us.

Wild Ireland! Through centuries of plantation, the Irish resisted. That is yet another reason why those imperial fantasies of colonists on plump smiling farmlands, near snug smug villages, solidified into such tortured facts. Packed in salt, pickled Irish heads were shipped to Whitehall. English settlers, men and women both, ran naked under blood-dripping Irish scourges to the gates of Cork. After Fitzmaurice retook the town of Kilmallock for the Irish, it was sacked, burned, and razed. Wolves lived there. Munster's lush grasslands were so badly damaged by conflict that they could not support an invading army (Berleth 60). The earth dried out with fire and famine.

Resistance. The *Shorter Oxford* shows *kern* as deriving from the Old Irish *ceitern*, a band of foot soldiers, a light-armed Irish foot soldier, one of the poorer class among the "wild Irish." Then the *Dictionary* quotes Shakespeare (again and always, their Shakespeare), whose Richard II in 1394 shouts jovially to his men,

Now for our Irish Wars:
We must supplant those rough rug-headed kerns,
Which live like venom where no venom else,
But only they have privilege to live (II: 1, 155-58)

Voluble of hierarchy, are they not, these royal pronominals *our* and *we*, the verb *supplant*, the adjectives *rough* and r*ug-headed*, the nouns *venom* and *privilege*? Surely the latter is ironic.

When I tell the Lower Fourth or Upper Fifth about yet another resignation from the cabinet (I doubt that Labour will survive October 25), or M de Gaulle's gains in the recent French elections, or the honourably heavy British contingent, second only to that of the Americans, in the UN effort in Korea – when I tell thus and so, a mistress stays in the form-room. I am not privileged to be alone with the girls. This is not because I am a male while they are young and presumably virgin females, but because Mr Greene cannot keep order. Therefore he cannot *teach* a class. The fact is widely known.

Another option in selecting a mark for Amanda's work was to reward her daring. But did she even dare? Her picture sprang from the page. I gasped. Such a reward would be unprecedented, but Mr Greene: Specialist in History and Visiting Lecturer, could confer such an honour. Eight out of ten, even nine, I could allot for those powerful colours and lines. Trouble might ensue, though. Some little girls, on receiving sevens and fives for their limp full-skirted ladies smiling beside pallid fields, might cry. They might lodge official complaints.

In my long-ago youth, even though I never once felt confident or safe among the other pupils, I dreamed of standing before rows of worn neat desks, faced by small attentive countenances. In my dream, each child had pen in hand. Each wrote down, carefully, tongue sticking out at the corner, my words. Together we turned clean pages. Together, my pupils and I memorized imports, exports, the changing names of political parties. We located battlefields and capitals, charted royal genealogies, weighed the terms of treaties. We drew beautiful maps. Our voices in recitation were low, our handwriting neat on the blackboard. I was the only man.

Never in my life have I seen such a classroom. Where do these ideas come from?

My Anglophile mother shipped me from Ireland to England after a neighbour in our town told her that I would soon *make a fine young Kerry-man*. Perhaps, by repeating to my mother what she wanted to hear – *I am a good teacher* – I came to believe that else-where, soon, after more experience, in other buildings or with differ-ent people, the assertion would gain substance. It would become real. Also I had faith that when I was ten, or fifteen, or twenty-one, or thirty-three, I would be able to stop biting my nails.

All girls giggle. Even Amanda did when, as I neared my perora-tion on the new Great Powers Partnership of Britain and America, Miss Trout's voice cut across mine.

"Questions, girls?"

Amanda asked, "Mr Greene, why don't you ever talk about Canada?"

The giggles turned on her when I replied, "It is not an impor-tant country." For a moment I was happy.

The sad sequence of my non-Roaring twenties, in which I lost two teaching posts and left two others, led to my less sad but still Depressed thirties. In that decade I uncovered my true gifts, such as they are. To wit: I tutor rather well if permitted to work with one pupil at a time, for a child alone does not laugh at bitten nails or balding head, and I give a rather good lecture if someone else will keep order while I deliver it. Thus I earn my living. The old Irish hedge-schoolmasters, those outlawed peripatetics with books on their backs – I am their reincarnation, or simulacrum, or travesty. For Mother I embellish somewhat the social standing of the girls' schools I visit each term. Describing our conversations on the Great Lawn, I substitute sherry for tea. I suggest that Fitzgerald, the butler, came to St Mildred's from a stately home in Wiltshire, and that Miss Flower attended Roedean.

She is gentle of demeanour and soft-voiced. She is not slight, however; she eats her pudding with enthusiasm, and solid round-nesses lift her twin-set. I intuit that she too would gasp fearfully at Amanda's picture yet feel driven to award it a high mark. Miss Trout, I am sure, could understand none of the subtleties of my dilemma.

But I must stop this, go back to my Notes. How dare I speak of these women thus contemptuously, when one has crossed so terrific a border?

A hooded schoolmistress has left the sanctuary of her room at night to move by silent stairs and passages, on grass and path and gravel, herself half-naked, to a target within the walls of School. Never have I dreamed of such a thing. Even to such a one as myself these feminine communities do bring invitations, for although I am not a master and have no residence and cannot teach and am in appearance unimposing, I am a man. Such messages are coded yet clear. At times I have gone so far as to show appreciation of the tongue spoken, but have never responded.

As for my early forties, they were The War. I worked on codes, not at a high level nor at the lowest. Weekly I received and read Mother's fusillades – pages and pages of her crazed script about the Republic's neutrality. Everyone fought his own War.

The modern term *guerilla* probably approximates *kern* or *wood-kern*. The *New History of Ireland* quotes a seventeenth-century Fermanagh undertaker as complaining that "although there be no apparent enemy, nor any visible main force, yet the wood-kern and many other (who have now put on the smiling face of contentment) do threaten every house, if opportunity of time and place doth serve" (Vol. III, 205). The *NHI* further claims that the image of the Londonderry colonist "with the sword in one hand and the axe in the other" was universal throughout the successive plantations. Thus the wood-kerns, though uprooted and pushed ever westward, fought to regain what had been theirs. The Flight of the Earls occurred in 1607. Heartbroken, corrupt, those defeated giant kerns fled the struggle.

Nightly, in rain or moon, I flee St Mildred's to walk this rectangular external pathway. On its other side lie either flat market-gardens or the lamplit fringes of the city: the canal, the railway, and the length of road where the country buses stand all night. From previous visits I know that solitary women will be standing by the notice board that displays the bus timetable. In similar locations not far from Miss Rammell's, The Gates, St Stephen's, such women wait. Our occasional activity does not take long. Money, not much, is the key. To these women, my inability to exercise authority is unimportant, as is my provenance. They open to my insinuation. Relieved, I resume my round. Water-needles fall athwart the rows of kale, and decomposing vegetable matter scents the air. The odour is not unpleasant, not unlike that of mown grass after rainfall.

In this mild October, red-faced Fitzgerald continues to mow the Great Lawn into subjection, making beautiful stripes of dull green and silver. He mows and rolls, rolls and mows. Carrying a short spear, he stabs at sweet wrappers, newspaper, lost bits of prep. Sometimes, when we meet, I point out a missed target. He nods, I nod. The girls call him *The Oirishman* and laugh at his brogue.

Standards are essential. Amanda's picture did not meet mine. It was outrageous, ludicrous. Never have I seen such a thing. Historians write and Mr Greene speaks admiringly of the planned abundance created in the Munster plantation, of bog drainage, wall-building, renovation of the peel-towers – in short, of sweet English order supplanting Irish anarchy. A failing mark would have been quite justified. O that I had given her three out of ten! Even four. Such a reprimand Amanda could not misconstrue. She would have felt humbled. She would have known who was stronger.

Evidently I hold contradictory positions on this matter. How very Irish.

The historical literature also unravels the knots of feelings about the Irish in the bosoms of the planted undertakers, servitors, tenants, and under-tenants. Their emotions included gratitude for the natives' skilled tutoring in their land and climate; scorn for their religious beliefs, hygiene, architecture, bards and rhymers, diet, dress, language, techniques of farming, hairstyles (the *glib*, or long forelock worn by men, was outlawed because it concealed facial expressions); fear of their rage; bewilderment at their lively humour; and anger at their higgledy-piggledy furtive bloody erratic ineffectual yet unceasing resistance. My Notes on these matters cover many pages.

Returning to St Mildred's three nights ago, I crunched wetly past the sainted dormitory houses, St Anne's, St Hilda's, and downhill to the main school, a converted Victorian mansion. That pathway is plain earth. My steps were silent in the rain.

This building during the day houses geometry, needlework, Greek, chemistry, and other intellectual enquiries. Here Trout and

Flower, Lincoln and Wilmer and Gregson and the rest have untram- melled access to those major ports of entry: eyes, ears, mouths. The girls sit in ready rows, up to the neck in their uniforms. At night, though, this building sustains only me, the only man. From one side protrudes a small two-storey addition, originally for a gardener or chauffeur. In a space below, the daygirls store their bicycles. An over- hang shields me from the rain as I insinuate my key. Inside, a stair rises to a second door, this one to my brief residence, my booley.

As always, I locked both portals. My tiny domain, dark and close, smelled of burned wood. The fire was out. I hung up my damp coat. Then, drawing the curtains, I saw, below, a hooded cloaked form, hand raised to knock.

My return had been watched for.

Ports. In Ulster, Coleraine was chief. Other notable orifices of the Irish body politic included Cork, Cobh, Lough Swilly. Through these moved the colonists, heading inland along few roads and many rivers. Modern historians distinguish three patterns of expanding settlement in Ireland: direct plantation, internal migration, and colonial spread. Were these modes experienced differently by the Irish? No one asks. Irish ways of moving about the land – creaghting, and transhumance or booleying – were despised, the lat- ter "on the ground that it provided hiding places for outlaws and malcontents . . . and [was] conducive to laziness and licentiousness" (Butlin, 152-3). Few historians discuss how the planted tenants felt, in the new land, about their own essential Englishness or Scottish- ness. That Sir Thomas Smith in 1573 forbade his tenants and sol- diers to take Gaelic wives shows that some must have wanted to do just that (Canny 24). Many did marry the country, in spite of such prohibitions.

And yet, in the twentieth-century Republic, my widowed mother, whose forbears came to Ireland almost two centuries ago, as under-tenants (on her mother's side) and Methodist evangelists (her father's), insisted that she and her son were *English*. "Never forget it!" This woman painstakingly and frugally contrived to send her only child far away, to school *at home*. Before I left, the barber clipped my hair close. Red curls would not do. I have maintained that style, though on my visits to Ireland Mother complains that I am not as nice looking as in boyhood. By now probably my curls would be grey, yet the mirror still shows a boyish look, a colonized child.

Someone had been waiting for me. Who stood outside my temporary door? In darkness I made my way down the stairs.

As I opened to the wet night, a sweet sharp scent met me. Lavender. Instantly there was a rough hood, a damp smooth cheek, a trembling hand pulling mine to a naked breast, its nipple stiff to my palm. My other hand met nakedness to the waist under thick tweed. Her perspiration smelled of lavender. Dark water dripped from the overhang. Awkwardly her head turned, the hood flopped over her face, my nose was in her warm hair, and the pit of her mouth opened under me. Fingers searched for purchase in my own hair, so short it offered no resistance.

In the 1641 rising or rebellion or revolt (the term chosen depends on the historian's politics, and it is marvellous how diverse the presentations of an historical event may be), the Old English – but no. Here I must stop, to make a Note. That term too may need definition for my audience, if ever I find one. The so-called *Old English* were women and men descended from the Anglo-Norman invaders of centuries earlier. In 1641 they allied themselves with the Irish against the (newer) English on a two-plank basis of unity: Catholicism and nationalism. Events occurring in 1642 England, though, doomed those Old English. Repudiated by what Clarke terms "their mother country," they tumbled down the social scale until they were "*submerged* in the eighteenth century peasantry and became *indistinguishable* from the native Irish [emphasis added]" (45). I wonder. For centuries, the Old English had been born and raised and lived their whole span of life in Ireland. How much more indigenous can one be?

At my booley, after two long deep kisses my visitor startled, though I had heard seen and felt nothing but her. She left, ran in fact, her cloak swaying down the path into the dark rain. Lavender lingered on my jacket.

The next day, as I walked up to the Dining Hall for luncheon, Amanda was emerging alone and late – the gong's echoes had ceased

– from a belt of pines west of the playing field. Several such plantations dot St Mildred's grounds. Though not large enough quite to conceal a person, they afford some privacy. The child must have felt explanation necessary. "Those trees smell kind of like the ones at home," she said. "And the dead needles too." *Kind of.* Then she ran away from me.

Dining Hall: odours of mutton fat, sweat, bitter Brussels sprouts, Bisto. A roar of eating girls. Clack of cutlery on plates, splash of water pitchers. The Irish linen cloth at High Table had been darned, *passim*, by an unskilled hand.

My inhalations canvassed all the mistresses near me for a fragrance, my eyes sought any hint of blush. As Guest Lecturer, I sat between Miss Pringle and Miss Hodgson. They smelled of Pears soap. Their bosoms drooped to their belts, and their heads bore dry knots, not clouds of living hair. At the sight of high-breasted Miss Lincoln, my scalp tingled, but the roses in the geographer's cheeks are obviously unnatural. I had smelled no cosmetics the previous night. Widowed Mrs Wilmer of Maths was surely faithful to memory. In any case her blouse lay flat on her chest, unlike Miss Flower's and Miss Trout's. Religion or History? I hoped for Religion.

The next night, I was just poking at the lumpy mattress of my single bed when a knock sounded, below. In disbelief I looked out. Not a fancy, not a dream. Another knock, soft but purposeful. O who? O Miss Flower, gentle, holy! Surely not my fishy protector, not that screeching common laugh on the soft night air?

Historians also speak of ideas being *in the air*. A late fifteenth century Scot wrote that a local crime involving the mutilation of animals was so awful that even "wyld Irisch and savadge people" would not have committed it. And, to a seventeenth-century English observer, the Irish were "more uncivill, more uncleanly, more barbarous, and more brutish in their customes and demeanures, then in any other part of the world that is knowne" (Perceval-Maxwell 15). Thus he left open the possibility of finding even worse behaviour in territories as yet unexplored.

My own discoverer stayed long enough in my world to untie the cord of my olive Paisley dressing gown. My two hands held her firm breasts. History? Religion? She touched my key. No rain or wind startled us, but again she fled.

A long time passed till I slept.

Yesterday, as usual, luncheon at High Table began with a disquisition from Miss Pringle on the King's rapidly failing health. Then it was Miss Maywood's turn to introduce a topic for general edification, and she put forward *The value of the Greek Myths in modern life*. That bulbous bosom would overflow my palm. Miss Munro of Music and Miss Fielding of Games – too tall. Miss Michaelson's face bears the scars of acne, while pretty Miss Pruitt is bone-thin.

Out the window of the Dining Hall, I watched Fitzgerald push the roller slowly across the Great Lawn. His wet face reddened with effort.

Miss Pringle and Miss Hodgson smile upon that man. I have seen this, heard their warm compliments. He grins, touches his glib.

To exert wholehearted dominion in Ireland, the planters and undertakers defined themselves in polar opposition to the native people. Their aim was money, either directly, as rents, or mediated, as grains, wool, beef, lace, timber, barrel staves, linen, butter. Their strategies included abolishing the land tenure systems formed by Brehon law and erecting primogeniture on the crushed bones of the clans. Their means was force. The state is a body of armed men, as Lenin stated so plainly. Yet ". . . the Crown had never sent a force to Ireland which was not eventually reduced 50% or more by desertion, defection, and an erosion of patriotism" (Berleth 22). *Hibernia hibernescit.*

Miss Pringle served the pink blancmange. As my plate arrived, something more than obvious occurred to me: I am *not* the only man in the School. There is Fitzgerald. This nobly-named man of my age and nation rolls flat the English grass on which I walk with English mistresses. Unlike Munster, the Great Lawn is verdant, smooth.

Distant across the tables, Amanda gazed out the window. She had not yet received from me her picture and her paragraph and her mark.

The Classics mistress spoke of Cadmus and the dragon. I breathed attentively, hoping for lavender. Kindly Miss Hodgson asked if I felt a cold coming on. Miss Maywood speculated on Cadmus's motivation in throwing the stone. Did he fear that the creatures sprouting from the terrible seeds would see the sower as their enemy? Or did he just bloody well feel like throwing? (The Head did not of course use that term.)

Miss Trout enlarged the discussion by deploring the innate tendency of certain European countries towards civil war. Miss Gregson sadly noted the Balkans, pre-1914. Miss Pruitt attempted a further enlargement and spoke of the Mau Mau, which was not well received. High Table felt, generally, that this rather young mistress should stick with her poems and her grammar.

Ireland's current relative quiescence made any reference gratefully unnecessary. The island is, in any case, although not uninteresting, of no importance.

Yesterday afternoon, after I returned Amanda's work, Miss Trout asked me to "look ahead" in England's colonizing efforts, subsequent to the Tudor conquest.

Amanda burst out, "Why can't he talk about Ireland now? All this stuff is hundreds of years ago." This breach of manners drew mistress and pupil out into the passage for a low-voiced exchange. Miss Trout would be stern, I hoped.

Then, at tea in Miss Pringle's quarters, Miss Flower spoke to me of the differences between the classical Greek mind and ours. Did I scent lavender? She mentioned that the Canadian girl had been distressed about the tale of Cadmus as told to her Latin class by Miss Maywood.

Miss Flower had found her crying. "They all killed each other, and they didn't know what made them do it."

Religion's tenderness touched me. I almost reached for her hand. Instead I rose to hand round the plate of bread-and-butter and to sniff. Infuriatingly, the fragrance seemed traceable to Miss Pruitt and even to the elderly Frenchwoman Mme Dutheil.

Frustrated, I passed on to the company, in somewhat embellished form, what Miss Flower had said about Amanda's tears. Miss

Maywood and Miss Pruitt led the laughter. Miss Flower's glance at me did not show aversion to my forcefulness. If anything, Religion seemed admiring.

Last night came the third visitation of the unknown She. The October chill was decisive. Soon all rolling of lawns must cease. Waiting by the dark door, I opened before she could tap. Who? One gasp is much like another. I pulled her to me. I was naked under my Paisley, she half-so under her hooded tweed. My fingers tugged at fabric, my tongue found hers. We would ascend my steep stairs to mix wood-smoke and lavender. My key was hard. The way I held her was decisive, not bewildered. Yes, I used my strength.

As the teeth of her skirt's zip-fastener opened, torchlight flared onto my face.

Flaccid again, I stood talking to Fitzgerald after she had fled.

The watchman apologized. On his midnight patrol, he had seen a cloaked figure approach my door and, as he thought, force entry. The Irishman was doing his duty for the English girls and mistresses, for the Visiting Speaker and Specialist in Irish History. He was ready to do battle for us.

Elizabeth's plantation of Munster began in 1584. Fourteen years later, the numbers of English settled there may have been three or twelve thousand, depending upon whether single males or families are tallied. Another tentative statistic: during the planting seasons in Ireland over the centuries, a common expectation was that for every Irish farmer evicted an English colonist would be killed. Their deaths for their country were not *dulce et decorum*. Favoured Irish weapons were the battle-axe, broad-bladed sword, crossbow, and spear. In turn, hangings of Irish rebel leaders, at least of those not dismembered in their hometowns and villages in Ireland, were regularly featured at Tyburn. There also hung an English captain, Thomas Lee, who after years of service to the English crown turned Irish and became an outlaw in the wilderness, identifying himself finally as a "bog soldier" (Berleth 21-22).

Long past the time of the first Elizabeth, Ireland remained imperfectly surveyed. Better maps were available of the eastern seaboard of North America than of Galway or Donegal, so the English monarchs might inspect the paper lay of their lands in Virginia but not in Ulster. Even some modern historians include in their books no maps at all of the country, then or now. The place remains unknown.

That Fitzgerald might be at large in the night at St Mildred's had not occurred to me. I gained a new understanding of his work. Large and solid in his bulky mackintosh, wielding his torch as we talked outside my door, Fitzgerald stood strong. I myself felt unusually so. A woman had been seen to seek me out. This strong man had seen her. Respect rang in Fitzgerald's tone. He did not speak to me as factotum to Foreign Affairs.

"How's that fireplace?" he asked. I mentioned the smoky smell. "The damper, that'll be. It needs a good hard pull."

For this specialist information, I thanked Fitzgerald. Son of sword-wielder: the name is ancient, deriving from the French. Perhaps an ancestor landed in Ireland with the Anglo-Norman invasion of 1170. He resumed his dutiful passage through the woods and shrubberies, while I went back inside.

As I got into bed, Amanda's tears came to mind. Munster's 1598 insurrection did indeed lead the English and Irish to kill each other in large bloody numbers. The Irish at least knew exactly why: to regain their lands, animals, homes, and rivers.

Marks too have clear meanings. Five out of ten means Barely Passable. Seven stands on the way to Better; even six-and-a-half suggests a hopeful curving up from Ordinary. I did not give Amanda such a mark, nor the three or four that would say Very Bad Indeed. Touching none of these extremes, I inscribed at the bottom right-hand corner of her picture the numeral 6.

The mark of mediocrity. How appropriate for a colonial child!

In analysing the Virginia plantation, Nicholas Canny hypothesizes that because those "who arrived [there] with Daniel Gookin from Ireland in 1621 did not bear Irish surnames ... these were in fact Englishmen whom Gookin had, some years previously, *brought* as tenants to his estate in Munster and then *transferred* to his newly acquired property in Virginia" (25, emphasis added). Was anyone

---

already living on that property? Indians, I presume. I presume they then headed west. No matter. The point is that Gookin's people, possessed and controlled, were shipped about as cargo, rather like other loads then crossing the Atlantic, by slave ship. A kind of human creaghting may thus be seen in the Irish and Virginian plantations, in Amanda's case, and in my own. Transhumance is the English term.

While the other girls, giggling, compared their marks, Amanda stared at her vivid rows of earthbound people. Miss Trout reminded the girls of their good luck in receiving instruction from a Specialist in History. Most clapped. Amanda raised hate-filled eyes. Averting my own, I addressed Miss Trout *sotto voce* in a manner open to a flirtatious interpretation. In a sloppy way, her breasts shook with laughter. I am sure my visitor could not have been she.

At the final tea time this afternoon, I sat as Mr Greene of Foreign Affairs among the mistresses. My knowledge was held tightly in my head: my origins, my languages, the visitations, Amanda's picture, her questions, her mark, her look of hate, my own hate, my recognition of Fitzgerald, my many Notes. All were safe inside.

Mrs Wilmer said, "How the days draw in!"

"They do, don't they?" responded Miss Flower.

"O rather!" I agreed, rhyming the *a* with *maths*. Thus my sliding tongue gave me away. The chatter of the English ladies ceased. Their eyes observed, their ears decoded. A silence filled Miss Pringle's sitting room. Years ago, before I understood that I must meet pupils individually or else have protectors by me as I stood before a group, that silence of judgment came often. Laughter always followed.

I left Miss Pringle's sitting room. No – like the earls, I fled.

The rain had stopped, the clouds blown off. The wind said *Autumn*. Litter blew about the playing field, for the tuck shop is nearby, and the girls are wont to scatter brightly-printed cellophane. With his spear, Fitzgerald was hard at work. He had missed a scrap. I called, pointed. When he picked the paper off his spear-tip, his bony jaw split in a smile. I looked. The genitals of the tiny Biro-blue figures, his and hers, swollen and joined, were unmistakable, though not artistically rendered. We laughed, hard and long. Did he too now know that I am Irish?

Since then, I have sat alone in my this domain that is not mine, working on my Notes. The wood-fire is out. Tonight I expect no visitor. No English lady will lie with a non-standard accent. O that I had given Amanda ten out of ten!

Tomorrow, a cool grey October morning, will begin with porridge, tea, and toast at the High Table. Any lavender in the air will not signify. The mistresses will be polite, as to one incurably afflicted. Miss Pringle will speak of Confirmation classes, Miss Hodgson of delinquency with fees. Packing my case will be next, and then the perusal of the railway timetables, the booking of a seat, the purchase of today's newspapers for the journey so that on arrival at my next post I may be truly the *au courant* Mr Greene: Current Events, Foreign Affairs, Guest Lecturer.

No, I shall not go through this again. I cannot bear it. I shall use all my Notes. I shall write my book.

Tonight, the trees and shrubberies of St Mildred's shall house me. They'll shield me from the sounding rain, itself another shield, while I hide in the little plantation that Amanda showed me. I'll watch my back, lest she be on the loose with her stabbing lines and sharp colours. Then, practicing my woodcraft, I'll trail Fitzgerald as he does his midnight rounds. Perhaps I may learn where the other man sleeps his few short hours. Will a visitor approach Fitzgerald's secret door? I shall cry no alarm. In him there is no pretense.

Later, at two or at three, I shall leave the school, not walking down the drive itself but keeping within the ramparts of wet moon-dappled foliage. Who else will be in search? Whoever passes will not know at first that it is I who make the hollies crackle, the pebbles jump. She will peer about, not realizing that she peers at me. Shall I let her find and touch my body among the leaves? Shall I draw her to me?

Finally, I shall move beyond the official grounds and the dying vegetable fields and over the low hedges that separate the suburban houses. No one will expect me there. The dawn will find me awake, alert as I have been all night, resting by a bare espaliered peach or in a greenhouse. Food and drink I shall take from sill, doorstep, kitchen garden. In appearance I am not alarming. My good shoes are stout, my jacket well-cut, so no citizen will think *That man does not belong here.*

At Miss Rammell's, my failure to appear will cause only brief and mild concern. In the life of a girls' school, lectures on Foreign Affairs and Current Events, offered by a quiet nail-biting middle-aged itinerant hedge-teacher with little hair, may be easily substituted. Also, should Miss Rammell place an enquiring trunk-call to Miss Pringle, the news of Irishness will explain all. *Irresponsible, unreliable, I always thought, so did I.* Such a call however is unlikely, since I am not worth the expense. Where shall I go? I know exactly.

All England has been mapped. Cunningly, kernishly, night by night I shall move westward from school to school and shire to shire, from wooded grounds to shrubberies to fields, to pine plantations and moors and empty sheds. Against all dangers, my weapons are my wits and my knowledge of the English tongue. So armed, I'll reach the coast of the Irish Sea.

Tomorrow morning I must remember, before departure to the train station, to return this key to Miss Hodgson, Assistant Head. She handles such matters.

Religious Knowledge

S illy old virgin and martyr" – such is St Cecilia's designation among the girls at St Mildred's School. The saint's own Day, the twenty-second of November, this year falls on a Sunday. A weak sun shines.

As always the early morning brings peace to Miss Flower, especially after the night's tumultuous quest. Before matins she readies herself, spiritually and as a teacher, to begin the week. For her own Bible study this term, she has chosen Corinthians 1:13. *Charity suffereth and is kind.* Neatly she writes out this and other verses on slips of paper, to stash in pockets, handbag, prayer book.

After Lights Out in the dormitory on Sunday, the ritual of St Cecilia's Dirty Night will unfold. "Just wait until Dirty Night!" For weeks, Amanda and Helen have heard snickers and pleasurable sighs. "You'll see!" Amanda wants to discuss, to speculate, but Helen is silent.

Charity envieth not, Miss Flower writes, thinking of Miss Lincoln's nylons.

That night in the dark dormitory, on her back, Amanda Ellis lies naked. She gets an early turn, being one of the youngest.

Sunday mornings are also for devotional reading, the adjective used liberally: Richardson's *Preface to Bible Study*, novels by Rose Macaulay, Elizabeth Goudge's *God So Loved The World*. At *Screwtape*, Miss Flower titters anxiously. *The Lion, the Witch, and the Wardrobe* is more to her liking.

In late November the dormitory is still unheated, but the torches *flashlights* held by other naked girls warm Amanda's thighs. Her smooth private skin feels light, embarrassment, pleasure, fear.

Charity vaunteth not itself, is not puffed up.

Someone holds Amanda open. Fingers go inside a place she did not know existed. To expand the view, someone holds a pocket-mirror.

Little Gidding. More daringly, Miss Flower attempts this but is quite dismayed and lends it to Mr Greene in hopes he may explain it to her and notice her blue eyes.

Next in the dormitory drama, Amanda must walk down the aisle between the beds crowded with naked watching girls. Her heart thuds. The spots where no breasts have yet appeared feel huge, while the small territory between her legs, to date used only for pee and number two, has swollen to a giant three-spouted delta.

With *Murder In The Cathedral*, Miss Flower does better. Under all that poetry there is proper history, after all.

Bulging globes of flesh are Amanda's tummy and bum. The dormitory is one absorbed stare, though not urgently breathless as when pretty Tessa and prettier Rose glide by the peering beds.

At the invitation of Miss Gregson (who first asks Miss Pruitt to go with her but is rebuffed, for the Literature mistress finds Eliot obscure and in poor taste), Miss Flower even attends a local performance of *Murder*. She is upset, thrilled, puzzled.

When it is Helen's turn for centre stage, Amanda squeezes her friend's hand. Dew glistens on Helen's white forehead. ("Paleface!" Amanda teases her, when they play Indians in the beechwood.) As the torch-beams reach her eyes, Helen gasps.

Miss Flower studies today's appointed Lessons, turning with relief from Ecclesiastes' gloom and Malachi's curses to Paul, who delivers for the Hebrews a paean to faith's powers. Then, in prayer, she rededicates herself as a teacher. The Third Form is about to study a few of the Forty-Nine Articles, and Miss Flower whispers earnestly, "Please let them ask questions." She rehearses her introduction to the topic.

Helen has knotted the cord of her dressing gown, and when the naked girls snatch at the tassels she slaps them.

Miss Flower lays Bible and prayer book aside. In watery sunlight before the mirror she brushes her hair, which is thin and feathery. Again she thinks *Perhaps a perm*, although this strategy has never yet worked. Her crimped head always looks unnatural. Girls laugh.

Savagely, Helen kicks at the girls crowded around her.

Beholding herself in the mirror, Miss Flower raises a frilled blouse on its hanger before her slight frame.

By the time the girls get that first layer of fabric off Helen's body, she is biting and scratching as well as kicking.

City of mirrors. In Paul's writing days, that was Corinth. Burnished metal the mirrors were then and shimmered softly; they didn't fire back these sharp reflections. Miss Flower sees her white cotton vest as she lowers the frills. At the memory of how her hands touched that bosom while questing last night, a blush spreads over her chest. She raises a plain V-neck blouse and checks the mirror again.

Under Helen's pyjamas are her knickers and vest. Her shoes, their laces doubly knotted, still contain her feet. Bigger girls, more girls move in to control and strip her.

Yes, this blouse is more modest. Quickly buttoning up, Miss Flower refuses to recall where those fingers went last night.

When hands at last slip under fabric to connect with Helen's struggling flesh, she shrieks so loudly that a prefect, startled, falls back against a bedstead to split her lip and crack a tooth.

Miss Flower hopes that after general confession she may approach the communion rail inoffensively. She garters her hated lisle stockings. O for nylons! On go her grey coat and skirt.

Helen shrieks again.

At matins Miss Flower receives the wafer and the wine, followed in Dining Hall by boiled beef and boiled kale and roly-poly pudding.

She supervises the Third Form for their hour of writing letters home. This is a new duty. She watches the girls, some smiling as their nibs race, others labouring. Then Miss Flower writes too. She uses a larger script than that employed for her teaching work and leaves wider margins. Thus she fills out the blue Basildon Bond.

Yesterday at tea Kate Gregson showed her holidays snaps from Donegal and the Aran Isles. I told her about the old Druid beliefs, there and here in

England. Mr Greene is in School just now; he had a good deal to say about Stonehenge.

This week we shall select the girls for the Lower School's Nativity Play. Miss Hodgson suggests that the Canadian girl be Narrator, in spite of her accent, or perhaps indeed because of it, since the Commonwealth now . . . .

What else can she write, to her widowed mother? Ah, the weather. That takes Miss Flower well over on to the fourth sheet. *Love, Elizabeth.* There's duty, done.

Helen shrieks madly piercingly unstoppably.

On this St Cecilia's Day Amanda also writes about the Nativity Play.

Probably I'll be Narrator. I'd be "essential to every scene," Miss Hudson says. Wouldn't you be proud??!! In RK we are going to learn Articles. What a funny word. The Professor writes articles, doesn't he? Articles of clothing, articles anything! These ones are Of Both Kinds. Of the Unworthiness of Ministers. Of the Civil Magistrates. Funny!

In these lines Miss Flower notes a complete absence of humility. She goes on to Amanda's friend, Helen, sighing as she reads. A puzzle, this clever Helen who slouches about the school, indifferent alike to poor marks and athletic performance. Her prep is routinely *lost*. So is her cardigan, her pencil case. Miss Pruitt exclaims, "Helen does not even trouble to be a good liar."

Dear Mother and Father, Thank you for your letter. It came on Thursday. The weather has been quite nice. It has not rained much. Today was roast beef and carrots and steamed pudding. The Fifth Form is going to see As You Like It. Lucky!!! We won all our matches this week. In Latin, we have begun the fifth declension. It is hard. I hope you are well. Love Helen.

The ungainly handwriting ekes out these seventy words to a third page.

Miss Flower remembers once finding at home a drawerful of her own school letters, kept by her mother. The memory of their patterned paragraphs morphs into a dark angry wave. Back then, also, she hated to go home. The swells overwhelm the questions her brain is trying to raise about Helen's letter.

Helen shrieks. Throughout the dormitory building, mistresses hear her cries.

Miss Flower collects the girls' envelopes and the crisp aerogrammes for India, Malta, Burma. All are unsealed. The girls jostle out of the form-room, and Miss Flower reads what they have written. Elsewhere other mistresses do the same; only the Upper Sixth's letters are exempt from inspection. Then the staff lick and seal, lick and seal, for no letters are withheld from the post. "We are guardians, not censors," says the Head.

At Sunday tea in Miss Pringle's sitting room, all report on *anything untoward* in the letters. In these sessions Miss Flower is aware of the low status assigned to Religious Knowledge. Bitterly she acknowledges her own fault. Strong Science, know-it-all Geography in her peacock blue – if they were RK, the others would listen! But she is shy. No, she is weak. No, worse.

Hear how the Head raps the tea table so all the cups jump in their saucers! "Look between the lines. Girls know many, many ways to hide meaning." The Assistant Head takes notes as her spaniels, Fred and Nelly, slobber all over their biscuits. Often no action results from these meetings, for the Head relies heavily on *Time, the great healer*, but sometimes a trunk call is placed. Sometimes a pupil is summoned to Miss Pringle's office, on Monday.

Helen shrieks. From chairs, from desks, from prayer, from loos, from beds, all over the dormitory building the mistresses rise.

Not everything untoward gets reported, either. Once in a girl's letter Miss Gregson reads, *Mummy, make lemon pudding and be careful not to burn it*. Metaphor bangs in her brain. She confides in Miss Flower.

"Brilliant! I'd never have guessed."

When Miss Gregson lights a candle, lemon-juice writing under Waterman's Blue tells all. The too-communal loos at St Mildred's embarrass this child; she has become very constipated. For privacy she seeks out the few singleton cubicles, but mean girls follow and stand nearby, calling her names.

"She doesn't need any more publicity!" Miss Gregson exclaims, proposing that she and Miss Flower shoo the taunters away. They do, and deduct many conduct marks for loitering. "Problem solved, parents unalarmed," Science boasts. "And Miss P kept in the dark. *Time, the great do-nothing!*"

Helen's shrieks continue as the mistresses speed along the corridors and finally rush into the dormitory to shout amidst the naked shouting girls.

After Sunday supper, a solitary walk leads Miss Flower to evensong on the BBC, cocoa, curlers, book, bed, and no questing.

Helen screams until Miss Fielding slaps a cold wet flannel across her face.

Miss Flower has still not arrived. In her room with soft music playing, she is intent on the pages of *The Man Who Would Be King*.

Helen folds and falls.

The uproar finally draws Miss Flower to the scene. The dormitory is all lit up. Matron is everywhere at once. Limp on the floor, Helen stares, as if she were seeing someplace else. Miss Flower recoils. The prefect with the split lip weeps and smears her face with red. Girls scramble to don nightdresses, plead with angry mistresses. Miss Lincoln has laddered a nylon and is furious. The hysteria revolts Miss Flower. *With so many, I am not needed here.* She goes back to her book and the BBC.

Helen is carried off to the San by Maths and Games.

On Monday, the Third Form starts on the Articles. Miss Flower tries not to be annoyed at Amanda's questions, remembering her prayer that her pupils would show interest.

Also on Monday, the junior girls involved in Dirty Night lose their tuck shop access and hot water bottles on cold nights. Older girls lose pocket money and all town privileges. The prefects' badges are cut from their tunics and School hats.

An extra bed is set up in the Dirty Nights dormitory, and the mistresses rotate supervision duties there. Soberly the girls prepare for sleep. At Lights Out, the silence is immediate. During the night, girls who wake to visit the loo feel uneasy at the alien sight of Miss Maywood's lump, Miss Pruitt's sprawl, while in the narrow girl-bed each adult woman feels herself strange.

In the San, Helen curls up with her face to the wall.

Repeatedly Miss Hodgson visits. "What is wrong, Helen? For goodness' sake!"

Matron, run off her feet with influenza cases, has neither time nor inclination to cajole a sulky girl into eating.

Helen sips Lucozade when Amanda visits, carrying stale buns from morning break. To make her friend smile, she tells about Canadian oddities like Orange Crush, maple syrup, chocolate milk. Helen says hardly anything. Amanda longs to discuss Dirty Night and the puzzle of Article X, *Of Free Will*, but instead she brings her Indian box to the bedside, so Helen can smell the sweetgrass and stroke the bright quills.

To her staff, Miss Pringle declares that good tone in School will be most quickly restored if all lessons and games proceed as usual. "To restore the normal routine: that is our aim." This directive is perfectly congruent with Miss Flower's wish not to think about Dirty Night. Carefully she prepares her lessons, trying to predict questions about the various Articles. Routine. Her mother's response arrives.

What is Mr Greene's age? Remember, men do not like women to exhibit their knowledge. As the most attractive of the younger mistresses you may easily distinguish yourself. Remember that you are getting on.

Is it wise to feature a foreign accent in a traditionally English and indeed sacred performance? Will it not distract?

You do not mention in what company Miss Gregson travelled. Tramping about the mud and dirt of primitive islands does not sound very . . . .

It is just as well that Mrs Flower has not seen Kate's holiday snaps of a dozen youngish cyclists, women and men, who are wearing shorts and picnicking on headlands and beaches – Fanad Head, Inishmor, Annagry. They laugh to the camera. Their bicycles lie companionably nearby. None of these people, Miss Flower feels sure, is married or even engaged to any of the others. One photo shows a caravan where unkempt children cluster and grin at the friends.

"Gypsies, travellers," says Kate. Then, cheerfully, "Care to come along next time, Elizabeth? At Easter we're going to Kerry. Dingle Bay, the Lakes of Killarney. Wonderful cycling, I'm told, and ruined cathedrals galore! You'd be most welcome."

Miss Flower blushes, thanks, promises to think about it.

St Clement's, St Catherine's – the drear days come and go. Wintry rain whips at legs. At night, Miss Flower washes out her nasty mud-spattered lisle stockings. Helen lies almost speechless, but when Amanda runs in, red-cheeked after hockey, she says, "You smell of grass."

Amanda tries to describe the Muskoka smells of cedar and pine. The innumerable pine needles are brittle yet soft. They coat the earth and the pink granite of the Precambrian Shield. "You don't leave tracks, on needles. There's no sound when you walk on them, either."

"If we were there now, we could run away into the forest," Helen yearns. "We could be Indians."

But it is too hard for Amanda to imagine an English girl, even this one, in Muskoka. Instead, she leans near. "Helen, why were you so scared at Dirty Night? Please tell. I could help?"

Close up, Helen's freckles look like pepper on milk. She is silent. Amanda does not ask again, fearing her friend will turn away.

"In Yorkshire there are fells," Helen says then. "They go so far away they look like the ocean."

Helen grows thinner. At her substantial desk, Miss Pringle drafts a letter.

Dear Canon and Mrs Hepworth, Although Helen may not be writing home this week, there is no cause for alarm. Preparations for the Nativity Play have been perhaps too demanding. She is suffering I think from a little nervous strain and is resting in the Sanatorium. Matron is confident that our Helen will soon be her lively self once more, and we shall ensure that you hear from her then in her own hand.

The Head sets this draft aside with another, written to the parents of a new girl who tried to conceal a note in her letter home and hoped hoped hoped that supervisory fingers would not find it. They did, of course. Miss Pringle smiles. *Homesickness*, her graceful handwriting says, *is always temporary. There is no cause for alarm.* Soon, she knows, their daughter will learn to laugh at her own feelings.

Next day the Head hands over this letter about the homesick boarder to Miss Hodgson for typing, but she retains Helen's draft. *Time. Wait. See.*

Helen lies staring in bed. Matron says, "The look on that girl would sour milk."

Amanda sits by her and tells about the winding path in Muskoka that leads to the raspberry bushes. In July, the hot air is sweetly perfumed.

Now, girls who cavorted naked on Dirty Night walk singly and clothed to the doggy-smell office of the Assistant Head. As they confess, the spaniels sniff at their feet. Miss Hodgson, in the shorthand learned in her youth in glorious London, transcribes. "Speak up, Angela," she says. "Janice, go on."

When all have spoken, Miss Hodgson synthesizes their accounts in one terrible tale and carries this to the San. Three times she asks Helen to describe her own experience of Dirty Night. Silence, three times. Miss Hodgson sighs and reads her typescript aloud to Helen's back.

"In broad terms, do you verify this?" The blanket moves. "I shall take that as confirmation," and she puts her papers away. "The Head says you have been here quite long enough, Helen. Tomorrow, Sunday, you will resume your place in School."

Helen lies curled up tight, her back to the door.

Miss Hodgson places her report on dearest Viola's desk and then heads out with Fred and Nelly for a rainy walk. Passing the Gym, she overhears the Nativity Play in rehearsal. Amanda says pompously, "Then said Mary unto the angel." A long pause. Miss Hudson, Drama, calls out, "Your cue, Susan!" The Virgin whines, "How shall this be, seeing I know not a man?" At this the dogs bark madly. Miss Hudson says, "Again. And not so *loud*, Narrator."

After rehearsal Amanda arrives at the San, to amuse Helen by telling her how to disguise herself with sweet blackberry juices. Perhaps then she will be willing to talk? But her friend's back is turned. Amanda comes round the bed, to kneel by her. Only the top of Helen's head is visible. Mousy brown. Why is that supposed to be not nice? Helen's long hair is a very nice brown. It trails over the side of the bed, smooth as Muskoka stream-water. There is an odd sound that takes a moment to identify. Helen is sucking her thumb.

Amanda lays her head on the pillow. "Tell me. Do tell me."

Helen pulls the covers right over her head and murmurs.

"What?" Amanda puts her ear where she thinks Helen's mouth is. Through the wool her friend speaks seven words.

At an ordinary tea time in the Dining Hall, Amanda holds these words in her head as she eats. On weekends, the white marge does not appear on the table. Instead, the prefect skilfully divides a block of butter into thirteen equal chunks. The bread is dense and floury. There is marrow jam. The tea steams up Amanda's glasses.

Next in the routine is prep. She forgets about Helen's words in the interest of declining Latin nouns and doing her French translation, but in the long stomach-aching pauses of not knowing what on earth to do with the dreadful sums Mrs Wilmer has set, Amanda writes down in pencil what Helen said. Each word is common. In combination, they appal. She erases. That night in the dormitory, she stares into her mirror and wonders how she can look so ordinary.

In the letter-writing hour on the first Sunday in Advent, Miss Flower observes that Helen has rejoined her form. She droops. Subdued, yes – but to some degree so is the whole School, still. The girl's pen does move. And Helen is always rather pale.

When the girls have gone, Miss Flower skims through Janet's letter, Tessa's, Rose's, Belinda's . . . . Then she frowns and riffles back to Helen's gangly script.

But the Fifth saw *As You Like It* last spring. This term's *Merry Wives* won't open till next week.

But the lacrosse team is utterly wet; it's not won a match in a month.

But today was apple tart.

But there's been rain for the last five days.

After examining every downstroke and line break of Helen's letter, Miss Flower notes the address in Yorkshire. Suddenly there comes a knock at the form-room door. The Canadian girl. Annoyed at the interruption, Miss Flower hardly listens.

"Whatever do you mean, you can't say what Helen said?" She proffers a pen, and Amanda writes.

Reading, the mistress flares scarlet from scalp to nipples. She stammers. Waves of heat roll over her as she tucks the slip of paper deep in her prayer book. For reassurance, she touches Amanda's shoulder. "Leave this to me," she says fearfully.

Amanda hears the words only. Relief, relief! Her insides loosen so that she must run for the loo before she goes to look for Helen.

To her surprise, her friend takes no interest.

"But Miss Flower says she'll . . . ."

"You'll see." Listless, Helen does not want to play in the beech-wood, so the two girls just sit together in a corner of the junior common room. Amanda tells about picking blueberries. On the hillsides that slope to the lake, you must look down to notice the small bushes with their blue load. These berries are sweet yet tart. Crushed, the fruit makes a paste of blue and green, red-flecked. "You can play that it's pemmican," Amanda explains.

Helen smiles faintly. "How far into those hills can you go?"

"You don't need to go far. The berries are near. My mother makes pancakes with them, and blueberry cobbler." But her friend has no appetite.

At Sunday tea in the Head's sitting room, Miss Flower reports that Helen's letter is identical to last week's.

Miss Pringle: "You do recall the earlier letter exactly? Word for word?"

Miss Fielding: "She simply makes no effort at all, in gym or at games."

Miss Hudson: "Although Helen has little to do in our Nativity Play, even that little she does poorly."

Miss Flower wonders about speaking privately to the Assistant Head, who is much less frightening than Miss Pringle.

Just then Miss Hodgson exclaims, "Why, Helen has probably just mixed up Shakespeare's titles! I'm afraid I often muddle them too, especially the comedies." She gives each dog another biscuit. Miss Flower almost groans.

"The fifth declension!" Miss Maywood's face suggests she is smelling something nasty. "Little liar. We shall be lucky to reach the third, by Christmas."

"Nothing in haste," finally pronounces Miss Pringle. "Next Sunday, we shall see what we shall see."

Kate Gregson opens her mouth and closes it.

Of the other matter, of the words Amanda wrote on that slip of paper now folded in Miss Flower's prayer book, the mistress cannot speak, no, not before so many, though her weakness shames her, shames her.

After tea, as Science and Religious Knowledge walk to their rooms, Kate mocks the Head. *"We shall see!* The imperial we." A grudging laugh. "If Eliot had lady knights in *Murder In The Cathedral,* she'd fit right in. How she loves her temporal power!"

"I don't think I fully understood what that play is about, Kate."

"Free will, I'd say," but Science's attention is not there. "Hasn't it occurred to Miss P that Helen's parents will think it odd to receive the same letter twice?"

They may have received it more often than that, Miss Flower fears but does not say. Feeling for her room-key, she finds in her pocket *I will not leave you comfortless: I will come to you.* Shame burns. Once in her cosy armchair, she opens *The World My Wilderness,* but in her ears resound the only lines still with her from Eliot's play: *the torn girl trembling by the mill-stream,* and *This is the sign of the Church always, / The sign of blood.*

Miss Flower gets up, looks in her mirror and then out the window where in the lowering dusk the beech trees shake their ragged leaves, dark red. To wear such colours! She must see the Head. She imagines sunshine, herself in blue shorts astride an Irish bicycle. Unlike Miss Lincoln's legs, hers do not resemble those of a dining table. She must tell the Head what Amanda has told. At Christmas she may treat herself to nylon stockings, but first she must show that slip of paper. Can she do it? Miss Flower longs to quest. To go to Ireland. Can she *choose* to absent herself from home at Easter? To wear shorts? Mrs Flower never even rolls up the long sleeves of her dresses. Miss Flower has always celebrated Easter at her mother's side.

By mid-week, the mistress of Religious Knowledge has still not seen the Head. Surely Helen's parents, once they have read their daughter's duplicate letter, will write, or wire, or telephone? Someone will act. All will be well.

At table, she notices a gap by Amanda. Others notice too. Helen, found and rebuked for not taking her place in Dining Hall, says mutinously, "But I'm not hungry." Because she has *had rather a rough go*, this infraction of the rules is not pursued.

Amanda cannot imagine such a state. "I'll help you eat!"

Helen shrugs, but when she does appear in Hall the two friends giggle as they shove beef gristle around their plates or push rabbit bones under their cutlery. From the Dining Hall they sneak out bread and Marmite and apples, for playing Eskimos in the beech-wood. "A cache!" Amanda describes crossing trackless snow for days on end. As she listens to this narrative, Helen's ennui falls away, to Amanda's relief. She's been worried. Miss Flower hasn't said a word, will not meet her eyes. The silence distresses her as much as does Article X, but she can't say so to Helen.

Mrs Flower writes to her daughter again.

Soon you will be home with me! Of course I shall prepare, but I am not as energetic as formerly. I need you.

Before your return, Lucinda Jones will join me for a few days. With so few old friends now, I welcome her, yet guests are always a burden.

Prepare to be shocked at this year's decorations in the Parish Hall! Mrs Heath has got the ear of the new man, and support from my own Committee has been sadly lacking . . . .

Her daughter sets this aside, to reread a slip from her handbag. *Charity rejoiceth not in iniquity* is probably a Pauline reference to the notorious sexual corruption of Corinth. Questing would find a place in the city of mirrors, she knows. Paul would be furious, revolted, but she cannot stop, to her shame. Another slip. *Charity rejoiceth in the truth.*

Helen goes to see Matron, who reports to the Head. "The girl says she wants to *come back* to the San. Says she feels ill. Lies, nonsense!"

On Saturday night, Miss Flower takes her turn in the Dirty Nights dormitory. On Helen's dressing table she observes a photo of an unremarkable man and woman standing by a stone rectory. Beyond, the fells roll beautifully away.

She does not put in her curlers before the mirror. Instead Miss Flower kneels and prays for strength, with her feathery hair sticking up between her fingers. The girls, at first astonished by this behaviour, soon sleep. Then the mistress tries to read, but through *Descent of the Dove* the Hepworths stare at her. The mother's mouth turns down. Her stance sags. The Canon grins. Even now that man may be polishing his sermon, and tomorrow in public he will stand like Paul to speak in all authority.

On Sunday morning, the Head drops the slip of paper onto her oak desk. It looks very small, there. "You give credence to this – document?"

"Helen writes gibberish, Miss Pringle, she is terrified, doesn't eat, has lost a stone at least. This explains her behaviour, explains . . . ."

"No, Miss Flower."

"But –"

"No. You fail to understand. It is my task both to lead this School and to protect it. Some little girls have played nasty games." The Head's fingertips dismiss them. "But this business, Miss Flower, is different. Ours is a Church of England school. Do you propose that I go before the Council of the Church Education Corporation, to whom I am answerable, to say" – Miss Pringle inhales – "that I believe a lying and undisciplined child who accuses her clergyman father of an unspeakable perversion? Do you know the word *scandal*, Miss Flower? And how it can destroy a School?"

As she stumbles away from the Head's study, Miss Hodgson tiptoes fatly after her down the hall, a packet of sweet biscuits in hand.

"No, thank you."

"Helen *was* frightened on Dirty Night, Miss Flower. All the girls agree about that. Her clothes, you see." Between mouthfuls of chocolate wafer, the Assistant Head tells about the knotted dressing gown and shoelaces, the knickers and vest. She describes how Helen struggled. "It was as if she knew what to fear."

"Miss Hodgson, tell me what we can do?"

The Assistant Head's crumb-dotted visage shows surprise. "Do?"

During matins, Miss Flower does not care that the staff glance oddly as they move past her toward the communion rail, nor that her hair lies limp, nor even, truly, that Our Lady was conceived immaculate.

In the letter-writing hour she can't herself set pen to paper. Instead she reads in *Britannica* of Kerry's broken monasteries, of a standing stone circle with cromlech such as she has never seen. Did those chummy cyclists sleep under canvas irrespective of sex? She would need to buy a knapsack and boots. Would she look right? Sometimes Miss Flower wishes intensely for a girl's tunic or a nun's habit – a uniform. The comely stringent sameness, which says directly who the wearer is, attracts her. Pastel twin-sets and gathered skirts feel indefinite.

When the girls have gone, Miss Flower glances at Amanda's letter home. Little know-it-all, still fussing about *Of Free Will*. Helen's is the same as before.

"Nothing to report," she says at tea time. Does the Head relax just a fraction?

Later, in the privacy of her room, Religious Knowledge at last confides in Science by showing her Amanda's written words. Not for a moment does Kate Gregson doubt what a suffering child has told her friend. For this, Miss Flower is grateful. Science rages at the Canon, at Miss Pringle. She deplores and commiserates and shakes her head. Then she has nothing more to say.

"Kate, what shall we do?"

"Be kind to Helen! Hearten her. Comfort her." The tone is warm.

Miss Flower gasps. "But we could get in touch with her mother. We could go to the Council ourselves." Her voice trembles. "If we chose to, we could do a lot of things."

Silence. Then Kate says, "Two more years here – that's my target, Elizabeth. Not a word to Miss P, mind! But I can hardly wait to be off." Jolly. Kate sounds jolly.

"Off?"

"Oh, Australia, Canada, Africa. Anywhere that's still a bit wild. I've no plan, really. Just *away*." She rises, smiling. "That's why I take these cheap cycling hols, to save my pennies. Only two more years!" And she is gone.

That evening, alone, Miss Flower holds her pen poised so long over the letter-paper that the nib scrapes when at last she writes *Dear* and a fat drop of ink falls, so she must take a fresh sheet. The words rush out.

Dear Canon and Mrs Hepworth, Your Helen, who does so well in Religious Knowledge with me, has perhaps mentioned my name to you? She thinks you might permit her to spend time at Christmas with my mother and me. I do hope you will agree. Other girls will also visit, so Helen would have company of her own age. My elderly mother would welcome . . . .

In this Miss Flower counts five falsehoods, minimum.

Quickly she takes a half-sheet – *Dear Mrs Hepworth*, a line or two – and tucks it inside the letter to the couple. Praying hard, she addresses the envelope to Helen's mother. Then she writes rapidly to her own mother. To suppress any second thoughts, she pulls on her mackintosh and walks rapidly down the School drive to the pillar box. The envelopes tumble in. *I've done it.*

This week, Helen does not do any prep at all.

Miss Lincoln is sarcastic. "You *are* a pupil here at St Mildred's, are you not, Helen Hepworth? Or do you plan to live your life as an ignorant savage?"

Helen's smile makes Amanda uneasy. Still nothing from Miss Flower.

"Helen, I can help you with your prep. Except for arithmetic, I mean." Helen shrugs, and simply looks on while Amanda carefully draws a map.

"Why do we draw maps of Australia, here in England?" Helen asks. "What for?" These ordinary words sound threatening. Hurriedly Amanda seeks advice about colouring Queensland. Turquoise, yellow? Another shrug.

In her pocket Miss Flower carries *He forgetteth not the cry of the humble*, and in her mark-book *Thou hast destroyed the wicked*. These stones from her Advent reading do support her through the stormy water, but Religious Knowledge can't bring herself on schedule to teach *Of the Unworthiness Of Ministers*. Even though she is aware that the sacraments' efficacy is not less because evil men administer them, awareness does not suffice. Sad Helen stops her tongue.

Miss Flower prays that the Canon will not find her note, that Helen's mother will answer soon, and that her own lies to the Hepworths, being motivated by charity, may be forgiven.

Nothing comes from Yorkshire. Mrs Flower however is communicative.

On Tuesday: *Your extraordinary letter arrived a day late, which quite upset my week. You need to remember that I worry. What on earth are you thinking? What have these devious girls been up to? Women! I told you of the Committee's attempts to discredit me at St Timothy's, but you make no answer.*

On Wednesday: *You seem determined to bring trouble down upon yourself. You are getting on. Do you wish to end like Lucinda, keeping farmers' accounts and taking in mending?*

On Thursday: *Your agitation bewilders me! Why is this girl your concern? Elizabeth, no good can come of your attempts. None ever does . . . .*

Miss Flower imagines Helen as a guest. The young face bends over the breakfast table. The freckles, the thin young back. Miss Flower will prepare boiled eggs and offer salt, milk, buttered toast soldiers. In this fancy Mrs Flower does not appear.

On Friday: *I wonder whether you even read my letters, Elizabeth. An incredible invitation! Is our home to be a sanctuary for schoolgirls with foul imaginations? Remember your own father! But you are, of course, the breadwinner. You are, of course, in charge.*

Sanctuary. That is the word.

On Saturday night after questing, she dreams that Miss Pringle (hairy grey tweeds) is at tea with Mrs Flower (chestnut wool) at home. The tray, slices of lemon, and teapot are all as usual, but the ladies lift off their heads, laughing, and place them on each other's necks. Miss Flower herself is a Nice biscuit, paralysed in sugar on a daisied plate. Her distress rouses her. More questing follows, rapturous and exhausting.

On Sunday afternoon, the mistress writes a brief blunt letter home.

When the dreaded Amanda approaches her again, Miss Flower offers a much-practiced line. "Helen is not your concern any longer. We have the matter in hand."

Her hand rises, to oppose the child's still-open mouth.

"Please, about something else? Free will." Amanda is agitated. "If we can't be good unless Christ *prevents* us, why doesn't He?"

"Be careful! Sometimes we are so blind that Christ cannot reach us. We see nothing."

"But Miss Flower, Article X says we can't be *un*-wicked unless He helps us." Her eyes shine with corrupt enquiring innocence.

"Amanda, that is heresy!"

The child's eyes widen and gleam. Flustered, Religious Knowledge tries to explain, but her words sink into such a welter of anger and confused theology that Amanda goes away weeping in confusion. Miss Flower herself cries. To *bear, hope, believe, endure* – clearly she can do none of these. An utter failure in charity, she sees only darkness. She has not the most minimal capacity for virginity or martyrdom.

That afternoon, all the Third Form's letters go to the post unread.

"Nothing untoward," Miss Flower says crisply at tea time.

Other mistresses note that Helen's presence at meals, lessons, even morning prayers is ever more erratic. Miss Pringle frowns. Miss Hodgson takes copious notes.

On Wednesday, Miss Flower sees her mother's letter atop her post and sets all aside unread until the evening.

Then she sets her hair, sips cocoa, finally reads.

First, our Christmas is to be spoiled by the presence of this girl – and now in addition you propose to abandon me at Easter? To spend the holiest week of the year with strangers?

But that letter slips to the floor. There is unfamiliar handwriting on another.

Helen's mother says *Yes*.

Clear joy flows through Miss Flower. Overwhelmed by happiness, she sinks to her knees and offers deep thanks for being allowed to protect Helen even a little, even for a week out of a young damaged life. At Christmas the girl will eat her breakfast in Miss Flower's home. The child will sleep safely. She will sing carols of joy. Seven whole days. And, at Easter, might Helen too come bicycling in Ireland? Kate's good heart will welcome her, Miss Flower is sure. Then, next summer . . . .

Footsteps snap down the passage to her door. *Rap!*

"Helen Hepworth has not been seen since breakfast," states the Head. "Twelve hours. She has hoarded food, to take along."

Boiled eggs roll away over the fells, roll away.

"She" – Miss Pringle pulls at the ear of Amanda, wincing and red-eyed by her side – "has given her pocket money to Helen. Do you hear, Miss Flower? The girl has run off. Disappeared." The Head gestures towards the night beyond the windows.

"The Canon informs me that Helen's letter this week was only blank paper. His wife is too distraught, he says, to speak on the telephone. *You* wrote to her?"

Mrs Flower's hands tighten around her daughter's wrists so that she can never never touch herself again.

Amanda sobs.

"Further, Mrs Ellis has telephoned. It seems that this week Amanda's letter home told a very strange tale. You chose not to report on that, either."

The Head's eyes glare. Miss Hodgson and other staff gather in a rampart behind her, and the footsteps of still more mistresses sound down the dark corridor.

"Miss Flower, what have you done? And who do you think you are?"

Legs in shining nylons run away over green hills that dislimn in a moment, as do bell towers and blue cotton shorts and a bicycle.

Miss Pringle's Hour

Fatherless girls are a particular concern. There are fourteen in the School. It is a great loss, a great absence, and not all of them have sensible mothers.

Of course we mourn their soldier fathers who fell, but never think that these deaths and the terrible destruction of English cities were the sum of the War. *Cut is the branch that might have grown full straight.* Timorousness, a certain superficiality or frivolity, an unsuitable bravado, or an excess of conscience: in fatherless girls, these are among the fruits of War. The teaching staff must be aware of this and attempt corrective measures while the pliancy of youth still allows for change. *Mem:* Spk Michaelson re less crit Felicity's handiwork.

July 8th, House Tennis Match, won by St Hilda's. All the girls played very well, I thought. The tension of Speech Day has eased, and our usual healthy attitude is with us again. *Mem:* Commend Fielding.

July 10th, Talk on Social Work as a Career, from Mrs Edwards of the Jubilee Infirmary. Is it really 12 months since her last visit? She spoke well, although I wish she would refrain from jokes. Senior girls about to leave School do not need such enticements in order to pay attention.

Departing, Mrs E commented that the girls' uniforms "have such a pretty old-fashioned look." ??? *Mem:* Ask RH.

Perusing the pedagogical theories of Mr Neill at Summerhill, I recently came upon a tirade against uniforms. How little the man understands! Repeatedly I have seen their beneficence at work. Angela: when she came to us, shy and anxious, our uniform sheltered her from notice. Thus reassured, she was able to work. Term by term, she developed confidence in herself and her School. I can see her now, attaching her first monitor's pin to her tunic. Or was that Anthea? Such care and pride. Her posture is much improved. She has reached the Sixth. She leaves her sleeves rolled up after Games, sets her School hat at a tilt. Within sight of her General Certificate, Amelia treats her uniform casually, knowing she is nearly ready to discard it.

July 20th, Staff vs 1st VI Tennis Match, won by 1st VI. I am not sure that F was pleased at this victory, in part at least the result of her excellent coaching of the girls. She is after all still young herself, but.

July 25th, End of Term. All went well, with only the customary few confusions of missed trains and forgotten articles. RH this time required Fitz to take trunks to dormitories 3 days in advance, not 2, which made a great difference. Her attention to detail is only matched by her skill in overall planning. What would St Mildred's do without Miss Ruth Hodgson, Assistant Head? HRH! Efficiency contributes to the School's tone. It is much changed since the days of my predecessor, a kindly woman of small authority.

After tea, I began my inspection. Moss on the front steps has spread shockingly. Why Fitz has not attended to this I cannot think. Wear and tear are plain on the furniture in the junior and staff common rooms, but. As for the curtains, I chose them in 1936. The piano tuner must come. The forms, springboard, and mats in the gym are shabby but serviceable. I had thought G's complaints about her laboratory exaggerated but am compelled to admit she is right. I should not like any member of Council to see the present equipment. The Lower Vth's copies of *Illustrated History of Modern Britain* are a disgrace, full of idle markings, in pen. We cannot have this. Probably there will be no new edition for years. Not a decade since the War, and already such careless waste! The grounds look well. In this Fitz is meticulous. Re-roofing the main building was the right decision. I did not reach the dormitories today.

Mem: Emph frugality in welcome talk in Sept. To Council, emph rel betw eqpt/furn and qual educ, compare Clarendon. Spk Fitz re steps (muriatic acid?), Gwen S re abuse of Sr Common Rm piano, Trout re closer superv Vth. RH to enq re new climbing ropes, arrange tuner, cost lab eqpt, find fabric samples – chintz, toile de Jouy?

As I stand on the steps when the girls have left and look out over the gravel drive and the Great Lawn, the silence fairly echoes. Miss Percival, who stayed only a term or two just after the War, once joined me at this hour and said, "*Let the Irish vessel lie / Emptied of its poetry.*" All wrong, of course. Mr Auden spoke of a dead fellow poet, not of a busy school in England, nor do his lines rhyme, nor could most of our girls be termed poetic – yet I felt in accord with her. When full of girls, our gym is not shabby.

Within a few days the teaching staff will leave as well, and Matron, whose sharp tongue I shall not miss. Then, so much to do! As RH and I inspect, make lists, write letters, take inventory, prepare accounts and reports, there is hardly time to walk the dogs. Fred and Nelly whine, to remind us. In Mrs Howard's enormous kitchen, we cook scratch meals and take them like picnics into RH's or my sitting room. We prepare for my interview with Council. We ourselves interview prospective parents, girls, staff. A new laundry must be selected. We must renegotiate with the baker.

Our week in the Cotswolds is always enjoyable. The dogs love our country rambles, and each year we resume the happy hunt for our retirement cottage. This summer RH lengthened her bird list considerably. I had not been aware that there are so many different types of warbler. Our solitude brings us delight. HRH!

Returning eagerly to School, we once again feel urgency. The telephone rings, the postbag swells. RH spends hours with the time-table and I with the budget. Vans carrying tinned goods, lavatory paper, chalk, soap, sheet music, notebooks, bed linens, hockey sticks and foolscap come up the drive, displacing Fitz's carefully raked gravel. (Overlapping arcs are apparently the style in Dublin.) New teachers arrive.

September 20th, School reassembles. *Mem*: Spk Council Chair re overdraft, all teaching staff new GC regulations, Fitz not appear shirtless in term-time (a singlet at least), Matron manner to new girls, Mrs H kitchen shelving.

September 25th, The VIth and the Upper Vth attended the Old Vic's *A Winter's Tale* at the Royal. Meeting Dr Chapple of Clarendon at the interval, I was pleased at our girls' poise. Some of his boys were rambunctious. Dr C enquired re our university entrances. Of course Clarendon's size and endowments ensure a higher proportion than we can attain, but. The actors performed very well, I thought.

September 30th, News-talk by Mr Oliver Greene. Amanda Ellis interrupted, to ask a question. No one welcomes more warmly than I the post-war trend of arrivals from other lands in the Commonwealth, as we are now to call it, but the difficulties cannot be denied. The ways of life followed by persons from the Caribbean living in our larger cities, unfortunately in their poorer quarters, are so different from those of native-born Britons as to cause social disruption. Naturally there is nothing of this sort with Amanda, who is physically indistinguishable from her classmates, but.

Mr Greene is prolix. That man will end his days in some residential hotel, one of those eccentric dodderers crouched by an inadequate fire.

October 4th, Lantern Lecture, The Romans in Britain, Miss Laura Harvie, BA, of the Historical Society. Funds simply must be found to purchase new equipment for such presentations.

Corresp: Old Girl Rosemary Hayton (Clarke) '37 wishes to endow a prize for best Senior essay on a 19th- or 20th-century woman artist. Most generous. I cannot think why she should wish thus to limit the subject-matter.

Mem: Spk Ellis pts re elocution lessons Amanda? RH enq lantern costs.

October 5th, Yesterday was tiring, yet about 2 a.m. I was wakeful (too warm). At the window, my reverie was broken by the sight of Mr G crossing the Great Lawn and going down the drive. The girls call him Mr Grey. At that hour, where can the man have been off to? Only distasteful answers occur. Fitz, yes, but Mr G?

Mem: Spk Fitz, again, re suitable address – Miss Pringle, not simply Miss, which is appropriate should he need to speak to one of the girls. Such distinctions matter. Unlike Mr Neill, I insist upon outward manifestations of respect. When girls rise on my entrance, I am gratified, for in honouring my position they honour their own.

Oddly enough, it was Mr G who overheard the Chair of the Council speaking to Dr C. "Remarkable" – that was the term used – "remarkable, the improvement in tone at St Mildred's since Pringle became Head." RH was equally delighted. A good reputation among such men is invaluable to a small girls' School. Of course Mr G told me so as to curry favour. He may think I am unaware of that. The man is a poodle.

The mention of *tone* is particularly satisfying, for a school is far more than lessons. On Speech Day, we at St Mildred's do not only award prizes for learning. We show our girls at Games. We present them reciting, dancing, singing, acting, playing musical instruments. We exhibit their handiwork and paintings. The School Magazine, with its exciting news of our Old Girls, is handed out to parents. I almost pity those mothers and fathers. They know so little of their daughters!

Secret knowledge is not a small part of a Head's work. For example, Mr G is Irish, a fearful man, and rightly fears for his post here. In her bedroom, Miss Pruitt keeps a bottle of gin. Miss Lincoln is three years older than she owns to. As for Mrs Howard's little manoeuvres with Purchasing, they were quite transparent. I made myself clear to her, and we had no more of that. A good cook is an asset to a School.

Other private knowledge is different. Sadly, Mrs Wilmer's husband was killed in action. Although some widows have done well with us, I now believe she will not recover. In Maths, girls are at enough of a disadvantage without the burden of a distraught teacher. Pamela in Upper IV appears very able and must have first-rate coaching. Miss Flower has not grown up. There is a leaning to the sentimental (e.g., the Helen Hepworth episode), but her other traits of honesty, diligence, and piety are valuable, and not only in the study of Religious Knowledge. RH feels this strongly. HRH herself: another secret! No one has the great good fortune to know her as I do.

Mr Grey, Goody Two-Shoes, Primp, Lips, The Oirishman –
very apt the girls are, in nicknaming! L and P's foolishness does no
harm. If I thought otherwise, they would not be teaching here.
Human variety is valuable; we cannot all be serious scholars, and
both women teach conscientiously. They will not be long in finding husbands. For some, that is best. However, I confess to resent-
ing L. According to Matron, she remarked that RH's "frumpy
clothes" were pale copies of mine. Yet the girls do very fine maps, I
think.

October 22nd, Piano Recital by Miss Gates of the Conservatory.
She played *The Merry Peasant*. I remember Father humming that. I
hummed it myself, *sotto voce*, during the dreary music at his funeral.
November 1917 – 36 years ago! Poor Mother. At the Recital, some
girls' deportment was poor. Josephine slouches ostentatiously.

After walking Fred and Nelly, RH complained of fatigue and
retired early.

October 29th, Lecture by Mr Alan Howell of Australia House,
London. Many girls took a lively interest in this talk, plus a short
film, in colour. I do not want to think of their leaving England. Foolishly, I do not like them even to leave School, though as Seniors they
must and do. Can there be a fuller world than here? Few see the rich-
ness. Lips chatted with Mr Howell; the Lower IVth are studying
Australia.

Hodgson inevitably is Hedgehog. Pringle is Quangle. Hedgehog & Quangle. Like a pair of lawyers in Dickens, RH says! I do not
in the least mind a sobriquet derived from Mr Lear's charming nonsense, yet I see it as a rare failure of the girls' imaginations. Would I
ever exclaim *That very few people come this way / And that life on the
whole seems far from gay*? A Head is by definition amongst people,
and, while I would concur with Mr Longfellow that *Life is real! Life is
earnest!*, I am not sad. For my subdued clothing I make no apology.
Dr Chapple may affect vivid ties and socks – *Mutton dressed as lamb*,
Mother would say – but it does not suit for the Head of a small girls'
school so to display herself.

Mem: Spk Council Chair re overdraft, more talks on career
oppts in Britain, lantern. Spk Mrs H fish pie. RH GC examinations

and costs new piano. Review proposals for new prefects. Spk Josephine posture.

November 3rd, Half-term. I encouraged RH to rest. Much time spent on consideration of a rise in School fees.

November 10th, Visit from ten Old Girls for the weekend. As always, gratifying.

November 20th, GC started. Most will do well, although Miss Maywood is anxious about Gillian's Latin. .

It is a great responsibility to prepare girls for the modern world. Much change is underway in Britain, not all good, and confusing for the young. Materialism and lower moral standards are ubiquitous. At least we can now be confident in our Government, having made up for the embarrassment of the election immediately post-War. Such ingratitude! However, the stringencies of wartime have only slowly lessened here. We cannot do all that should be done. We can only do our best. Even with rising costs of living, however, parents do see some extras (riding, swimming) as desirable, which pleases me. A boys' school like Clarendon may raise fees without question, but.

November 29th, French Plays by III, Lower IV, Upper IV. As a girl, RH spent summers in France. She praised our girls' accents. I missed some of the byplay, gestures and the like. Difficulties with vision are perhaps inevitable with age. A settee from the drawing-room was on stage; the plot required bouncing about on this delicate furniture. Lesley was actually wearing tennis shorts. Girls must learn appropriate behaviour. I feel that St Mildred's makes this lesson easy, as the grace of our old buildings encourages good manners. Our integration of modernity must be respectful.

Complete fluency in French is unnecessary. We do not wish our girls to be mistaken for Frenchwomen.

Dr C once disparagingly remarked, "A pity that no scholarships are offered for sewing." Such a little mind! Quite apart from its traditional feminine value, needlework requires concentration, physical skill, commitment to detail, and perseverance in a demanding task. The sight of 3rd Formers engaged on their aprons and handkerchiefs thus gratifies me; the abilities involved built the Empire and will sustain the Commonwealth. Artistic talent may also be fostered. Dr C's remark was an insult, possibly intentional.

Mem: Appt eyes. Tell Council Secy put fees on agenda. Spk Matron re withdrawal of h-w bots unsuitable discipline, Hudson unauth use of settee, Amanda VITamin not VITEamin, Trout order in classroom, again. RH to revise Clothing Lists, enq new Maths, review menus with Mrs H.

December 8th, St Anne's House Party, a pleasant occasion, although the room felt insufferably warm. RH was quite comfortable. Later, she was perfectly so. HRH!

December 11th, School Nativity Play.

December 14th, Prefects and Seniors attended the Clarendon College Dance. No incidents. However, I shall not in future designate T as chaperone.

December 15th, Council Meeting. Fees to rise, not enough in my view. To my surprise, the Chairman wishes to consider rises for the teaching staff. I cannot agree. Anyone who enters this profession – a calling, as I see it – with a view to acquiring wealth is a fool. Careful management enables St Mildred's staff to live in simple comfort. Room and board are, after all, provided for most of the year. It was perhaps my annoyance that made me feel so hot. RH and I shall be glad to see the end of term. Her fatigue even follows exertions formerly seen as only pleasurable.

Mem: Appt eyes! Not done, in spite of my earlier note.

December 16th, Carol Service. Miss Flower remarked that the girls' veils, rather than lessening their individuality of appearance, accentuate it. Exactly. She went on, however, to compare nuns. I cannot approve. To withdraw so, to stand aside! No. Our girls must have opportunities to weave together all the strands of a full life – intellectual, vocational, social, domestic, even artistic.

December 18th, End of Term. Whether girls take advantage of those opportunities is to some extent beyond our control. Horses to water, etc. However, the personal qualities of the staff, as much as their teaching, may exert a powerful influence. Mrs Wilmer must go.

Snow fell. RH and I walked for an hour before tea. Such uninterrupted conversation is rare. She was quite puffed, and rested before dinner.

As usual in the holidays, there is much to do. A few days in London will be required. RH suggests a new School uniform! We shall visit Neals'. We may manage a visit to the Cotswolds. At least, weather permitting, we shall take daily walks together.

January 1st, The official New Year never seems as new as does September. Word of Father's death came on this day in '17, and of my brother's in '43. My poor Mother. RH noted blue tits, a chaffinch, blackbirds. The swans looked very white on the dark river edged with snow. They showed no fear at all when Fred and Nelly barked.

January 6th, Appropriately, the Royal's *Twelfth Night* opened tonight. RH enjoyed herself very much. All the actors did well, I thought. Neals' sent sample designs for new uniforms. Wrote Mrs Wilmer. RH – pain in arm.

January 12th, nr Burford. We may at last have found a suitable cottage. I hardly dare to write this. RH fully satisfied. HRH!

January 17th, School reassembled.

January 20th, Talk on Careers by Miss Macnaughton of the Ministry of Labour. Matron termed her *hard-bitten,* not a phrase I would myself employ, but her personality was certainly not engaging. A pity. Victoria, Janice, Eleanor, Anne simply ceased to listen, yet Janice has a genuine interest in veterinary medicine.

Today Eileen again set my hair very nicely. Truly her accent is dreadful. How glad I am that no St M's girl, barring disaster, will ever need to earn a living thus.

Dr Ingram recommends spectacles. I returned to School feeling quite depressed. RH as always was solicitous. Twice, which is now rare. HRH!

January 31st, Lantern Lecture on Britain's Fascinating Geology, by Mr McKee of Cambridge. Our new equipment does enhance such presentations, esp on a topic not of automatic interest to girls. That young man truly opened vistas. Valerie had several questions. Of course Lips and Primp were at him, moments after he concluded. I should not be surprised to see Valerie come back to St Mildred's one day, to teach Science. I have often predicted which Old Girls will return, which will send their daughters here. Not all these women by any means were prefects or prize-winners in their day.

Mem: Birthday present for HRH.

February 10th, Lecture by Miss Penelope Seaman on the Mary-hill Missions in Kenya, Rhodesia, and Nigeria. The name smacks of Catholicism, yet this is fine work. We are of course a long way from *They call us to deliver / Their land from error's chain*, but Africa *is* in a bad way. To help is our duty. For the girls to see this is important. I think we were all alarmed at Miss S's comments on the Mau Mau. The ingratitude, after all the British have done for Kenya, is shocking.

I regret having written *smacks* of Catholicism. The Romans are simply at the furthest point on the Christian spectrum.

RH is delighted with her camera!

Mem: Spk Council Chair re uniforms, all staff Spring morale slump, Vicar Conf class, Trout classroom atmos, Josephine posture, Wilmer replacement. RH to arr GC exams, cost new gym eqpt, draft fees letter to pts.

Really, a new science *building* would be most desirable.

February 15th, News-talk by Mr G. Could the man be any more dessicated in manner or appearance? Undeniably, he is very well-informed.

RH and I hardly speak of Burford, except re agent, bank, etc. To have one's heart's desire! Speech is not enough, we agree.

The new uniforms engage me greatly. RH is right that it is time for a change, to make the girls' dress better suited to the 2nd half of the 20th c. Daily we consider Neals' sketches, over coffee or before retiring. Of course the School colours will not alter. But how best to introduce the new clothing? Should an incoming 3rd Form be the first outfitted, and so lead the way up the School? However, not all girls enter in the 3rd. A parti-coloured effect would not look well in the Photograph or at Away matches. Morale would suffer. I would not wish parents to have the expense of 2 uniforms during a daughter's years at St Mildred's, but.

RH thinks I am going through the change. I am most reluctant to write these words, remembering how my poor Mother became so red and distressed.

February 21st, House Dancing Competition, won by St Anne's. All the girls danced very well, I thought.

Colds and a nasty influenza have filled the San. Matron does better in a demanding situation than when there is little illness. On the whole, this is not a good trait for those whose work is in institutions.

A talk (our third) with Mrs W today. I wish a different decision were possible. I shall of course provide a good reference. As a tutor, she may do well.

If new uniforms were introduced this Sept in the 3rd, the whole School would be newly clothed by my retirement at 60. *Mem*: Try not to dwell on age. But why should Dr C be able to continue as Head of Clarendon for 5 more years than I at St Mildred's, simply because he is a man?

The purchase of the Burford cottage has been achieved. HRH!

There is no reason for me not to continue. Never have I seen more clearly what St M's needs! Some plans, also, simply require time to reach fruition.

HRH. Without her calm, I should be even angrier. The cottage garden offers such potential pleasure for her. Surely occasional visits should be possible in term-time? We shall be there, and here. We shall.

March 1st, Gymnastic Competition, won by Upper VI.

If I must retire at 60, I shall not see Valerie's return to our Science laboratory.

Hair appt today. It does not hold a set as formerly. Neat appearance is essential. Eileen has booked me for appts at 4-wk not 6-wk intervals.

March 2nd, Half-term. To Burford. We attended what will be our church. Later RH asked me why, since I do not believe, I sing the hymns with such enthusiasm.

On the village war memorial, she noted two cases of a father dying in WWI and a son in WWII, as in my family.

Buds are visible on the trees and shrubs. The Windrush is a very pretty little river. RH took many photographs.

March 20th, Good Friday. The Senior Prefects read the day's Lessons very well, I thought.

Interview with L and P, who feel entitled to the same salary as the junior masters at Clarendon.

RH tolerant as always. I admit she is right that young women do well to consider their financial future, but. Alone, neither RH nor I could afford our cottage. I positively dread the little residential hotels one sees all over England. Such a terrible terminus that would be for HRH! Yet a school like St M's simply cannot pay such salaries. Always, the good of the School must be paramount.

I enquired of L and P whether Flower, the other junior mistress, took their view. They affected ignorance, but I feel sure she would not dare to put herself forward thus.

To become accustomed to spectacles takes time. RH declares they look well on me. I doubt this but in the moment was not able to say so.

Mem: Once more – T, no order in classroom. We really cannot have this.

March 25th, Spk Council secy re agenda items: uniforms, salaries, *New Eng Bible*, poss Science Bldg, Speech Day, applic from Nigerian businessman/Manchester for his daughter. Drains – do not forget! And GC of course. It is regrettable that the new GC only records a pass, however good an individual mark may be. To level down, rather than to encourage aiming high, is most unfortunate.

RH indisposed. Pain in upper arm again.

March 28th, Lecture on the Mystery Plays by Miss Ellen Hurrell, MA. Dr Chapple attended, with a friend, as did the Vicar and Curate. Mr G is here this week, as well. Our little reception afterwards was thus lively. L and P were quite beside themselves. For some reason I introduced P as Miss Percival. An annoying slip.

Dr C says that he regards Clarendon's Speech Day as *the crown of the year*. I cannot agree. A School then *displays* itself most fully, but *is* not most itself.

On certain days in the year's cycle, St Mildred's runs at full tide – the first At Home match in the autumn, the Carol Service, the spring sitting of the GC, the annual School Photograph. Sometimes

I must make an announcement in Dining Hall, as when our King died. Then the School is one. This is my hour. Or an individual girl may do something which says *St Mildred's*. A new prefect tells me of an untoward activity in her dormitory. A 3rd Form girl in a battle over nail-biting shows me her clean hands, or one in the VIth writes an essay so good that a scholarship able to transform her life moves within reach. Parents do not know such moments. I may pass through the main school at half-past ten of a weekday, when Latin verbs murmur in the Lower IVth and needles flash in the sewing room. Mme Dutheil is giving a *dictee*. In the laboratory, beakers tap and chink. Someone is practising scales on the piano, tripping over B. No one sees me. All my girls and staff are here, at School. That is my hour, my year's crown.

Retirement at 60 means that I will not likely see the Science Bldg complete.

Dr C, speaking of the Mystery Plays, said *quaint*. In that context the word could only be pejorative. I do not favour such a light-hearted dismissal of Xnity's profound expressions. Just as girls should refrain from shorts in the drawing-room, they should respectfully inhabit the house of their country's history – which includes Xnity.

As I told RH, I do sing some hymns, or parts of them, with enthusiasm. For example, *When Duty calls, or Danger / Be never wanting there*. The dangers incurred in running a School are great, given a Head's responsibilities for the future of youth. Duty is more prominent, to the lay eye. *Jerusalem* and *St Patrick's Breastplate* are stirring.

April 2nd, first Confirmation Class, 11 to participate.

Passing the Lower Vth's classroom, I overheard P conclude her exposition of Iambic Pentameter – *Look ON my WORKS, ye MIGHTy, AND desPAIR!*

Mem: Write acceptance for Nigerian girl. –

April 3rd, End of Term. Two hundred girls plus mistresses and staff departed successfully. HRH!

After five terms it is clear that T cannot maintain discipline. *If* – a large *if*, in my judgement – she can make progress, this must occur

167

elsewhere. I regret it very much. T is an Old Girl who takes a lively interest in her subject but alas is too inclined to a girlish enthusiasm that cannot command respect.

In RH's view, almost a decade post-War we must repaint the dormitories; it is not good for the girls to inhabit such shabby quarters. Kindness itself, my RH.

F wishes the girls to elect their team captains. No one appreciates more than I the advantages and burdens of democracy, nor of the need for youth to gain experience in both, but. However, RH is in favour.

At Burford, we discuss these matters and much else. Holiday too short! Nelly and Fred and I enjoyed the walks, though sometimes had to rouse RH to come too. Father used to jolly me along when I moped, so thus I encourage her. Better to hearten! Greater spotted woodpecker, snipe, pipit. RH made pleasing photo studies of our new home. None of this change nonsense for her, naturally, too young, but a visit to the doctor may be in order. NB binoculars, next b-day.

Returned to School to find Neals' firm estimate. Prices have unaccountably risen since Christmas. We cannot have this. I hope to present the designs on Speech Day.

Fencing by daygirls' bicycle shed needs repair. Has a tramp been sleeping there? Fitz disclaims knowledge. We simply cannot have School grounds used by strange men so incapable of managing their lives that they have no home. Lawn & flower beds immaculate. Fitz wishes to enlarge two borders.

Frequently I mislay my spectacles. RH suggests a cord.

Interview with T, who took it like a true St Mildred's girl.

My final talk (I trust) with Mrs W made it clear that, since she has never signed any contract with the School, her hopes for legal redress must be slim.

Mem: Fitz re kitchen garden, kale, rasp canes, peas, reduce sprouts. Dormant oil to damsons. Agree borders. Mrs H, summer fruit *not* always stewed. RH place adverts Maths, Hist.

May 1st, School re-assembled.

May 7th, Piano recital by Mr Andrew Mornay of the Conservatory. Handsome is as handsome does.

May 9th, Talk by Reverend Geoffrey Hart on the Church Pastoral-Aid Society. The man gave last year's talk verbatim.

At Staff Meeting, Nigerian girl subject of lengthy discussion. I spoke of the C'wealth and of oppty, indeed duty, to share the very best of England.

Mem: Spk Council Chair re Speech Day, Old Girls Assn funds for new Science Bldg, Vicar Conf class, Mrs H inferior quality of bread/change baker, Head Girl and prefects whispering during Hart's talk.

RH to tel secy of CP-AS and speak frankly.

May 15th, School Photograph. The event went very well, I thought. A little cloudy today, so probably fewer girls than usual will be squinting.

May 19th, Lantern Lecture on *The Brontes of Yorkshire* by Mr Leslie Morton of Oxford. He was, I think, rather older than anticipated by L and P – amusing! New eqpt again most satisf. Branwell B appears to have been an utter wastrel.

The Spring weather is delightful. I find though that I spend term-time almost entirely indoors. RH walks dogs daily.

May 20th, Old Girls' At-Home. Very satisf, although RH retired long before the evening reception was over. Her arrangements made all smooth. HRH! After our guests were gone and all was still, I joined her.

Mem: Spk Fitz, again, re wearing singlet. His bare chest not suitable for exhibit.

May 26th, Talk by Mrs Rawlinson of the Royal Jubilee on Nursing as a Career. A most capable administrator, she makes a fine impression. Nursing is not the profession which I most gladly see our girls enter, but. To my annoyance, Mrs R's name slipped from memory as I was about to introduce her. I cannot have this.

June 1st, Half-term. Hair appt. Eileen looks forward to a visit home to Galway. Her manner is most pleasant.

Interviewed 3 poss Maths, one a man! Cannot understand how this happened. RH also at a loss. An inoffensive young person, but. To men as visitors to the School I do not object, for they can bring other and valuable perspectives. And 2 poss Hist. An easy decision, for really Miss Birkenstall might as well be an Old Girl.

Corresp: Letter from father of Nigerian girl. Her arrival in September will take careful handling. RH and I will discuss at length, at Burford.

June 10th, all music students attended perf by London Philharmonic Orchestra, on tour. RH enjoyed this very much.

June 16th, GC started. Most girls will do well, I think.

June 20th, Expedition by motorcoach to Abbey ruins, L and P in charge, T assisting. Many girls truly learned, I think, yet for disciplinary reasons I saw no fewer than five in my office afterwards. We really cannot have this.

The School Photograph includes only one squinter, Josephine. I am certain that this was deliberate. RH looks very well.

June 25th, Confirmation, 10 girls not 11. Flower & Vicar felt that Jennifer's muddle re consubst made her an unsuitable candidate. Next year? Her mother is RC, possibly the root cause. RH says Flower handled this rather awkward situation well.

The Bishop took tea on the Great Lawn with the candidates and their parents. RH and he spoke of her father, in old age a petty canon at the Cathedral where the Bishop began his career. RH was touched at his recollections of her father singing, off-key.

Hard work from now until end of term will enable us to spend almost a fortnight at Burford. HRH! Only the major enterprise of Speech Day remains. Netball, tennis, and swimming are well in hand, and the elected captains of the senior teams are those I would myself have chosen. The uniform project is underway. Very few parents are in arrears, RH confirms. The Chairman of Council tells me that a new member takes an especial interest in Sciences since his own daughter is a chemist; he is said to be enthused at the prospect of a Building. Several times weekly, Mrs Howard presents attractive dishes of fresh fruit. Pamela's mathematical abilities appear exceptional. Maywood reports that 3 girls in the Vth show real promise in not only Latin but also Greek. The Upper IVth is, claims Michaelson, the most competent group of needlewomen seen since 1938.

All in all, it will be a pleasure to make my Report on Speech Day.

June 29th, House Tennis Match, won by St Anne's. All the girls played very well, I thought. St Hilda's was gracious in defeat.

The cord for my specs is most helpful. HRH!

Mem: spk Council Secy re new Tennis Cup. There is scarcely space left for engraving any more winners' names.

July 4th, Ruth Catherine Hodgson died in her sleep. Her heart failed. At sixteen minutes past six I awoke to find her dead.

July 8th, Her funeral. The School Choir sang most beautifully, I thought. Everyone was most kind. The Bishop was most kind. Of course I had not expected to see him again so soon. He spoke of God's will. I cannot agree.

July 10th, Speech Day. Although the Chairman spoke with warm appreciation of all that the Asst Head did in her many years of service, this Day remained, as HRH herself would have wished, a celebration of St Mildred's School. More parents than ever attended. Dr Chapple was most complimentary.

July 11th, 1 wk.

July 18th, 2 wks. Daily, Matron takes Nelly and Fred for a long vigorous walk. I have misjudged her. They do enjoy their biscuits.

July 25th, End of Term, 3 wks. I shall not leave the School this summer but rather attend to the Burford sale from here.

Lincoln offered help in inspecting classrooms, gym, dormitories, grounds, etc. She would be ready to rearrange her holiday plans. With thanks, I declined. I have misjudged her also. Misjudged. HRH. HRH.

Fitz has found a good home, on a farm, for Fred and Nelly.

September 15th, 11 wks. Misses Hunnicutt and Birkenstall, new Maths and Hist, arrive today. Cutt & Stall. Hedgehog & Quangle.

New secy's arrangements already prove most unsatisf. At the train station the Nigerian girl waited an hour, alone.

Mem: Arrange VIth attendance at Old Vic *As You Like It*, always an RH favourite.

Spk Council Chair re mtg agenda, all teaching staff School spirit, Hunnicutt Pamela, Fitz repoint kitch garden wall, prefects set example punctuality.

RH – no. No. New secy check fees arrears, cost new tablecloths, arrange removal RH furn & paint office.

HRH. HRH.

Also, prep Dining Hall seating plans.

Learning to Dance

The Sixth Form girls were to attend a spring dance at Clarendon, the boys' school some miles away. As a treat, juniors might gather in St Mildred's courtyard to watch the seniors in their finery board the charabanc. The light, on that late Friday afternoon in early May, was just softening into dusk, so the long party-dresses held their colours as they swayed in the cool air. The girls giggled and exclaimed. Some moved from hand to hand the unfamiliar accoutrements of cloak, bag, and evening gloves.

"Cloaks on!" called Miss Lincoln. Against objections, her voice rose. "Your frocks must stay clean. Not a spot! And you don't want to take a chill."

All the pinks and forget-me-not blues disappeared, candles quenched. Some girls spun round, smiling as dark wool flared out over pale yellow taffeta or rose sateen. "When we reach Clarendon, of course you film stars may uncloak before you step off the charabanc." About to give the order to board, Geography frowned. "Molly O'Brien, what *are* you wearing?"

Over this girl's shoulders hunched her school uniform coat, thick, graceless, its sleeves flapping like a double amputee's. "I haven't a cloak, Miss Lincoln."

"Nonsense! They are required, for the Sixth."

Chin up, this Molly – who was tall, slender, and doubtless pretty when not white as wax in public crucifixion – spoke softly. "The School List says they're Optional. Except for the choir. I'm not in the choir."

Molly's hair framed her cheeks in shining black parentheses. Her eyes were brilliant, her dress pale green. A susurration carried her words to the rim of the watching circle, where they were glossed and annotated till even the youngest girl grasped that Molly O'Brien's parents hadn't the money to buy their daughter a cloak.

Geography, swishing her peacock blue taffeta, joined other mistresses on the steps of the School. They conferred. Then Religious Knowledge detached herself from the cluster and entered the building. Silence. After some minutes this dogsbody returned, carrying a dark something. The mistresses removed the ugly coat from Molly, whose arms and throat shone pale. Velvet flowed over her, black water.

"Fasten it! You've kept us waiting long enough."

Molly's fingers twitched on the frog closings.

"Stupid girl, don't cry." Miss Lincoln took over. "This is Miss Pringle's own cloak." Gasps ruffled the spring air. "Yes, our Head wants St Mildred's to look her best! On board now, my Irish beauty. Right to the back of the bus. Take great care."

As the mistresses urged Molly up the steps the velvet flapped, revealing ivory silk inside. Shortly the charabanc rumbled away with its nubile cargo of almond and lilac, ninon and voile.

The bell now rang for the evening meal. There was brown Windsor soup, and Hovis plastered with Marmite.

Talking little at first, the left-behind girls contemplated Clarendon. How would it be to dance not in the gym by day, after Arithmetic and before Art, not with known girls but with boys, and at night? Not country dances, either, but waltzes, foxtrots. Boys. Terror for some, like Amanda's vanished friend Helen. Nervousness, for many. Kay, the dead ballet dancer, would surely have been fearless.

The table talk turned to rumours of a film the Lower Fourth was soon to see. Its unique subject matter, *Health*, dictated watching it in the gym – after lessons, blinds drawn, Matron and the Head present. The word *Health* generated knowing snickers as the steamed puddings arrived. No custard! That sent the gabbling voices right back to Clarendon, where Refreshments were to be served. The girls speculated. Might there be *melons icy cold / Piled on a dish of gold*? They scraped their plates clean of stodge, not a spot, and went off to Drama practice.

The Lower Fourth was helping to present Christina Rossetti's *Goblin Market* for the Spring Entertainment and Reception To Follow. These, said the official Notice, were "designed to give pleasure to parents and friends of the School." Each girl would narrate part of the poem, while older pupils took the major roles of the sisters and the goblin men. For now, chairs set on the stage represented these others. Queuing up to recite, the twelve-year-olds jostled in the mirror by the barre. Their tunics and blouses were rumpled at the school day's end, their ties twisted out of true.

Amanda was not the only girl who found *Goblin Market* strange. What to make of it? Laura and Lizzie are enticed by goblins who sell the familiar English tree-fruits and berries but also oranges, citrons, figs, pineapples, dates, melons. Laura pays, with a lock of her golden hair, and eats to surfeit. Next day she is frantic for more, but the merchants and their fruits are now invisible to her. Desperate Laura grieves, starves, nears death. To save her sister, Lizzie bravely visits the goblins. She pays money but won't eat, even though the goblins attack violently and try to force fruit pulp into her mouth. At last they retreat. Joyful Lizzie goes home to Laura, who frantically licks and sucks at her face . . . and is revolted. She loses consciousness. Nursed by devoted Lizzie, she wakes next day fully recovered. The sisters live out their lives happily.

Yes, puzzling. Amanda overheard scraps of talk among the popular girls, but to her that discussion was closed. She focussed instead on Rossetti's novel words – *obtuse, bullace, cankered, lamentable, ratel, succous* – and shared this pleasure with her father.

"Yes, whatshername's diction is very rich," reflected Mr Ellis. "Though not very original, in comparison to Keats's. It seems forced. Excessively archaic – is that what I mean?" He reached for the *Shorter Oxford*.

Amanda's recitation included

Laura stretched her gleaming neck
Like a rush-imbedded swan,
Like a lily from the beck,
Like a moonlit poplar branch,

Like a vessel at the launch
When the last restraint is gone

She learned her lines easily, scorned girls who needed a prompt from Miss Hudson. What was hard about memorizing poetry, especially with Rossetti's thumpy-thump rhymes? *Cold, gold, hold. Forbidden, hidden. Tasted, wasted.* Pronunciation was another matter. *Branch* and *launch* were tricky, like *bath* and *mall* and *secretary*, for Amanda's English accent was not under perfect control. *Raunchy* and *controversy* she did not yet know. Mercifully, Drama had read the whole poem aloud before the girls got at it, but Amanda's mouth did not want to say *branch* as the mistress did. By Lake Muskoka the pines, cedars, and poplars made their own sounds on August days as wafts passed through their leaves or needles, and in September thunderstorms when the wind sawed roughly at their limbs or wrenched them off. Canadian trees didn't have *brawnches*.

Tonight Amanda made no error, and soon Miss Hudson read Lizzie's disapproving words to the chair representing Laura.

Let us get home before the night grows dark;
For clouds may gather
Though this is summer weather,
Put out the lights and drench us through;
Then if we lost our way what should we do?

Slowly the girls ground through the poem. At the end, all the narrators were to circle the principals, stretch out protective arms, and turn to reveal the triumphant and virtuous sisters, entwined. Tonight, Drama's judgment was as usual.

"Girls, I am not satisfied. Do you not understand this dance?" Their circle had been irregular, their stretches ill-matched, the moment of revelation blurred. "A new life, of the spirit, not the body, is to be born. You are opening the way."

After all that was over, Mrs Ellis picked Amanda up and they drove home to The Green House. Spring rain fell, harder and harder. As the little car moved north on the Woodstock Road, the windshield streamed and water pummelled the roof.

"Amanda, the School says you must have a dress for the Entertainment. There are swatches in my purse. Take a look. The dressmaker will need to work quickly."

Purse. Nearly two years in England, and Mrs Ellis still didn't or wouldn't say *handbag.* Infuriating – yet other matters crowded Amanda's mind. Had the charabanc reached Clarendon before the rain? She imagined the coloured dresses belling out like flowers to float on the dance music. Would Molly's green look like leaves?

"Listen! You must choose." At the hotel, Mrs Ellis snapped on the car's interior light and insisted that her daughter look at fabric samples then and there. Some minutes later, she got out and slammed the driver's door. "Very well. We'll have to shop for a ready-made dress."

She still didn't say *frock,* either.

"Mum, I'm hungry."

Mrs Ellis herded her daughter inside. "You've had your dinner. Get up to bed."

All through Saturday and Sunday, although images of Molly and her velvet cloak swelled inside Amanda, she did not release the story to her parents or to anyone else at the hotel. St Mildred's dormitories would be in ferment with tales of the dance; she longed to hear them. Supposedly doing her prep, Amanda lay on her bed with a book splayed out on her chest, daydreaming about Clarendon as time stretched, contracted, stretched again.

Ordinarily the day-girls held inferior rank within the School, but on that Monday morning they were welcomed back. The boarders were like parent birds, their crops bulging with undigested matter that they must urgently regurgitate. For once, seniors and juniors gossiped without distinction.

"Molly O'Brien ran off with a boy. No one could find them, not for hours."

"She got Miss Pringle's cloak filthy."

"They went out in the night and rain."

"Pringle gave Lincoln a fearful wigging."

"Lincoln called Molly a guttersnipe."

"The charabanc wasn't back till two in the morning. Janice saw."

"They did it."

"Philippa says Molly's in the San. Matron's keeping guard."

"She'll be expelled. Gwen says her people are coming to get her, today."

"Will Jeremy be expelled?"

"Not likely." This Fifth Form expert played on the second net-ball team. "He's cricket captain at Clarendon. Anyway it's worse for a girl to do it."

"They didn't get back till dawn."

Amanda's stomach hurt. Without Helen or Kay she was deeply alone, and longed for friends with whom to translate this language.

The day dragged by. Giggling and reprimands marked each lesson. Sometimes food could bring down the fever of school rumours, but today the hissing continued after morning buns-and-milk, and even after lunch. Not having done all her prep caused trouble for Amanda. Fractions sank her even lower than usual, and in Latin she was only lucky not to be called on to conjugate. Lacrosse went on and on and *on*. During one drill, the Lower Fifth laughed themselves scarlet as they tipped the ball from basket to basket, whispering, "Molly! Jeremy!"

Then came the shopping trip with her mother. Amanda had forgotten.

"But I don't feel well, Mum. My stomach aches."

"Nonsense. There's nothing wrong with you."

The shop was large and pillared and carpeted, its atmosphere serious. The smiling assistants quietly made their availability known.

Amanda stood in her uniform before a rack of frocks with cap sleeves, Peter Pan collars, gathered waists. Mrs Ellis noticeably restrained herself from suggesting either plain colours or Liberty prints. Her daughter's hand did not reach out to any dress.

Then Amanda noticed, through an archway, a showroom of grown-up clothes.

"Dear, those are too old for you."

She walked slowly to that next room and took down three dresses.

Her mother then selected a fourth, in a rich mauve, and insisted on joining her in the dressing room. "You'll need help, dear."

Amanda's first choice was a pale green wool, with a zip-fastener awkwardly at the back. Mrs Ellis yanked it up for her, and they both looked in the mirror. The dress was too tight. Below its hem stuck out sturdy bristly legs in socks. Above the graceful neckline were pimples, spectacles, chipmunk cheeks, and hair unbrushed since morning. Tears, violent, choked back, subsided into hiccups. Mrs Ellis quit patting her girl's shoulder only a second before she would have been slapped. The zip surrendered. Amanda peeled off the wool, scrabbled in her tunic pocket for a handkerchief, and flopped down on the spindly chair provided.

"Such a fuss. And don't sit like that, with your legs open." Mrs Ellis's voice grew urgent. "Amanda. That spot. On your under-pants."

The girl saw red. "*Knickers*, Mum!"

So many times Amanda had imagined this jubilant discovery, this arrival at the promised land – but never with her mother stealing the moment. Exclamations followed, a tearful hug that made her cringe. Then Mrs Ellis hurried off to purchase *supplies*.

Silence, solitude, until a shop assistant's whisper slid through the louvred door. "Miss, are you managing in there?" The tone told that the secret was no longer hers. Death by shame felt imminent. When Mrs Ellis returned, those familiar hands touched her flesh till Amanda nearly screamed. Just before they left, her mother held up the mauve dress against her own body. "Nice," she said vaguely to her shining reflection.

Once in the car, she began eagerly to review the facts of life. "So important now, for you, dear, but do understand that it's *all* perfectly healthy and normal."

Amanda, strapped into a pure white elastic harness and her first ST, sat stiff and horrified lest her ears have to endure *egg* or *sperm*. When a careless driver swerved near the Morris, Mrs Ellis honked and swore and forgot about life's miracle. Still Amanda's fear grew. Vivian Clyde, her mother's confidante – she would be told, for sure. As for Mrs K and Miss Talbot, Miss Tilly and Mrs Ledington, even

179

Celia the maid, her mother was quite capable of publicly announcing to them that her daughter was now *menstruating*. Privately she might even tell Professor McGeachie, or shy Mr Penrose. Of course Daddy would know. The news might take his mind off Keats and Shelley; he was hard at work, her mother said, trying to finish his book. Still, he might talk to her.

To see the hotel's empty lobby brought relief. Soon Amanda was on her bed. Mrs Ellis brought a hot water bottle, and an extra pillow for comfortable reading.

"I don't want to come down for dinner, Mum."

"That's fine dear. Just turn up for coffee in the lounge, after."

The coverlet beneath her felt cool, smooth. Amanda slept.

When she woke, the pain in her belly registered but then she was right back in her dream of Clarendon, where a boy's arms encircled Molly under the softness of Miss Pringle's cloak. The rain sang. They stood, they sat, they lay, black velvet their protection. In all the glamorous tale, the most alluring part for Amanda was not the kiss, not whatever other strange things those two had done with their bodies. What she imagined repeatedly was the moment when Molly and the boy exited the school building. Within its walls there must have been alcoves where those two could be together, an empty study, classrooms even, but instead they opted for the chilly night and rain. Molly just walked out. She stayed out. For hours.

She was endangering her egg. This was so clearly and horribly her mother's voice that Amanda at once got up. Rinsed her face. Brushed her hair. Wanted to pee but dreaded the sight of her ST. Started downstairs toward the communal coffee-hour.

On the landing she realized it was No Go. Between her legs felt wet. Touching herself anxiously behind, Amanda found dampness. In her room she saw that her coverlet was spotted. And the blanket underneath? Clean, thank goodness. She let out her breath, collected supplies, and went down the hall to the loo.

The ST's once neat white rectangle was a sodden red twist. All the crotch of her knickers was stained, the new sanitary belt, her inner thighs. At least her tunic, being dark, would not show anything once the blood dried. Blood fell in the toilet, too, when she peed.

The blood felt almost lumpy, emerging. As best she could, Amanda cleaned her body and struggled into a fresh ST. Now what? She wanted to be alone and go to bed but was hungry. Also, she didn't know what to wear. Should there be knickers under her dandelion pajamas, to hold the ST in place? Did pajamas also get bloody? What did women do?

She gave up and went to find her mother.

At the lounge door, Amanda quailed. Stood. Did nothing, did nothing. Peering in at last, she met several pairs of eyes, but her parents' backs were to her. To reach them would expose her to everyone. Could she call out, "Mum, Mum"? Impossible. Amanda pulled her head back, stood still, then heard the sounds of chairs moving and of female laughter. She ran up to the landing to hide on the curtained window seat, just as footsteps started on the stairs.

"She is rather ill-mannered." That was gentle Mrs Ledington. "Nor does she keep her nails clean."

Mrs K exhaled. "Spoiled rotten, ladies. And messy! You should hear Celia go on about the state of her room."

"She boasts shockingly about her marks." Miss Talbot. "Too clever by half."

Mrs Ledington added, "I'm afraid she is rather greedy."

"Remember, Amanda's only a little girl," Miss Tilly pleaded.

"Be good, sweet maid, and let who will be clever." Miss Talbot again.

Even Miss Tilly tittered at that, as the residents went up step by step to their silent rooms. Mrs K laughed, hitting the baize door to the kitchen. Her smoke oozed up and in between the curtains to Amanda's nose.

Rude, spoiled, messy, greedy, boastful, dirty . . . . To this string of pejoratives Mrs Ellis soon added gauche and graceless. "To poke your head into the room without a word! Why on earth? These English already think we're strange."

Her mother then subjected Amanda to examination, and in the bathroom made her kneel in the tub to soap and rinse herself. "Thoroughly!" Then there must be not one but two STs for overnight, a thick awkward wad, and two pairs of knickers. At first brusque while directing her daughter, Mrs Ellis gradually calmed down. When Amanda was ready for bed she produced oatcakes, and triangles of cheese in silver paper, and Ovaltine. Tears and eating followed. Then sleep came so fast that Amanda gave hardly a thought to Molly in the spring rain. She gave none at all to her prep, untouched.

Next day, though, in the Trout's History lesson, Amanda had to resort to her ruler. This device, one of the tools of her trade, bore inches along one edge and along the other the dates of all the kings and queens, plus Cromwell 1649-58.

The Trout noted the line of Amanda's gaze. "I will not have cheating!"

Accusation, conviction, sentence. She must write one hundred lines.

Then came Geography, with Miss Lincoln even more snappish than usual.

"So, Amanda, as usual you were swotting up long words for English and couldn't find time for the principal exports of our industrial North?"

In fact, Miss Pruitt's lesson that day was worst of all. Her glance, when Amanda had nothing whatever to say about the absolute's syntactical independence, was sorrowful. The girl winced. Everyone laughed. Also, yesterday's blood-soaking made Amanda scrupulous about checking her ST, but she must not visit the loo so often as to draw notice. Anxiety was constant. Still nothing was as bad as the not-there-ness of Helen and Kay. Amanda longed to tell about her bleeding, and to share her terror of the hot-breath talk that would follow discovery of her new situation. To know herself spoken of was unbearable, unless there was praise, or envy.

The invisible Molly O'Brien still ruled the lunch table.

"Wendy says she'll go to a Borstal."

"No, a convent. Miss Flower said."

"Matron's force-feeding her. Like the suffragettes."

"Honestly, Molly just has a bad cold. She took a chill."

"That's not all she took!" Shrieks of laughter.

"Miss Lincoln says Molly's black Irish." Silence, incomprehension.

"Aren't the Irish RC? Why's she even here, then?"

Another silence. Then, "What's RC?"

"Honestly, Alice, you're hopeless! Pass the gravy."

"Did you hear? We'll see *Health* next week. Matron said."

The afternoon was little better.

Finally there came another practice for *Goblin Market;* the dress rehearsal was now only forty-eight hours away. Impatiently Miss Hudson said, "Girls, this is no time for poetic expression," so the recitations amounted only to a gabbled run-through. Mostly the narrators knew their lines. A different problem arose, though, after the scene of the strong sister defeating temptation.

> *White and golden Lizzie stood*
> *Like a lily in a flood;*
> *Like a rock of blue-veined stone*
> *Lashed by tides obstreperously . . .*
> *Like a royal virgin town*
> *Topped with gilded dome and spire*
> *Close beleaguered by a fleet*
> *Mad to tug her standard down.*

When the next girl started in with *One may lead a horse to water / Twenty cannot make her drink*, Miss Hudson raised an imperious hand.

"No, Stephanie. Make *him* drink."

"But Miss Hudson, it's Lizzie."

"The masculine pronoun is always used in the general sense. Recite, please." But Stephanie could not get the line right, and cried.

As for the circle at the poem's end, the girls tried it until their arms ached. "There is no grace in you," declared the mistress. "I sincerely hope for better on Thursday, when all the cast is here."

As the bus heaved through the rain toward The Green House, Amanda tried to do sums in her head.

How far down the fortnightly mark-lists would today's performance drag her? She was always near the top of her form, though never first because of Arithmetic. Each of her efforts produced a different answer. Later, her prep complete and her one hundred lines written out neatly (though what on earth did the Trout's line mean? *A few honest men are better than numbers*), Amanda did more calculations, this time with pencil and paper. Eventually the sums did turn out the same. The usual helpless shame oozed through her body.

She went then to her parents' room, for her bedtime snack, and came through the door just in time to hear her father say, "Rachel, I can't bear to go back to that country."

"Not now, Gerald."

During cocoa-making, Amanda described the problems with the end of *Goblin Market*. Gradually her father began to ask questions, her mother to relax and even smile.

"The way it ends isn't a patch on *St Agnes Eve*. Why didn't Miss Whatsername choose Keats?" He sipped his brandy.

Rachel Ellis giggled. "Well, I suppose *These lovers fled away into the storm* wouldn't be entirely suitable, would it?"

"One thing's certain," and her father took another sip. "No Canadian school would dream of performing either. A cultural wilderness, that place."

"Gerald!"

"Don't Gerald me, Rachel! My life's work is the Romantic poets. Who in Canada cares for them? Name one person."

"Time for bed, Amanda. And remember, we must find you a dress. No nonsense this time, either."

In the loo, she was surprised to find less blood than before on her ST.

On Wednesday morning, her lessons went better.

At lunch, a crescendo of exclamation met Molly O'Brien's entrance into Dining Hall. She blushed faintly but remained calm. In any event the communal furor subsided moments after Grace, for the giant pan of food delivered to the prefect at each table held a loathed melange termed *Resurrection*. Forensic analysis absorbed everyone. Not until the girls were heading back to lessons, Molly with her form, did details emerge.

"The cloak wasn't ruined. Just muddy, at the hem."

"I know! Matron told Hilary. And Pringle was furious with Lincoln."

"Alice, old cheese! Everyone knows *that*."

"Poor girls shouldn't even be here. They don't belong."

"Molly can never be a prefect now."

"Where there's smoke, there's fire. I don't believe she didn't do anything."

After school, when Amanda arrived at the hotel, her mother was waiting. Mrs Ellis wore a particular smile, enthusiastic and intended to dissolve objection, that meant she had done something related to her daughter without consulting her.

On Amanda's bed lay a matching jumper and skirt, in royal blue.

"For you, dear," said Mrs Ellis redundantly.

The colour would become her. Amanda saw that at once. The outfit was not childlike, nor meant for a grown woman, but exactly suited to her age and station. She hated the clothes. She loved them. She hated her mother for buying them.

"But you said we'd go shopping again."

"Put them on, Amanda! We'll show the others, at tea downstairs."

"No! You'll call them *duds*, and everyone will laugh."

"No, I won't."

The jumper and skirt were a perfect fit.

Still, when she stood by her mother to be exhibited to the residents taking their tea in the lounge, Amanda felt herself looming like a woolly prize sow, shameful, overheated. Professor McGeachie and Mr Penrose offered only a smile and a nod, but the women touched the garments. "Charming," they murmured, "sweetly pretty." Their fingertips scorched Amanda. A small animal rushed madly around her brain in search of any exit from the inferno.

Released, she took a chair by the Professor, who asked his usual question.

"And what have you got up to at school, of late?"

Did he wish she were a boy at some famously savage public school? He affected sorrow when she had no canings to report, no tirades from the Head. Today, Amanda did have Molly's story. *But he would like it too much.* Her face grew hot again.

"I had to write a hundred lines." Amanda's mother, across the room by the Talbot sisters, lit her cigarette with a flair that said *I heard that.*

"Indeed! And did the mistress set you Cicero or Caesar?"

"It wasn't Latin at all. It was just *A few honest men are better than numbers.*"

The Professor startled. "Oliver Cromwell? Whatever was the woman thinking?"

Amanda explained about peeking at her ruler.

"The rapist of Ireland," said the Professor, not listening to a word she said. "Those criminal hands wet with innocent Scottish blood." His voice gained strength. "Odious Cromwell!" His full tea-cup tumbled. The saucer broke.

While Mrs K took the Professor up to his room and Celia mopped up the spill and Vivian Clyde smoothed over the upset by chatting with the Talbots about the weather, Amanda felt the needle of Mrs Ledington's glance pierce her waist, where the blue jumper and skirt met. Her scalp itched with sweat.

"This isn't a *frock*," she whispered, when she could get her mother's attention. "I can't wear this at School. Everyone will say it's Canadian."

"Nonsense! It looks just like a dress. And what was that about writing lines?"

"But it *isn't*, Mum. Everyone will laugh at me."

Mrs Ellis considered. "Well, perhaps a belt, to tie things together."

"Milly has a pretty one!" Tilly, nosing near, delightedly made the suggestion. Her sister's eyebrows went up, but Miss Talbot did leave the lounge to fetch the belt.

It was indeed pretty, soft braided leather in blue and red. With its twining clasp, the belt fully concealed the lack of union between jumper and skirt.

"Say *Thank you*, Amanda." Rachel Ellis's tongue grew a serrated edge. "Now, are you finished fussing? Are your new duds okay?"

Amanda cried and ran and tripped over the carpet by the lounge door.

The Englishwoman, emptying their teacups, tut-tutted to Mrs Ellis, not unkindly, about *that difficult age*. The mother apologized. She noted the moodiness of menstruation. She thanked and thanked Miss Talbot.

When the old sisters closed their room's door, they said to each other, "*Really*. Did you ever?"

At Thursday's practice for *Goblin Market*, Miss Hudson issued no judgment on the belted outfit, and Amanda saw that in fact it did not greatly differ from what other girls were wearing. Relieved, she could focus on her ST. Bloodstains weren't now a concern, the flow being reduced, but the thing's outline might show under her new skirt, so much slimmer than a tunic. Again she wished for her friends, but for reassurance could only twist herself about before the mirror in the gym.

The dress rehearsal began.

The costumes designed by Miss Michaelson were based on Arthur Rackham's illustrations of Rossetti's poem. Thus, the sisters wore loose trailing gowns that emphasized but did not expose their breasts. Laura's dress was the insipid blue shown in the book, Lizzie's a richer mossy green. Like the shade Molly O'Brien had worn to the dance at Clarendon, it contrasted well with her dark hair and pale skin.

To turn girls into goblins, Amanda's form had stitched felt caps just like Rackham's, bright orange-red with pointed crowns. With Mrs Tonelli in Art, the Lower Fifth had fashioned papier mâché nose-masks. Held on by ribbons or rubber bands, some masks had whiskers, like foxes or rats, but most were just long fleshy protuberances, all bulges and lumps. Makeup enlarged and slanted the goblins' eyes. The oddly-tinted yet familiar faces, the costumes, the hot lights excited and distracted all the girls. Miss Hudson, annoyed, had to prompt several narrators.

After Amanda's recitation, the mistress raised a hand to delay the next girl, who was starting on *Backwards up the mossy glen / Turned and trooped the goblin men*.

"Wait, Joan. Amanda, repeat after me. *Brawnch. Lawnch.*" Pause. "No. You are exaggerating. Try it again." Pause. "Is that the best you can do? Once more."

To stop the goblins staring, Amanda spoke as directed. Miss Hudson's look said *Such disobedience won't be forgotten*. The rehearsal went on.

In the attack on good Lizzie/Molly who in her virtue braved the wicked goblins, what a hubbub on the stage! Ringing her round, the girls nuzzled her and shrieked. They clawed at her shoulders, shoved papier mâché bananas and pineapple at her lips, tried to trip her. At the mob's centre, Molly was exactly Lizzie. Still as a statue, she seemed far from the glazed eyes, the tossed hair, the noses that swung and wobbled and wiggled.

"Too loud, girls! And too long. You will delay the narrative." The goblins conceded the battle and huddled, grumbling, near the wings. Then Lizzie, moving to the rhythm of her own recitation – *Did you miss me? / Come and kiss me* – ran eagerly across the stage to heal her fallen sister Laura.

"Not so fast!" Molly slowed. Her green gown pooled at her feet. "Remember, you're not galloping to meet some boy at Clarendon."

Molly stopped. Silence.

"Go *on* now!" Drama cried. "Continue, I say!"

But eventually the mistress must surrender and finish Lizzie's speech herself.

Never mind my bruises,
Hug me, kiss me, suck my juices
Squeezed from goblin fruits for you,
Goblin pulp and goblin dew.
Eat me, drink me, love me;
Laura, make much of me:
For your sake I have braved the glen
And had to do with goblin merchant men.

Then the rehearsal went on. Molly's voice did sound again, but toneless, expressionless right to the poem's end. She moved like an automaton.

The Lower Fourth were not allowed even to attempt the dancing circle and the revelation. "You're not capable of such discipline," the mistress shouted. "You'll simply have to stand there in a silly row, like the silly little girls you are."

That Saturday night, after St Mildred's Spring Entertainment was over and the reception had duly followed – hundreds of girls plus mistresses and parents all jabbering and feasting on Battenburg cake, orangeade, and tepid coffee – Amanda and her parents were driving home to the hotel. From the back seat of the Morris, their heads were silhouetted against the windscreen.

"Yes, Rossetti's diction is richly sensuous. But Keats had a much better story to work with than this concoction of the poetess." Her father exaggerated the *ess*.

"You didn't say, Amanda, that a teacher would be acting. She was terrible. And Miss Hudson says you have not been co-operative. What did she mean?"

As expected, Amanda's mother did not grasp the badness of publicly treating *launch* and *branch* as half-rhymes, only the disobedience itself. She would return to the topic, no doubt, but Amanda was so happy that she did not care.

Her Anglophile father did hear the nuance. "Dear girl, I hope you don't lose your beautiful English accent when we return!"

Silently she vowed to speak Canadian only.

"Gerald, haven't you got anything else to say about Amanda's behaviour?"

Evidently not. After a while, Mr Ellis opened the passenger window and the night air poured in, fragrant, nearly warm.

With pleasure Amanda lost herself in re-imagining the Entertainment.

Molly had not appeared. Her absence from the dressing room (vibrant with the heat of agitated girls, sweet with powder and acid with sweat) grew as huge as Miss Hudson's anxiety. Searches and enquiries produced no news. The girl was gone.

At such short notice, no other Sixth Former would agree to play Lizzie. "I can't do it! Honestly, Miss Hudson, I just can't!"

The Headmistress, summoned to the crash scene, over Drama's strong objections assigned Geography to take the role. Miss Lincoln was as tall as Molly but thicker. To make the green gown decent, she had to be bound about with ribbons. Of course she could not speak her part but had to read from the playscript. The goblins, gob-smacked, dared not attack authority with any vigour. They only patted at her. Laura flinched from her dear sister's embrace and mangled her own lines.

Soon the strained applause subsided.

When the cast of *Goblin Market* had got itself off the stage, spontaneously all the girls ran out of the School building, to laugh and squeal in the dark fresh air. "How weak! How utterly weak! Did you see Pringle's face? Wasn't Lincoln awful?"

Happily Amanda drifted over to the beechwood, the trees that she and Kay and Helen had once defined as theirs, and under their budding branches she imagined what her dead or vanished friends would have said about tonight.

Then, turning to go in search of her mother and father, she saw Molly O'Brien slip out of the gym's side door.

How had she disguised herself during the performance? Had she laughed silently at the mistresses' humiliation? Was Molly going to meet her cricket captain? Or would she go back to her dormitory, to lie quiet in her bed until "found" by the returning girls?

These questions fully engaged Amanda, curled up in the back seat of the car. She had not said *brawnch*, and the blood was all gone, and she was comfortable for the first time in days. Next week the film on *Health* would be shown, but she already knew everything. No one could laugh, even if she got a word wrong. *Lounge* or *sitting room*, *bathroom* or *loo*. Who cared? She didn't, not any more. Or not much.

"Derivative," said Mr Ellis. "Is that too harsh a term?"

"Gerald, what are you talking about?"

"I am speaking of Rossetti's inferiority to Keats."

Past her parents, the car's lamps made long yellow cones on the road ahead.

"Yes, derivative. Lacking all originality." Amanda's father rolled up the window again. "I may use that."

"But what has it to do with Shelley and Keats?"

When they reached The Green House, he took out his pen and insisted on making some notes then and there.

After Amanda was in bed, Rachel Ellis came out again, to find her husband asleep in the Morris Minor. Leaning against the windscreen, she put her head in her hands.

The Promised Land

C aptain George Belland was too old to be an undergraduate. Even Amanda could see that, when the Bellands' taxi pulled up at The Green House. They had rather a lot of luggage. He was tall and big-featured, with thick honey-dark hair, a man to claim space in any room. Mouth wry. Forehead scored with lines. A thoughtfully confident manner, the kind that good looks can bestow. Something was wrong with the Captain's lower half, though. He moved unevenly, as if his knees bent both ways.

"Not young." Why did her mother so often state the obvious?

His wife, Eleanor, had a moony face. Just before the taxi left, she retrieved from it something that looked like a crutch. She stayed only one night at the hotel. "Off to Devon again." The Captain smiled as if this explained something.

He made a lively addition to after-dinner coffee, urging Mr Ledington to describe the black-headed grosbeak and the Talbot sisters to reveal anagram tricks, but at times he fell silent amid the chat. Reviving, he asked Mrs Ellis which Great Lake was her favourite. Abruptly he limped out of the lounge, leaning heavily on his blackthorn stick.

"I've never thought of the Lakes in those terms," said Amanda's mother, later. "Never even seen Michigan. Such romantic looks that man has!"

"*Il Penseroso*," said Mr Ellis. Amanda did not ask, simply pleased that the wife was gone, but her father insisted on explaining that *reading Greats* meant studying philosophy and classics. "In the spring Belland will take his viva voce. He's anxious."

"Why?" asked Mrs Ellis.

Amanda too was puzzled. To sit in a hushed classroom and read

191

the exam questions, their Parts and their Either-Ors; to feel her brain marshal its contents and cast up phrases; to notice others examinees struggling; and finally to write – this was high pleasure, unless numbers were involved. Perhaps Captain Belland had not done his prep and revising? Surely such a wonderful person could not be lazy.

At the hotel, curiosity sparkled. Professor McGeachie checked with his few extant academic connections. "Belland's brilliant. Sure of a First, they say. But moody. They say that too." He shrugged. "Not an advantage at a viva, moodiness. And why so late? Where's the man been, since the War?"

Celia told Amanda's mother that Mrs Belland had complained about the towels, and a lampshade, and the lavatory. "Insulting! I use a full bottle of Harpic every week." Stacks of Paton knitting patterns stood on Mrs Belland's night table, Celia reported. Also scrapbooks. They were full of clippings: cribs, chests of drawers, infant chairs. Under her side of the bed were cases full of handmade baby clothes.

"She's knitted enough for triplets," Mrs K confirmed. The proprietor had also got the dope on Devon. Mrs Belland's parents lived there. So did she, in part. Like a schoolgirl at half-term or quarter-term, she would regularly take the train from Truro to Oxford. A married woman with no home: a middle-aged student with no degree.

"He needs to study. To concentrate." Mrs K made these verbs conspiratorial. "But it's not proper, Mrs Ellis. They want their own front door, that pair. He must do well." He certainly worked. Right after breakfast, he grasped his blackthorn and heaved himself up to their room on the top floor, or hobbled out to take a bus to the Bodleian.

Quiet Mr Penrose, in a laconic exchange with Belland about their respective Wars as sapper and submariner, learned that the Captain's parents had died in the Blitz.

"Big brother and little sister, all alone in the world," Mrs K mused enjoyably. "So romantic. I wonder if she's pretty?" Arabella lived in London and was to visit soon. "A pretty name," said Mr Ellis.

"But Gerald, the parents must have been stone deaf! Bella bella bella."

"But Rachel, isn't her name Ellen?"

"How can you be so forgetful? Eleanor is the Captain's wife."

"But isn't she getting married? The sister?"

Mrs Ellis sighed. "Yes. To some Canadian oilman."

Mr Oil was rich now and would be far richer. With his off-balance smile, the Captain had told Mr Penrose so. And Mr Oil had bought Arabella a large diamond ring.

"My goodness." Mrs Ledington's uncertain glance went to her husband.

Milly Talbot's expression did not change as Tilly said, "So exciting!"

Furthermore, Mr Oil was buying Arabella's entire trousseau.

"What's that?" asked Amanda.

Mrs K said that in Ireland it was improper for a man to offer a single woman, even if he were shortly to marry her, gifts of clothing.

"Why?" asked Amanda.

"I've lived in this country thirty years," added Mrs K, "and I believe the English see it the same way. What about in Canada, Mrs Ellis?"

"I bet he'll buy her a dress, too. For sure, the Captain couldn't foot the bill for a fancy wedding."

"Rachel, Rachel," sighed Mr Ellis. "Little whatsername and the oilman aren't interesting. The brother is the one worth talking about."

Silent, Amanda agreed. There was no competition. *A wounded hero.*

One evening, she sat in the window seat on the stairs to the first floor. She liked to gaze out at the quiet North Oxford street, with its hedges and the evenly-spaced plane trees towering above. Sometimes, as the light changed, the air in this city view developed a luminous quality that gave her the same feeling as Port Meadows.

Against the dusk, a bus heading north up the Woodstock Road was brightly lit. The few passengers who got off were shadowy, but the Captain's limp identified him at once. *My wounded hero.* The blush rushed to Amanda's hair. But Tilly Talbot was waddling along-side. So boring for him!

Entering the hotel, the two laughed companionably. At what?

"Perhaps tonight we shall see that film about Canada."

"If Mr Ellis has remembered to collect it, in London." Tilly's silly giggle. "He might bring another, too. A Canadian filmmaker, McLaren? A funny film about war."

The Captain lost all jocularity. "That is not possible."

Stupid Tilly.

When the first of the Captain's mystery women made an official visit to The Green House, she settled in with the ease of a lifer. To Amanda Mrs Belland looked just like all the mistresses at St Mil-dred's, old and plain with faces like puddings or hatchets, but in fact this wife was a decade her husband's junior, not quite thirty. She favoured floral print dresses or tweed costumes; these showed the heft of a bosom fated to solidify into a bolster. Everywhere her creamy flesh offered signs of more to come. Amanda hated the rim of Eleanor Belland's cheeks, where the jowls were forming.

Now each day the Captain left the hotel after breakfast, without his blackthorn, while his wife spent the morning in their room. "Lit-tle busy-nesses," she murmured, smiling. "You know, Mrs Ellis."

Amanda's mother hadn't a clue. To her, as the family's sojourn in England wore down, a day spent inside was a day wasted. Her Letts diary swelled with explorations of the city, the county, and beyond.

Each day, after lunch and after advising Celia on what to do dif-ferently and better, Eleanor Belland took a good walk.

"What would a bad walk be, for an Englishwoman?" wondered Rachel Ellis, who loved driving fast along England's narrow twisty roads.

Amanda's father considered. "Not walking?"

To spend as much time as possible in the same room as the Cap-tain, Amanda worked furiously at her prep before dinner. Then she lived the coffee-hour at the card table in the lounge, a little apart from the grown-ups. From the Professor she had a book of a hun-dred solitaires; she would try them all. Half-curious, half-bored, fully embarrassed by her parents, she moved the cards about and sucked Callard & Bowser toffee till her molars ached, while waiting to hear the Captain's warm low voice.

On a weekend, Mrs Ellis might report that she and Mr Ellis had visited Ely that day, or Chipping Norton, or Bury St Edmunds.

"So far!" Miss Talbot.

"Imagine, there and back in one day." Mrs Ledington.

The Captain sighed. "This country's so terribly small."

"But so old!" Mr Ellis would cry. "Wonderfully old." Yes, Amanda's parents were always on the roam for ancientry, through castles cathedrals keeps towers abbeys chapels forts minsters barbicans priories monasteries and all their stony ilk.

"And so beautiful!" Amanda's mother enthused about east windows, flying buttresses. "Lovely, marvellous!" Such awful adjectives. "Those amazing gravestones for babies, so touching!" At Bury St Edmunds, the martyr king, so amusing, the attenuated monarch stuck with Danish arrows. "Like a pomander with cloves!"

The mouth in Mrs Belland's moony face opened. "The stained-glass in the lady-chapel there is very fine. Unusual too. Mostly from the fourteenth century." She turned a page of her scrapbook. On the table by her stood clippings, paste, scissors. "Our English glass is much better than the French." Mrs Ellis was about to yelp *Good gravy, what about Notre Dame? Versailles?* But Eleanor Belland was not done. "Darling, do you prefer green or blue?" She held out a coloured advertisement for two wing chairs.

The Captain turned to Mr Ellis. "What about church architecture in Canada?"

At home, Amanda's parents (*Hypocrites!*) never entered a church except for weddings or funerals, and expressed scorn for all goings-on therein. Mr Ellis's response was brief, yet the Captain was attentive. His solid bulk filled the chesterfield's corner.

In the Ellises' room later, with Horlicks for Amanda and brandy for her parents, her mother declared, "That man wants to emigrate, but Mrs Stick In The Mud doesn't."

"A dreamer," said her father. "How can he think of leaving this country?"

"Didn't you buy any more?" Mrs Ellis searched the drinks cabinet. "Talk about dreamers." She tipped her glass for the last drops. "He says England's finished, Gerald. Finished. Did you notice he won't use his cane when his wife's here?"

His stupid wife. Amanda sighed. "Mum, it's a walking stick." Her mother still didn't use *cawn't* for can't, *Nay-oh* for No, either. Had she even noticed the difference?

Thus Mrs Belland after a few visits became familiar to the hotel. However, when the unknown sister finally came – by herself, with no Mr Oil on exhibit – the Ellises missed her. Just then Amanda was boarding at St Mildred's, while her parents were off badgering at a stately home whose new American owners aimed to *revive* its glories – an orangery, a folly, a conservatory whose three score windows had been shattered in the War. Also on tap in this particular stately were a few Sheets & Kelly letters.

"Second-rank material, really," said Mr Ellis. "But wonderful. A great deal could be done with it."

"Which you will do!"

"Dear Rachel!" Amanda's parents hugged. She turned away.

To the Ellises at coffee-hour on their return, Mrs Ledington confirmed that the diamond ring glittered brightly on Arabella's hand. "Such dainty fingers she has."

Mrs Belland beamed, proprietorial. Amanda hid her own bitten nails.

Mr Penrose said, "It's really rather something to think about, that beautiful thing coming from deep under the earth. Don't you think?"

"A sweet English rose," was the Professor's ruling. "But what about her brother? Those missing years. D'you suppose he cracked up, after the War?"

The next day when Celia was doing out the Ellises' room, Mrs K made her way there with an extra jar of furniture polish. Amanda sat by the window, half-reading *A Traveller in Time*, while her mother darned her father's socks.

Mrs K assessed Arabella as a very pretty little thing. "Madly in love, of course. She'll be hoping to start a family soon."

Celia put the unneeded polish away. She reported that Arabella's underthings were exquisite but not her nightdress. "Ragged, really. Torn." Mr Oil's photo on her night table showed a plain man, "rather heavy," with a strange haircut.

"Handsome is as handsome does," remarked the proprietor.

Briskly Mrs Ellis said,"It can be hard to tell how a husband will turn out. What's his hair like, then? Oh. That's a brush cut. What the French call *en brosse*."

"I wouldn't know about that," said Mrs K, "but surely Mrs Belland will take it hard if the Captain's sister gets off with a baby right away, while she must wait."

"Mrs B's not a girl any more." Celia would never see fifty again.

"No spring chicken," Mrs Ellis agreed. "Best to act soon, before the eggs go off."

Appalled at this language, Amanda left the bedroom.

A silence grew there. With concentration, Celia applied lemon oil.

"Sometimes husbands need managing," offered Mrs K.

"Time for guile," said Rachel Ellis. "I'll talk to Eleanor."

"I hear tell some won't let themselves be managed," said Celia. "But then I've never had the bother of one." The pungent liquid dripped on to her cloth.

Hearing the staff move down the hall towards the Talbot sisters' room, Amanda set her revulsion aside and went back to her mother. "What did you mean about the eggs?" She had to admit the information sounded solid.

In the evenings while she played solitaire, the Ellises and the Captain were at another game. If they could get him to talk about England, that was a goal for them, while he scored if they talked of Canada. Anything about the country interested him: the proposed St Lawrence Seaway, motels, popsicles and Eskimo pies, Red Fife, the Orange Order and the Fenians, mining and totems and Doukhobors in British Columbia, schools, streetcars, pears on the Niagara Peninsula, a Shakespeare festival for Stratford.

"It won't be very good," said Amanda's father. "Not like the real Stratford."

"Why not?" The Captain also asked about the Group of Seven, and a novel called *The Loved And The Lost* that the Ellises hadn't even heard of. And Halloween. Mrs Belland cut Amanda's description short.

"Children begging door-to-door for sweets? Not very nice, if you ask me."

I didn't ask you. Blood heated Amanda's neck and cheeks. Back to solitaire – but as her face cooled she began to wonder. Could she still be a witch or a gypsy and cry, "Shell out!" when she went home? Thirteen: no longer a child. All the while Mrs Belland's snip-snipped round a small refrigerator and a gas stove. Her deft fingertip touched the paste. Without a smear, the images took their place in her scrapbook.

Most of all Captain Belland liked to hear *about the geography* – not the kind Miss Lincoln at St Mildred's taught. Canada's vast land mass fascinated him, the greatness of Lakes, the enormity of forest and prairie, Shield and Icefield, the extravagantly long rivers that could wrap Britain round three times and tie a bow. Mrs Ellis found a last-year's calendar for him, featuring dark and sticky-looking reproductions of Carmichael, Lismer, et al. The Captain studied all the images closely and asked more questions than the Ellises could answer.

He was bewildered by how they spoke of their summer home on Lake Muskoka. The biggest wild animals, Mr Ellis told him, were raccoons and skunks and porcupines.

"No bears? What about moose, or elk?"

"Oh no, not for decades."

Her mother noted the well-stocked butcher, baker, grocer in nearby Port Carling, but complained that the township was slow to repair the gravel roads, buckled by the heaving of the frozen earth. Captain Belland shook his head, smiling. Amanda told how a farmer supplied ice for all the cottages up and down the shore, travelling by horse-drawn sleigh over the solid lake. He piled up the blocks, sandwiched with sawdust, in the dark ice houses under the pine trees.

"He charges too much. It's just lake water," said Mrs Ellis.

Amanda told how to carry a block of ice, with big tongs, to the pump by the back steps, for a rinse, and then to the ice box in the kitchen, and how you could even tell time, sort of, by the slow dropping of melt-water into the pan at its base. She emptied it daily. The Captain liked all this very much and got her to tell it again when Mrs Belland returned from fetching more paste. She was unimpressed. The news that the Ellises' cottage lacked indoor plumbing did move her.

"How primitive!"

The new page in her scrapbook showed dining-room furniture, tiny paper shapes in Regency style. Mrs Belland had already completed double-page spreads of what Amanda's mother called, laughing, Chippenwhite and Heppledale.

"Some nerve that woman has, Gerald!" Mrs Ellis was near admiration. "In this country they run hot-water pipes outside, and then act all surprised when they burst."

Mr Ellis made no reply.

"And have you noticed that she doesn't do the baby pages, in public?"

"Who cares?"

"That's slangy, dear. And vulgar."

Once, when Eleanor Belland was away in Devon, Amanda brought down her Indian box to show the Captain. His reaction was naturally perfect. He gazed with delight at the scarlet and white quilling and the slender braids of grass, turned the box in his hands, took off the lid, smelled the inside, and smiled right into her face.

"Who made this?"

Amanda told about the orange-crate stand in Port Carling.

"Would she be of the Ojibway tribe? Huron? Algonquin? Is the reservation right by the town? And by the way, what does *Muskoka* mean?"

Sister Arabella's second visit to the hotel was unheralded. She arrived in that shapeless hour between tea and dinner, when the residents hunched in their rooms to search their souls or dab benzene on a spotted jacket or write appeals to their bank managers. Amanda was in the window seat as a taxi pulled up, so close to the door that she couldn't see who got out.

The bell. Celia's surprised voice. "Why, Miss Belland!"

"Is my brother here? Please find him at once." But that day George Belland was taking dinner in college. His wife came down instead, and led the tearful Arabella upstairs past all those closed doors.

The two women sat together at dinner, talking quietly.

Arabella was indeed pretty. No one had mentioned that she and her brother looked alike: the honey-dark hair, the off-balance smile. Amanda did not care for the female version. Although the spring evening was warm, a pink cashmere shawl was folded over Arabella's sloping shoulders so that her arms were concealed.

Wife and sister attended coffee-hour only long enough for Arabella to greet everyone and to meet the Canadians.

Mrs Ellis put her hand on the small of Amanda's back and pushed. "Our daughter, Miss Belland. And our congratulations to you, on your engagement."

Arabella's small fingers slid out from under the cashmere as she registered Amanda's pimples, inkyness, flopping shoelaces, loose belt.

"Thank you, Mrs Ellis. How sweet." Arabella turned to Eleanor "Shan't we . . . ?"

"Yes, we shall wait up for George, in our room. Arabella is very tired. So kind, good evening, good night."

The Bellands' room was above the Ellises'. Next morning at breakfast Amanda's mother reported crossly. "Quite a chin-wag those three Bellands had themselves last night. Up to all hours."

"Didn't hear a thing." Cheerfully Amanda's father marmaladed his toast.

Arabella did not appear in the dining room.

"Gone up to London again," said the Captain, in the lobby as the residents left the dining room. He was pulling on his Burberry, to head out. Mrs Belland hovered nearby, her moony visage expressionless.

"Such a short visit." Mrs Ledington's faint voice.

"So very, very pretty," Tilly Talbot gushed.

Her wounded hero limped badly, Amanda saw. His face was tight with fatigue. Why wouldn't he use his stick in front of his wife? How irritating. No. How stupid.

The Captain smiled. "Ladies, my little sister got the idea that she didn't want a wedding after all." He took up his bookbag. "Silly girl. Mr Oil will tell her what to do." But his wonderful voice, the lines by his mouth, his hands . . . . Amanda gazed at the Captain until the door closed after him and the women started to exclaim.

Talking to the Ellises about England, the once-submariner told stories of arduous walking tours he'd done, "when I was young" or "before the War."

"Of course Captain Belland really means before his legs were wrecked." There she went again, saying what Amanda had known for ages, simply ages. Sometimes, to see the Captain's hands make their slow gestures, she set down her cards, even if her solitaire showed a promising hierarchy of black and red.

George Belland and his friends had tramped through the Lakes, the Dales, the Dorset moors, all country that the Ellises had toured. These chums were climbers, too. As the Captain spoke, his big torso moved about on the chesterfield as if to embody the efforts then made. "Nothing like your Rockies, of course," self-deprecating. "Not *real* mountains." On every trip, it seemed, there was an injury: a sprain, a torn ligament, a cracked clavicle. Some climber, all bloody or else white with sweated pain, got carried off the rocky slopes by the others.

"Just part of the fun!" The beloved smile. He himself had broken his left ulna. It poked through his skin. Still his account ended as usual. "So a rough slog we had of it, that day." Captain Belland recrossed his legs, awkwardly. Amanda felt sick.

"You make me wish we could see again all that we've seen." Mr Ellis sighed. "For us, Yorkshire was just the Brontes. Dorset was Hardy."

Once the Captain told a different tale, about a fox hunt he'd witnessed as a boy near Peterborough, not far from the abbey.

"We loved that place!" exclaimed Mrs Ellis. "Amazing."

Perhaps because of his War, the Captain was able to invest his account with both strategical and tactical detail, and Amanda abandoned her knaves and queens for the tremulous pleasure of hearing the deep voice sound on and on. The pulse in his neck beat steadily through the tale, from the first sighting of a plumy orange brush to the leaping thunderous horses and the yawping hounds and at last, hours later, to the jubilant huntsman holding aloft a string of furry gristle, bloodstained and torn.

At the Ellises' discomfiture, the Captain was surprised. Rachel Ellis managed some phrases about Amanda's bedtime, and shortly the family left the lounge.

"Peterborough! I can never think of it again. Gerald, d'you suppose it's because of the War that he can speak so?"

"Morbid. The man is morbid."

"No. Cruel."

Amanda rejected both terms. She saw only a boy who ran with the dogs and horses, ecstatic, fleet and strong, every muscle flexing as per its flawless design.

A month after Arabella's visit, George Belland left Oxford and went up to London for several days, to meet his wife and attend his sister's wedding to Mr Oil.

Then the couple returned to The Green House together.

Mrs Belland told at length of the church, the garlands, Mendelssohn, Vivaldi, the bridesmaids' gowns, the wedding dress itself in full darling detail of fabric and overskirt, lace and covered buttons. Then she described the reception, the cake and champagne, the toasts offered one by one by one. All The Green House ladies had questions. She was delighted to expatiate.

When they were done, Captain Belland commented, "And for this I lost three full days in the library!"

His wife's countenance produced a ripple, as if a spoon were to touch a pool of cream. "Darling, we had to be there! Your sister's wedding!"

He shrugged. Mrs Ledington asked again about the lace overskirt, at which point Amanda put her cards away and left the lounge. Behind the curtains of the window seat, she went into *Swallowdale* for the umpteenth time. Roger, Vicky, Mother.

Feet on the stairs. One pair stepped steadily, one didn't.

"Darling, won't you come to Devon with me next time? Being there without you feels strange. People ask questions."

"They'll ask far more, Eleanor, if I don't get at least a Second."

"But George, you're getting a First! Everyone says so."

His voice sharpened. "Not if I waste my time in chats with Mummy and Daddy."

A gasp, a halt. Then the two went unevenly on.

Amanda did not tell her parents. To keep things to herself, to re-imagine them privately – these enjoyments grew in her. Much better than telling was to watch the Bellands eat their porridge and to recall that indrawn breath with the catch at its finish.

At coffee one evening, Amanda's father showed a short film from the National Film Board, brought at last from Canada House in London. Everyone was eager. Mr Ellis was at his most genial, and the ladies basked in his gentlemanly attentions while in the role of technician Mr Penrose beamed, setting up and testing the projector. Vivian Clyde was his assistant. For a screen Mrs K provided a sheet, slightly creased.

"Such a treat!" Miss Tilly cooed. "O when did we last see a film, Milly?"

"*A Christmas Carol*, not long ago."

Mrs Ledington surmised that with so many people now emigrating to Canada, England might soon be empty.

Her husband said, "I don't expect there will be birds, Ellis?"

"I'm sure Canada's full of birds!" Miss Clyde smiled warmly at Mr Ledington. "In any case, now we shall see for ourselves what our emigrants find, in Canada."

Professor McGeachie said, "By definition, the promised land is not as expected."

"Now now, sir!" protested Amanda's father. "No Celtic gloom this evening!"

Miss Talbot grimaced. Mr Penrose turned off the lights. *Clack-clack* went the turning reel.

A clock swung round through 5, 4, 3, 2, and a loud male voice stated *In days of yore from Britain's shore / Wolfe the dauntless hero came*, just as *The Dominion of Canada* burst onto the wrinkled sheet. Hastily Mr Penrose lowered the volume. A map of Canada appeared, blank except for rivers, lakes, and mountain ranges. Gradually names wrote themselves on these. Dotted or solid lines defined colonial and then provincial borders. Guns meant forts, puffs of smoke were wars and feathers Indians, and circles showed villages that swelled into towns, then cities. Fat black inchworms, heading west, were railways.

All this was engaging for Amanda, but the animation soon ceased. Boredom took hold, briefly lifted by a painting of Lake Superior's north shore, the same one as at the Bank of Montreal on Bloor Street. She could smell the leather chair where she used to wait for her mother. That picture melted into actual land and lake, black branches on black trees, trunks pressed down by the wind. Bent pine. Water, water, grey rocks. Water. Rock. Pine. Still the boring voice-over. The Great Lakes, so great, great . . . . Just when continuation felt intolerable, the camera left earth behind and soared to show nothing anywhere but the dark steel of illimitable forest nicked by the lighter steel of a thousand lakes, all the way to the grey horizon's curve.

Mrs Ledington said, "My goodness, how the country does go on."

"Not cosy!" Miss Tilly giggled.

More boredom. Then the West, where Amanda had not been. Strange heads frowned and stared from totem poles. There was a supermarket in Park Royal Mall.

"Incorrect pronunciation," snapped Miss Talbot into the dark.

The camera roved the endless shelves, crowded with tins of all sizes, with boxes canisters jars bags packages bottles, and along the produce counters loaded with a hundred grey vegetables and fruits. The English watchers gasped. Among the cereals Amanda glimpsed *Red River*, and her tongue slid over her teeth in search of flax. Now a jolly butcher pointed to his display case of abundant steaks chops roasts bacon sausage and slabs of fat black liver. Another gasp. The camera dove into the freezer, full of boxes stacked against the smooth gleam of snow.

More dullness then, and then *God Save The Queen*, very loud. Everyone in the lounge rose to join in the anthem. Mr Penrose switched on the lights.

"Rachel, it's wonderful." Vivian Clyde sounded stunned.

"Oh yes!" sighed Tilly. "How I wish I could go."

Miss Talbot said, "Everything in Canada seems new. How very odd."

Mrs Ledington had hoped for a grizzly bear. Her husband couldn't get over the sight of ten thousand snow geese on a Saskatchewan farm. For Mr Penrose, all that meat was a bit much. "Makes the old tum uneasy!" He fitted the metal lid over the film.

"Magnificent," said the Captain. "Thank you, Ellis, more than I can say."

The two men shook hands heartily. Mrs Belland gathered up her scrapbooking materials, tonight untouched, and at the lounge door waited calmly for her husband.

On another evening, it was the Captain who produced something Canadian to look at: a map. "I wrote away for some information," he said. "To Canada House. Brochures. That sort of thing."

Like a pointer, Eleanor Belland raised her head and held it rigid. Then she pasted in a coffee pot and a graduated set of sauce-pans.

Toronto lay unfolded on the coffee table. Never having seen her city in map form, Amanda took a while to find the Annex.

"Don't you know your own town?" enquired Mrs Belland.

It's a big city! At last she found their street. But the house had been sold. Where would their front door be when they went home? Her parents pointed out the university, the legislature, the art gallery, the museum, the conservatory of music.

"Is Toronto near Calgary? Arabella will live there."

Amanda did not even try not to snicker. Her parents glared and explained.

"So far? An even greater exile." Mrs Belland looked sadly at her husband, who was intent on Toronto.

"What's this river?" he asked.

Amanda's mother set her hand alongside the blue wriggle. "East of the Don, that's social suicide." Mrs Belland's face crinkled with suppressed laughter.

Her husband asked about teaching in public schools. Awkwardly Mr Ellis explained the meanings of *public* and *private* in the Canadian educational system.

"Isn't that funny, darling?" The scissors sliced around a bed with spiral posts.

"It doesn't matter what they're called, Eleanor. I keep telling you, this country's all washed up. We've got to start over. So – what I'd seek would be a post at a good private school for boys." He uncapped his fountain pen, and Amanda's father started in with Upper Canada College, Ridley, St Andrew's. The angular black script ran quickly along. "I've heard there's a St Michael's?"

"RC," said Mrs Ellis.

The Captain closed his leather notebook. The two men moved into their umpteenth discussion with the Professor about the value of studying Latin, while Mrs Belland spread out her current page right over the map. She arranged and re-arranged the bed, two nightstands, and an ugly kidney-shaped dressing table with a skirt.

Later Mr Ellis reflected. "Rachel, I just can't see Belland in Toronto. Tempered clay, he is. The Canadian louts would eat him alive, even if he were at a private school."

Mrs Ellis grinned. "Picture her in a Scarborough split-level!"

Next day when Amanda came home from school, she found her mother and Mrs K in the lobby. They were looking upwards. Eleanor Belland's progress on the stairs was slow, and her face, glimpsed as she made the turn, was not cream but grey.

"Many a slip twixt cup and lip." Mrs K headed for the baize door to the kitchen. "I'd best see to dinner. Lord knows what mess Celia's made, this day."

"Mum, what's wrong with her?"

"Manners, Amanda! Don't point. And for goodness' sake, say the name. Mrs Belland. What's wrong? His viva voce didn't go well."

Ice formed in Amanda's stomach. "Did the Captain *fail?*"

"Fair to middling, your father says. A low Second. Not what he hoped. Not at all what everyone expected of him."

Once more the small animal ran wildly about Amanda's brain, seeking an escape. "Can't he write the exam again?"

"Write? A viva is an oral exam, Amanda. Spoken," redundantly. "Things don't work like that in life. Mostly there's only one chance to do well."

As the residents that evening waited for Celia to open the dining room, they did not stand in silence as they had until Rachel Ellis arrived at The Green House.

"Good evening," they said to each other, bowing slightly.

"Another fine spring day."

"I do believe I heard a warbler, by the pillar box."

"Were you able to match the silk for your embroidery?"

Mrs Belland looked tired, but the Captain, courteous as ever, offered his crooked smile all round. Amanda got one just for her. This almost made up for her humiliating ignorance about vivas. Then they all moved to their own tables, the Captain first pulling out chairs for the Talbot sisters.

Private talk began as Celia brought the soup, fawn-coloured, made from powder out of a giant tin on the kitchen shelves. Martha had shown that tin to Amanda. Long ago. When the Ellises first came. When she was only eleven. Some lumps of undissolved powder remained. Then came pale veal, cauliflower, potatoes, and for sweet a trembling oval of junket. The Captain ate everything, Amanda saw, plus Mrs Belland's sweet.

"You needn't stay long at coffee, Eleanor." The Captain's voice was tender as the couple came in. She stuck it out, however, through the Professor's discourse on Scottish beef (superior) and Mr Penrose's analysis of the hotel's new guttering (doubtful).

After his wife left, the Captain remained. Listening, mostly. Smiling at Mr Ledington, who seemed set to talk all night about moor-hens. Winking at Amanda, once. Her insides swirled. She put down a black king, not a red. In time Miss Talbot, as the senior lady present, rose to declare the evening over. Everyone moved slowly towards the lobby, so the Captain could go first and get his battered legs upstairs alone.

McGeachie spoke, his voice thick with an old man's satisfaction at the ruin of the young. "I've got the whole story now. Belland cracked at his viva. Mixed up the *Dialogues*. By God, he mixed up Plato and Aristotle."

"Good night, Professor," said Miss Talbot. "Come, Tilly."

Once in his pyjamas with brandy at hand, Amanda's father was warm in his admiration. "The Captain held on to the bitter end! Kept the old flag flying."

Mrs Ellis sipped. "That poor woman. I feel for her."

Why? Why on earth? She hadn't failed a crucial exam.

Later Amanda lay in her bed unable even to drowse, for what seemed an extremely long time. There followed a kind of blank stupor – that must have been sleep. Then angry grown-ups began to shout. Somewhere nearby. Above.

Amanda got her glasses. Got up. Opened her door a crack, then six inches.

A shriek.

Eleanor Belland came into view, descending from the uppermost floor of the hotel. Sobs. Nightdress torn. Face red, much redder on one side. Eyes staring. Hair wild. Sob sob sob. Her right hand cradling her left arm.

Mrs Ellis's foot lifted, to start up the staircase towards her.

Captain Belland was invisible on the top landing. His voice was rage, savagely beaten back. "I'll not be manipulated by women. Not by you, not by Arabella, and not by you, Mrs Ellis. Eleanor, don't you ever try to trick me again. Your Dutch cap doesn't belong in the night table."

"But it's natural, George!" cried Mrs Belland. "For any woman!"

The Professor's door snicked. A needle of light showed at the sisters' room. "Natural?" The Captain struck the door jamb so hard that the hotel's bearing walls resonated. "If nature ruled, we'd all starve. Can't you grasp that after today no one will want me? If you've started one, Eleanor . . . ."

"I'm sorry, I'm sorry, I'll go away tomorrow, back to Devon."

"If you have, there'll be more of what I gave you tonight. Come back here."

Mrs Ellis turned away from her and she went up, sobbing.

Amanda jumped back into bed. There was just enough time to get her breathing regular and slow, before her parents tiptoed to her side.

"Thank goodness," murmured her mother. "She thinks the world of that man."

Amanda smelled her father's familiar hair tonic, bay rum.

"Rachel," he whispered, "what did you say to Ellen? What did you do?"

Mrs Ellis winced. "Her name is Eleanor!"

Next morning, Mrs Belland's luggage was piled high in the lobby. She did not take breakfast. A taxi arrived, and the Ellises never saw her again.

What was a Dutch cap? Amanda searched every dictionary in St Mildred's library. Was it related to foolscap, on which both Canadian and English exams were written? Such a puzzle. As for *Il Penseroso*, or the eager boy who followed the fox, they simply would not coalesce with the midnight man who hit the door and hurt Mrs Belland's face. Would not.

The Captain himself was jocular about his less than brilliant viva voce. "Put the kibosh on – isn't that what you Canadians say? Emigration is beyond me now, Ellis. I'm too old. And a wreck!" For comic emphasis he waved his blackthorn, now in constant use. "And too English." His sights were now set on a little prep school. "Not the first rank. In the Shires perhaps."

Amanda's father argued with him.

"But Rachel, I couldn't get it across that at home any fool with an Oxbridge accent can land a teaching job. No, of course I didn't put it like that!"

Amanda's mother exhorted the Captain too, with like results.

When she took her frustration to the ladies of The Green House, Tilly Talbot spoke gently. "Mrs Ellis, the Captain has tried and failed to scale the peak. Now he's going to settle in the valley."

What pray tell was heroic about that? Nothing. Nothing at all.

The Arrival

S itting on her bed at The Green House, Amanda opened her Indian box.

Iridescent shells from Lake Muskoka and a few coins lay covered by prize ribbons (Latin, French) from St Mildred's, playing cards, stones from thirteen English rivers and the North Sea, a theatre program for "The Mousetrap," souvenir pins from Edinburgh and Aberdeen and Inverness, chocs and toffees in bright paper, a postcard of a Dali painting (the drooling egg) in the big gallery in Glasgow, and a signed card from P G Wodehouse, pictured with his favourite basset hound. At the bottom lay the torn pink address book, long unused, not even looked at.

Her father saw Amanda counting her English money.

He gave her a sovereign. "Think of the history in that golden slice! The weight of the past." He dropped it on her palm. "You won't find anything like that in Canada."

"Dad, I need the others too! I've only pennies and thruppence and a shilling."

Happily Mr Ellis searched his wallet, box of cufflinks, shaving-kit.

"Gerald, haven't you got anything better to do than look for a half-crown? We leave this country in one week, and Amanda's nearer ready than you are."

The hierarchy complete, from farthing to guinea, Mr Ellis laid the coins out for his girl.

9 September, 1953

The Ledingtons had gone to Port Meadows. So beautiful, so green. Recently at coffee Miss Talbot had quoted from a young Welsh poet, something about *the simple light*, about *spellbound horses walking on the fields of praise*. Not quite – the phrases teased Mrs Ledington's memory. The air whistled with wings; the autumn migrations were underway. Thousands and thousands of birds touched down there daily. The couple planned to stay out on the shining expanse all morning, saying goodbye.

In his room, Professor McGeachie was re-reading Tennyson's *Ulysses* and marvelling again at the sentimentality of the English. Burns was much to be preferred. There was a man who gave a plain farewell, with none of that killing self-importance.

At a meeting of St Margaret's altar guild, Tilly Talbot was creating lilies of the valley. Her eyes stung, working at the little flowers. The day before, the sisters had fought over whether to open their bedroom window. At dinner Milly spoke only once. "Matilda, have you sufficient mustard?" As for Miss Talbot herself, she was just now on her way to see a new house on the Banbury Road. The architect was known to her from the Brocklehurst years. She walked briskly, wiping her cheeks from time to time.

High on a ladder against The Green House, Mr Penrose inspected the new gutters. Inferior, as expected. The old wooden ones with their bevelled carving had served a century before the rot won. Ellis would have liked that bevelling.

Vivian Clyde sat in her solicitor's office, reviewing the papers. Rachel had found the house. Semi-detached, near the train station – perfect for a bed-and-breakfast. She had carefully not asked Jim Penrose to look the place over for her.

The Captain and his wife were walking slowly through the country cottage that St Osbert's School provided as their dwelling-place. The master previously resident there had been unmarried. The dirt was simply disgraceful. Mrs Belland's fingers itched.

Waiting, the Ellises stood in the hotel lobby as Mrs K upbraided Celia about the scones at breakfast. "Butter! D'ye think I'm made of money? My lady at the castle wouldn't waste like that." Behind the green baize door, the maid's comeback was inaudible. "And two bottles of salad cream, in only a week."

Then the Green House was all quiet. The lounge was closed. Who could tell that, at coffee the previous night, tears had been shed behind that door? There had been embraces. Now autumn sunlight shook on the patterns of the lobby's tile floor. The umbrella stand and the hall table gleamed, testaments to Celia's good work and to Martha's before her.

The taxi arrived.

To the station, for London.

To the boat-train and Liverpool.

On boarding the *Empress of France* (Mr Ellis regretted not sailing on the *Britain*), the family found their cabin at one end of a long passage.

Amanda ran excitedly right to the other end, up a staircase, along a corridor, along another, and down to her own deck again. There she met a young steward, busy about his work. He smiled. Twice. She slowed. Together they saw in the distance two elderly gnomes, bent over so their coats stuck out as they fussed over their bags. When doubtfully the pair checked labels, their hats bumped. *Ridiculous!* The steward assumed a patient look. Settling his white jacket trimly on his shoulders, he headed for her parents. She followed slowly.

Mrs Ellis smiled. "Thanks for bringing back our little girl!"

Now the steward's face was all respect.

When the cabin was arranged just as Mrs Ellis wanted it, the ship's whistle sounded. At this, Amanda took out *The Code of the Woosters*. Her parents objected only a little before they left her alone and went eagerly up on deck, to savour with sadness and joy the moment of severance from the dock. Then they planned to find the bar and drink a long series of toasts.

With her Indian box and her jacket, Amanda got onto her bunk. En route from Canada two years earlier, she'd run up and down that ladder a dozen times a day, loving the crisp mitred sheets and the taut red wool blanket. The porthole was right there, too, the big eye seeing the ocean under bright sun or in the dark dark blue of night. Right now, ragged white lace was splashing over grey-green.

She emptied the box, filling all the pockets in her jacket and the two in her skirt. There were still things left over, so she tied them in a scarf.

Up on deck, she went astern through the crowds of passengers to watch the churning wake of the *Empress*. Some time passed, because of the collective excitement at departure, before she could act unobserved.

Amanda felt light, floaty, as if the brisk wind might blow her away. Her father would be sad, her mother angry. Not yet. All was drowned now, gone, clear, clean. The Irish Sea glittered. Among the hundreds and hundreds of strangers, her parents were invisible. The engines throbbed through the deck's timbers into her feet. She'd forgotten the feeling. That resonance, so persistent and steady yet gentle, and often not even consciously heard, was the music of the long week at sea.

17 September 1953

After six days the great windy openness developed an edging, to the west. Still the ocean was as round as if the *Empress* were sailing across a bowl.

Before nightfall that pale edging grew dense, grew dark, and revealed itself as the black-green of conifer.

Amanda slept past Newfoundland.

On waking, she couldn't get her bearings, and went to look at the map by the Purser's office. The ship was well into the St Lawrence; the river's sword struck to the core of the stupendous continent.

Now the *Empress*'s narrowing passageway was steeply walled by millions and millions of trees, already (yet this was only the edge of the fringe of the country) far more trees than in all Britain.

Amanda went up on deck to look astern. The liner's slower

214

speed had much reduced the tumbling fountain of her wake. No ocean. An unimpressive vista.

Going forward as far as possible, she gazed at the rain and at the grey river that was flurried about and so decisively split by the prow.

Only hours ahead lay the inevitable landing-place. If this was home, if this was Canada, why was she so strange?

1953–1957

At Amanda's new school in Toronto there were no boarders, but the girls were still sorted into three "houses." The school's anthem crescendoed at *For Cartier, Brant, and Grenfell let us say-ay / Jubilate De-e-o!* Amanda was in Grenfell. The popular house was Cartier. Because of her higgledy-piggledy handwriting she constantly lost marks. She longed to go back to public school.

Enthusiastically Rachel Ellis re-entered the fullness of her Canadian life. At dinner parties she told lively stories about *our amazing English years*, and these not only amused people but stemmed their enquiries about Gerald's book. It was not long, however, before Mrs Ellis became deeply absorbed in her Canadian story, especially the chaotic and disturbing chapters of Amanda's teens. Her correspondence with dear friends in England began to dwindle. After only a few years, a cordial exchange of Christmas cards was all that remained.

Every term, however, Captain Belland wrote a long letter to the Ellises. He reported on the cricket team at St Osbert's, the revised Eleven-Plus, his pupils' struggles with Ovid and Virgil, the *New English Bible*, and a surprising rumour that the Romans might abandon the Latin mass. *That of course will put paid to the classics. However, I rather think that* amo amas amat *will see me out.*

In loving detail he described the Bellands' garden and their cottage. *With all Eleanor's handiwork, you can imagine how pretty and cosy it is!*

"I shudder at the thought," said Mrs Ellis. "Can you write back, Gerald?"

"Don't I always, Rachel?"

The Captain wrote to tell of their child's birth and of the many changes in their life that followed. Rachel Ellis airmailed an expensive set of knitted bonnet, jacket, and bootees. Eleanor Belland's note of thanks was sent by return of post, but something about it suggested insincerity.

"English babies don't wear peach, I guess." Always the editor, Amanda's mother sieved through the letter's syntax, trying to locate the negative intonation. "Or maybe store-bought isn't good enough?"

Amanda, in despair over her fat loathsome stomach and her tiny horrible breasts, did not bother to say, "A *shop*, Mum. They call them shops."

In 1957 Captain Belland wrote a very different letter to his Canadian friends.

Arabella, in Calgary with Mr Oil and two little girls, appeared on the Ellises' Christmas card list, but otherwise there had been no contact. Nor had Captain Belland's sister gone back to England to visit, and naturally on his salary he could not take his family across an ocean and a continent to see her. *Arabella is to be with us soon, though*, he wrote, his handwriting urgent across the aerogramme's blue. *I only wish the circumstances of her arrival were otherwise.*

Mr Oil with his hair *en brosse* had turned out to be a wife-beater. Even a fiancée-beater. *Needless to say, we knew nothing. Arabella never told of this. He has even harmed the little ones.* Somehow, the Captain had managed to gather funds for Arabella's flight and to send the money to her secretly. At the Toronto airport, mother and daughters must wait an hour before boarding the plane for Heathrow. *Would it be possible for you to meet them there? And if there were to be any delay, any difficulty . . . ?*

In the black Plymouth on its way out to Malton, all three Ellises were silent as they listened to the voices and laughter from the lounge in The Green House. They smelled Bisto, cigarettes, and wet umbrellas in the lobby. Tilly giggled, and cried, "Oh my!" Celia battered the gong, Mr Penrose set a single flower at his own table each Sunday, old Mrs Bracegirdle cried when the Brownie snaps came of her granddaughter on the farm in Manitoba.

Guilt filled them, guilt for the Captain's little sister mauled by a Canadian.

"But Rachel, why did she marry someone like that?"

Mrs Ellis signalled for the airport exit. Having taken the curve expertly, she looked at her husband as though she and he had never met before.

Arabella, heavily made-up and glancing nervously all round, looked less like her brother now, for she had lost weight, and her face was almost vulpine. Still the Captain felt present among them.

To Amanda's delight, his sister did not recognize her.

Arabella's thanks to the Ellises were profuse. After that the talk stayed close to *How very nice to see you again*, and *George will be so happy to meet your dear girls*. These daughters, dazed with fatigue, were reluctant to drink apple juice in the airport's restaurant. One had a cast on her arm.

After forty minutes the flight to England was called.

Back in the parkade, Amanda ran ahead to reach the driver's door first, and gripped the handle until her mother gave her the car keys. Her father sighed. He took his place in the back seat.

The Captain's letters kept on coming.

Eleanor and George's child, severely retarded, required much care.

With more courage than wisdom, as their choice was then viewed, the pair went ahead and had two more babies, a son and another daughter. Both were normal.

His three children were, the Captain wrote, all his life's joy. He underlined *joy*.

Acknowledgments

My thanks to John Metcalf, for encouraging me to
complete *The English Stories*.

To English friends, for information and comments:
Sheila Dunnachie, Jo Evans Priestman, Jan Lancaster,
Anne Morley.

To Penny Goldsmith, for decades of counsel on literary
matters.

To Edna Alford at Banff, who responded to an early draft
of the book.

To Jane Kanya-Forstner, for suggesting *Marche Militaire*.

To Stephen Ng, for advice on how to live.

To the editors of various Canadian magazines, for
publishing earlier versions of some stories: *Descant*,
Canadian Forum, *Event*, *Geist*, *Prism International*, *Quarry*,
CNQ: Canadian Notes & Queries.

To Dean Sinnett, for all his love and support.

* * *

The crossword in "The Usual Accomplishments" appeared
in *The Times* on 3 March 1952 as Puzzle No. 6,848.

About the Author

Cynthia Flood's stories have won numerous awards, including The Journey Prize and a National Magazine award, and have been widely anthologized. Her novel *Making A Stone Of The Heart* was nominated for the City of Vancouver Book Prize in 2002. She is the author of the acclaimed short story collections *The Animals in Their Elements* (1987) and *My Father Took A Cake To France* (1992). She lives on Vancouver's east side.